T0266385

Cleans Up Nicely

Cleans Up Nicely

Linda Dahl

SHE WRITES PRESS

Published 2013
Printed in the United States of America
ISBN: 978-1-938314-38-4
Library of Congress Control Number: 2013933096

For information, address:
She Writes Press
1563 Solano Ave #546
Berkeley, CA 94707

She Writes Press is a division of Spark Point Studio, LLC.

*For all the women I've known who've faced up
to difficult truths.
Especially for Martha and Katrina.*

THE CLEAN UP

Her destination, that summer of 1977, is a luxury apartment building, upper Fifth Avenue, a slice of New York life completely alien to her. After the doorman confirms she's expected and nods her toward the elevators, Erica crosses a sumptuous lobby tastefully decorated with white leather couches and stainless steel tables covered with lavish flower arrangements. She is shaking. She awkwardly recites the all-purpose, three-line mantra that Addie McC. has assured her will always help get her through any situation. In the paneled elevator, she rides to the floor below the penthouse, where Addie McC. ushers her into an apartment with yet more expanses of white; it feels like entering a thirties movie set—there's even a French bulldog to go with the expensive view of Central Park.

Addie hushes the little dog and stretches out her arms. Erica submits to her hug. She is beginning to get used to hugs from all those meetings in church basements. Or no: It's more about being accepted. Erica knows she is not at her best. She's pumpkin-faced with bloat yet skinny. Her paint-stained blue jeans are limp at the waist, her Che Guevara t-shirt sags, her good old Mexican sandals are kept alive with duct tape. Because these are the clothes that she's down to, now that she's hit bottom. Erica remembers, looking around Addie's glamorous apartment, nights when she could still pull off glam, and not that long ago. Midnight at a Harlem nightclub with Scotty Jones, smooth alkie and hustler, qualities hidden behind bow ties and British-borrowed West Indian manners, taking her arm after she had stowed her secondhand Army-Navy cloth coat. Moth to butterfly in the simple, perfect black designer sheath that would have cost, what? Hundreds? Thousands? Erica had found it orphaned at the Salvation Army store in the bowels of the Lower East Side and paid her own small fortune, forty dollars, for it. Scotty had said, "Don't you clean up nicely?"

Well, Erica thinks, sinking into a pearl-toned linen chair in Addie's living room with the view, *I'm a complete mess. I'm probably having a nervous breakdown. So why not do it here in the lap of luxury?* God knows she can use a little. She watches Addie pour coffee into pretty porcelain cups. Erica has two cups, a Marlboro with each, and Addie lights a thin, jewel-toned cigarette, a vivid turquoise. Its elegance banishes even the idea of cancer.

"So how are you doing today?" Addie finally asks. "Really," she adds.

Erica doesn't have a fucking clue how she is doing. "Day thirteen."

Addie seems to understand this. "I used to sit and cry at my kitchen table when I was getting sober. Should I have Wheaties or corn flakes? I couldn't even pick out a breakfast cereal without crying. But 'it gets better.'"

In these two weeks without drinking, Erica is already getting used to this strange new A.A. culture, with its slogans for every occasion and serenity prayer and in-group lingo. She already knows she is Addie's "pigeon," a raw new recruit to the sober life. People don't talk, they "share" or "dump." That drunken travel is "taking a geographic cure." That alcoholics don't drink again, they "pick up" and "go out." Sitting her raggedy ass down in this luxurious apartment with a woman who's told her she was a mobster's moll, smokes jewel-colored cigarettes and of course, speaking of jewels, wears them—a diamond and ruby ring that for all her stunned fog, Erica lusts after—is just part of this new deal of not drinking and going to meetings.

Addie is short, with a perfect figure and a heart-shaped face, large green eyes with thickly fringed eyelashes, and chiseled red lips. It doesn't matter that she is no longer young. She will die gorgeous.

Erica met her in a church basement a few days before and then talked to her on the phone for hours. In the new basement culture, this means cutting to the chase, or the bone, a frightening and fascinating prospect, like facing surgery without an anesthetic. Erica gets that people in these basements raise their hands and talk about matters she is determined never to reveal. And then they reveal even more of it one-on-one to their sponsors. Erica is far from convinced this is a good idea, but she is entranced by their stories, and Addie's is a good one, a poor Jewish Cinderella from Flatbush, Brooklyn, growing up above the family's store. Dancing lessons scrimped and saved for and then paid off big-time, Addie in the chorus line, the apogee the glamorous Copacabana. There a mobster fell in love with her and bought her the great apartment and who knows what else. And then, more good luck for Addie, the mobster gets whacked and she gets to keep the goodies, she stops drinking and cleans up her act in A.A., then she falls in love with a proper man. There the Cinderella story ends. The proper man drops dead, boom, heart attack, and Addie ends up finally, alone. And sober. *How strange is that,* Erica thinks, *I would have gotten well and truly wasted. The proper way to mourn.* For reasons Erica does not yet understand, Addie not only did not "pick up," but seems eager to tell her such painful intimacies. Everything in this new world of sobriety that Erica has unwittingly entered is strange, possibly cultish, but also safe these days. *These daze,* she thinks, *my first joke.*

Addie McC. said last night on the phone that she'd be Erica's sponsor and invited Erica to lunch. Erica has walked, of course. Since she has virtually no money, she walks everywhere, all over the city to dozens of meetings. Or rather, all over the East Side. There are meetings at seven a.m., noon, six, seven, eight, midnight in some places in the city, and Erica is on her shabby way. She has always walked around New York, but this daily plod, anxiety prickling like an invisible hair, is different, because there's no escape from herself. Every day she slaps her hair into a pony-tail and maybe puts on some mascara and a t-shirt and jeans and dark glasses, then walks familiar busy streets and avenues, almost jogging at times to get to the meeting, as if her old self is trying to catch up with her and force her to duck into a liquor store or a bar.

Addie smiles now. "Feeling better than last night?"

"I guess so." And this might be true: Her sense of all the lights going out has segued into grey and even in this short time without the booze, the city seems to be expanding—she notices clouds scuttle across the sky now, a hot dog vendor laughing, and she smiles at a black street musician honking fart notes at a sour-faced grand dame who scuttles past him. New York, like her, just might be cleaning up. Really, they both have nowhere to go but up.

Erica follows her sponsor (what *does* that mean?) into the kitchen and sits at a round table with a beautiful Provençal table-cloth, a vase full of perfumed roses, and another slice of the park from a window. It is hot outside, the air heavy and sullen, but here it is cool and pristine.

Addie asks what she wants for lunch. Erica ponders. All she can manage is comfort food: eggs, bananas, ice cream, chocolate cake. And coffee and cigarettes, of course. She asks for a soft-boiled egg and a slice of toast.

Addie fixes herself a sandwich while the egg boils, makes toast, pours orange juice. "Here you go," she says.

Erica taps the egg with her knife. The shell splinters and she picks through chips of the shell; eating is difficult with her hands shaking.

"Want a sandwich instead?"

Erica's face reddens.

Some days later, Addie tells her she'd been drawn to her at once. "I could see you'd been hurt badly. It happens a lot to us women alcoholics." It seems the gangster had slapped her around for years.

Erica feels rooted to the floor of the current church basement, though this one's in a synagogue. It turns out there's a lot of Jewish alcoholics, too, at least in New York. Addie is at ease with her gangster abuser past, Erica can see that, but she can't imagine a time when she'll feel comfortable about hers. Let alone find comedy in the shameful/dangerous/ridiculous positions that alcoholics so often put themselves in, like many of the stories she's hearing at these meetings. Like the laughter when the fastidious, very southern Evert E., immaculate in jacket, bow tie, and matching handkerchief, drawls, "*Well.* I knew the end had come for me one morning when I woke up and—" (dramatic pause) "—discover that there I am, in bed between a little old wrinkled man and a little old wrinkled lady. Honey, even I knew I had to draw the line somewhere."

"When you're ready," Addie inserts, and Erica is back on track with fear and self-loathing, "You'll talk about the past. And learn to let it go. All the stuff that got you here."

THE RATHOLE

It is March of 1975 when Erica Mason moves to Manhattan. Mexico had been good for a while, a lot of painting got done, some of it good, but more of it mediocre. At the end, she'd practically lived in that hammock on the beach while she got off the 'ludes. And she knew it was time to go back. Tail between her legs, back to Mom and Dad's, broke again. Got some boring job as a secretary, went almost nowhere, saved. The old crowd was gone, one way or another. College, jobs, drugs. A couple of them got married. Larry Lopez, one of her running buddies from college, was still around. They'd meet at that Mexican bar and try to recreate the anti-war days, then give up and just drink. And Sandra, who'd managed to combine being a sixties freak (it was still the sixties, as far as they were concerned) with a career, of all things. She was fun. In fact, it was Sandra who provided the wheels that got Erica out of Milwaukee again. They drove to New York through snow and sleet, stopping only at rest stops, to visit Sandra's friend Karin, who agreed Erica could stay at her place for two weeks while she looked for her own place.

So March will always feel like New York to Erica. High, sharp winds with trash and newspapers whipping around, sometimes hitting you in the face, one more shock in this shocking city. She has never been so much at the mercy of the weather. She plays tourist with Sandra during the day, and with Karin after she's done with her Wall Street secretary gig at night. The best part is the wondrous assortment of bars, glittering up and down the avenues of the East Side. When they get home from these rambles, Erica and Sandra squeeze onto the floor around Karin's pullout bed.

When Erica arrives at the Port Authority bus station, she can immediately see that New York City in 1975 lives up to everyone's worst fears back home. She's a shade too old for the pimps waiting for strays from the heartland, though several young black guys try to get her attention anyway. Trash swirls and has fallen everywhere, and a bitter March wind stings as she leverages her hard-sided, avocado American Tourister suitcase (high school graduation present), stooped over from her heavy backpack and listing to one side from her overstuffed Mexican shoulder bag. All around is noise, crowds, ugliness. A newspaper headline from a kiosk all but shrieks, "ABE SLASHES CITY HALL," which she will too soon be able to decipher. The pint-size mayor cutting away the meat from the city, now that the fat is gone. New York City is teetering on bankruptcy. The results of which Erica sees without understanding on her first sighting of the city. A picture of hell: aged junkie prostitutes, winos, crazies, horrid-looking shops offering fried stuff, the "underworld" feeding off the huge bus terminal. "We are the lost," they might suddenly break out singing in some imagined off-Broadway musical. And Erica feels sorry for them.

She gets a cab, a long ride from this underbelly of New York to the part of the city called "the fashionable East Side." Thank God she has a place to crash for a bit while she looks for her own place. The building is a white-brick (or is it plastic?) high-rise, surprisingly unattractive but "safe, safe, safe!" points out Karin, the friend of a friend who lives there along with two roommates in the little bitty boxy apartment.

"Oh my God, the Port Authority, it is so, so bad."

"New York is bad, you'll see, it's this terrible money crisis. Oh God, but it's so exciting too!" Karin, a fresh-faced Midwesterner, pours out bad white wine from a gallon jug and they all puff away on Marlboros or Virginia Slims. Erica, who is truly grateful for a place to stay, even if it has turned out to be a makeshift bed on the floor of the tiny living room of a bunch of airheads, reminds herself to be polite. She puts on what she calls her "face," feigning interest in their jobs at PR firms, on Wall Street, as headhunters. Modest, entry-level jobs, but the roomies all have hopes. And meanwhile, there are tons of singles bars around in which to meet men.

When one of the roomies asks her if it's true she's an artist, she says pleasantly, "Yes. I studied art in college. And then I lived in Mexico and, well, it was fascinating. But I got homesick," she adds. *A strange word,* Erica thinks. She had been sick *of* home as much as sick *for* home. "I sold some paintings in a couple little galleries, and this writer—Jack Reynolds from *The New York Times*? He was traveling around and met a bunch of us expats, sculptors, potters, painters, so he wrote this article about us." As much as anything, that's why Erica has come to New York. Because of Jack Reynolds and that article. Even though he'd moved to San Francisco.

On the second Friday of her stay, Erica moves into a YMCA, pleased with herself for finding this cheap place. Her Spartan room doesn't bother her: She's stayed in worse in Mexico, and this is clean. And quiet. Karin's high-pitched laugh and Sandra and the other one's bovine acceptance of what would bore Erica to drink, deepen Erica's embedded sense of aloneness. Which, she knows, is tinged with hostility. To her, it is logical to be an artist, and she never thinks of herself as a "kook," as Karin had called her. As in, "Oh, you kook!" Time to move on. Her Y room has a bed with an iron bedstead, a wobbly table, a lamp, and a recess with a pole to hang her clothes. The bathroom is down the hall, the cafeteria in the basement. Her plan is to buy the *Village Voice* the moment it comes out, find some apartment deals, and jump on them.

But the Y is not in a convenient location; it's far from the singles bars and cream brick high-rises of the Upper East Side's friend of a friend's apartment. In fact, it's in the middle of nowhere; it isn't a commercial area or a residential area. It is, like so much of New York in the 1970s, a half-abandoned area.

Walking and walking. Looking at apartments that are too expensive or too horrible. Walking through icy water spilled from overwhelmed drains, through garbage fallen from heaped bins and also tossed by junkies and cabdrivers and white girls in car coats with long hair. Nathan's hot dog wrappers, empty cans of Coke, pizza boxes. The worst is walking back to the Y from the subway through the long, dirty blocks.

But it is not entirely an empty area. In fact, Erica is figuring out, Manhattan is a movie always being made, shifting sets of characters looming up and then fading back into the shadows. Like the men who hang out outside the Y talking passionately to the sidewalk. Some of them wave dirt-encrusted arms or crutches, shuffle-dancing, holding their sacramental wine up to the pea-colored, late-winter sky. Many have grocery carts stuffed with bags. Some of the men turn out to be women. One, a tall, pale black man, stands out, wearing (only) a black garbage bag like a debutante's gown and high-top sneakers.

Erica thinks that is the worst she'll see. No. Near the scabrous 34th Street subway exit from which she emerges into the twilight trash night, at six o'clock after hunting apartments, a man leans against an armrest of trash, a watch cap beside him with a penny in it, singing in a cat's screech, some gospel hymn. She looks at him: Filthy McNasty with an aging black man's white cap of curls. And she sees that the curls are *moving. They are alive.* She takes an instinctive step back and covers her eyes. She's seen lots of ugly suffering in Mexico, the expected cripples begging by churches, the various millions of Indian peasants scratching out Chinese-famine harvests, still believing that the scraggly corn seedlings they try to grow are their children. But that's the Third World, this is America, this is New York. And, she thinks, she should do something.

What she does is go to one of the liquor stores that hardily remain in this blast zone after all the other stores have fled. She is exhausted and drinking cheap wine to blot out the sight of the moveable hair seems the most reasonable thing in the world to do, the only thing, really, snug in her tiny room. It has taken her a while to figure out that the Y is basically a repository for some of the crazy people who throng the streets. Maybe she'll run into the guy with the moving hair in the basement cafeteria.

At last she finds an apartment on a street between neighborhoods. Like all such border towns, it feels lost and nameless, with the ennui of nowhere places. Erica's building is an old brick walkup overlooking a vacant lot full of rubble, no trees. The people in the building are unremarkable, or so she thinks at first. Later she learns the colorful lives some of them live behind the closed doors of their apartments. The Puerto Rican janitor down the hall who, when she went to borrow a cup of sugar, opened his door resplendent in a red dress with a plunging neckline, silver heels, and a blonde wig. The super, who turns out to be a hallucinating mole drinking and shouting from his lair on the ground floor. A couple on the third floor who have thumping fights and visits from the cops regularly.

Once again she's landed in a strange land, this time near Spanish Harlem. Still this apartment is better than the YMCA way over on 34th Street, filled with crazies. Used to strangeness after living in remote Latino places for two years, Erica tells herself she can take whatever New York throws at her.

When she first saw the empty apartment in the old building, she remembered old photos of immigrants in the 1800s, pouring into New York with dirty faces, big staring eyes, caps and scarves, crowding into "cold water" flats with no plumbing. A hundred years later, progress has meant indoor heat and plumbing, a toilet and sink carved out of a tiny space, a bathtub in the kitchen. The only charming, even beautiful, things about her apartment—besides the very cheap rent—are the old wooden shutters that lattice the light into the square little living room. They make her want to paint.

She'd tried to after she moved back from Mexico to her parents' home outside Milwaukee, but the room allotted to her there (her mother had made a sewing room out of her and Claire's old bed-room) was in the finished basement with a permanent underwater effect: an anti-studio. During the week, her time was dully occu-pied at the new nearby mall, standing at the cosmetics counter at Sears, a job from which she added her piffling pay each week to the New York getaway pile, except for the percentage needed for gas and smokes and beer at the Mexican bar with Larry or the singles place with Sandy. What had saved her sanity was a studio class on Sunday mornings at a local arts center, and the paintings she'd produced, which jump-started her return to American themes. At the art center, among estranged teenagers and housewives, she'd produced one picture she'd valued from those months in exile at her childhood home, which she thought of as Lucien Freud meets Beatrix Potter. A strange (to her) mess of layer upon layer of pearl and white and bronze skin tones, scattered eyes, a body pared down to near skeletal, and a long, drooping, fluffy foxtail: A joke of a self-portrait, but somehow it worked, this *cri de coeur* of a self-portrait, which now hung on the wall of her apartment.

Erica moves in with no furniture, but there is a card table and two metal chairs and a bed frame left behind. She goes to the phone company office and is amazed to get a phone within a week; in Mexico, this would be impossible without big cash handouts. She calls everybody with her new number. Almost immediately, her old college running buddy Larry Lopez calls her back.

"Can we crash at your place for a few days?"

"*We?*"

There's a big solidarity rally up at Columbia for Cesar Chavez and the Grape Pickers Union, Larry says. He promises the guys will be "respectful. And we'll pay you, chica."

April awakens and suddenly the weather is a lot nicer and the guys, four of them, arrive the next week, their sleeping bags, beer cans, pizza boxes, and manifestos filling the empty living room. Because she's Larry's friend, the other guys are polite to the white girl and even help her move some thrift shop furniture up the five flights of stairs.

They come and go from the tenement, smoking joints and laughing at the Puerto Ricans hanging around just a street north. "They talk like they got hot marbles in their mouths, man." A couple of them score some weed off the dude on the corner and they all sit around cracking up in Erica's funky apartment, home-sick for Texas where their *abuelos* came from, until Larry grabs Erica. "Hey, man, let's go check out this New York." He means just him and Erica.

They go down to the Village and debate about the Vanguard – no, too expensive. Walk around and look at what Larry calls the "fags," find a little Mexican joint. Once upon a time, Erica was in love with Larry for about a month. He has smoldering brown eyes, looks like Pancho Villa, and dresses like the assistant profes-sor he is destined to become, in neat chinos and a blue work shirt. As soon as they slept together, she knew they were destined to be friends. In that new-normal, sixties rule-bending kind of way.

Over their combo plates, they drop the Grape Pickers poli-tics and loosen up over beer, *Tres Equis* this time. "Remember Fuzzy?" Yeah. "She's pregnant now." Wow. "Pico's getting his law degree, and Candido is still an organizer." OK. "And Frenchy got busted." For how long? "He got some time. Dealin' coke."

She's looking down at the table. One of those metal tables like they had in Mexico, with "Coca-Cola" all over it. "That's bad." And it could have been her.

"You doin' OK here, Erica? I mean, New York is *heavy*, man. And that pad, up with those crazy spics? You should get a man, you're a good-looking chick."

"I can take care of myself." Erica laughs. "Larry, we chicks are liberated now. Haven't you heard?"

"Yeah, that's what Flora says."

"And how is she?" Erica's glad to change the subject.

"She's cool. Taking care of little Larry."

And more power to her, Erica thinks. But she *needs* to talk, so she says, "I am kind of freaked out about my place. But it's so cheap. And it was time, Larry. This is where it's happening. Oh you know me, I don't give a shit about 'making it,' but it's just—if I'm going to be a painter, seriously, I have to be here. For a while at least. And I'm going to paint. I just need to get a job and then I'm set."

Larry surprises her by reaching over and taking her hand. He's not coming onto her, he's showing he hears her. "We both have that fire in the belly, chica."

"Yeah, you're gonna be the first Latino President," Erica says.

"President Lorenzo Lopez." He smiles. "That's a ways off. It's gotta be somebody black before they'll let in a Chicano. Hey, let's have another beer."

The guys leave the next day and Erica finds an envelope on her kitchen table with a stack of twenties in it. She's surprised by how lonely she feels once they've gone. She's used to being alone here in New York. And of course, she's met people like the cross-dressing janitor, shopkeepers. But on the street, she has picked up on the deal: Don't make eye contact, no unnecessary chatter. There's a constant shuffling of people everywhere, a hyper-vigilance. And she feels at a disadvantage here, like a foreigner. She's still a little tropically slow and dreamy. And behind that, tense, here in this slum—with a bathtub in the kitchen that has this cover where you can set your dishes, when you're not taking a bath.

Decadent. Even in her cheap college days, she'd always had a proper bathroom. Even in Mexico, she had a shower. But this place has a little closet with a toilet and a sink, and the bathtub in the kitchen. Also, climbing up and down the dimly lit stairs of her building is exactly like being in some black-and-white horror movie where a junkie-monster might jump out at you at any time and demand your money, even your life. It happens all the time in New York these days, heroin and cocaine addicts twitching around all over the place, mugging people. And then one night, the fear ratchets up. Erica's taking a bath in her kitchen, which has a useless window that looks onto an abandoned building. She hasn't bothered covering her window. She climbs out of the tub, one of those great old claw-foot numbers that weighs about a thousand pounds, and grabs her towel, thinking about making dinner: perhaps some broiled chicken, a salad, bread. With wine, of course.

A movement, a flicker of light across the way, catches her attention. She makes out a flashlight and is that a face? Staring at her—some deviant prick has got a front row view into her kitchen in that empty building next door. Erica shrieks and drops to the ground, and on her hands and knees makes it to her little bedroom where she wraps her robe tightly around her and sits on the mattress on the floor, rocking slightly, then bursts out laughing. What's so scary here, does she think he'll what, pole vault over to her window and crash through? But, this is New York and strange things routinely happen here—Erica's just beginning to get this.

AZURE BAR

One evening a few days later, combing through the latest *Voice* for jobs, Erica sees a little ad for a jazz club down in Chelsea. Why not go there and keep it to one drink maximum since that's all she can afford. Must keep finances together. It's the first time she's out on her own for a New York nightlife adventure, the real beginning of a new life, she tells herself.

She takes the subway, gets out, and realizes she has the usual long walk to the club. Cold mist usefully blurs the dirty streets, taxis pass in a dazzle of lights, she catches the crusts of conversations as she walks, like dialogue from a play: "You *know* I do, you *know* it," and three feet on, "No fuckin' way, motherfucker, that's *all?*" Spanish too, a bitten and staccato island-variant that doesn't penetrate her Mexican-accustomed ears. A Chinese delivery guy on a bike flies past barely missing her; a child's arm is yanked by an angry mother. A slice of pizza whips past, thrown from a window.

She smokes a cigarette in the drizzle and walks on, still on the old tropical time, not impatient and staccato like the New York girls. She's wearing her shabby raincoat left over from college days, over a purple sarong skirt, black boots, black turtleneck, her wild curls still bleached from Mexican sun. She has to ask two people before she makes it to the place, at the ass-end of Chelsea, another neglected remote part of the city. And there, edging the

West Village, is the Azure bar, doors open although it's not at all warm out, music, old blues, light. People.

Erica knows what to do, how to handle herself. What a surprise, this rusty skill remembered. She chooses a stool at the end of the bar, takes her shabby coat off and sits patiently. *The beer is cheap, so why not have two?* The female bartender darts in with it, after a wait. There's a crowd to deal with, a tide of drinkers to hold back. Erica drinks calmly, feeling the nightlife around her.

She likes the music – Lightnin' Hopkins, B.B., Herbie Hancock. Everything moves along like a well-rehearsed play; everyone knows their parts, the questing men, the women weighing their choices, the barmaid tossing cracks. Lights behind the bar cast a soft glow, making Erica feel expensive, worthy of attention. The haze from cigarette smoke thickens like incense.

She has another beer and then—welcome change! —a cognac bought by a red-haired man with a Beatles accent. He calls imperiously, "Donna! Remy," and immediately a brimming goblet appears. The Beatles guy introduces himself to Erica as Robbie Shaw, immediately taking a stance so that no other man will approach her. He is one of those men who are a force of nature, she can see that, and she soon learns that Robbie Shaw acts like the king because he owns the place. He is short, the way Erica imagines all working-class Englishmen are: stocky and pugnacious, the cool accent, not handsome but forthright, an attractive quality in a man. Dark blondish-red long hair he combs back off his face.

He's delighted that she likes Remy Martin too. Erica smiles into her frequently replenished goblet. It starts to get late and she finds herself a little wobbly on a trip to the restroom. The rhythm of the bar has changed; it is not as crowded, the old black men with guitars sound louder over the speakers. Girls with shrieking voices, as if they are protesting, their good time running out.

Robbie says, "You're different, eh? Not a New *Yawker.*"

Erica fills him in briefly.

"Artist, eh? Starvin' artist? You know what, I need somebody behind the bar weeknights, Tuesday through Friday, early shift, 6 to 12. Donna's good but she can't do this alone. My partner usually works the bar then but he's off in England for the moment, letting me do the dirty work over here." He laughs. "So how about it then? Say a week's tryout. You come in tomorrow at five, Donna can show you where everything is. The tips are good, try it on, eh?"

Erica nods. "I used to work at a bar. In college on the weekends. Tips were good and there was this smokin' piano player that nobody's ever heard of 'cause he refused to travel. We had these Playboy Bunny-esque costumes, except ours had a tail like a cat, only I refused to wear the tail, I said customers kept pulling it off." She raises her goblet. "Score one for women's lib."

Robbie snorts. "Women's lib, too bleedin' right. None of that dangerous radical talk here, me girl."

Since he must be joking, Erica smiles.

"We got a great piano player on weekends," Shaw goes on. "Dime a dozen in the Big Apple, you know? Under your feet, all of them good and all hungry for work. Like artists, eh? Need three people to handle the bar then. But my weeknight girl packed it up last night." He makes a face.

After several nights of working behind the bar, Erica is surprised Robbie hasn't fired her when he realizes her deep ignorance of mixed drinks. Instead, he has the afternoon "bird," Toni, meet with her. Toni shakes her Afro and bark-laughs as Erica writes down what she explains to her in a spiral notebook. "Baby, this ain't college."

"I've got to memorize these. All I ever drink is Remy, wine, or beer," Erica explains. "I did the same thing when I learned poker. People thought I was cheating."

Toni snorts. "You just a little slow, seems like. But Robbie, he got eyes for you."

Erica turns away and looks at her notes. It is her parents' generation that likes "mixed drinks," martinis and so forth. Plus here in New York, people want exotic concoctions. So she gets everything down on note cards in alphabetical order, and still gets them screwed up. Tonight, for example, she put cognac into someone's Alexander and the customer let her know, loudly, that an *Alexander* wasn't a *Brandy Alexander,* airhead, it's got gin in it for fuck's sake. And Erica knows she is slow. She peers at and stirs the liquids she pours into glasses, carafes, snifters, as if she is mixing paint, aiming for a precise, pleasing shade of, for example, amber and gold of brandy, or of straw-yellow vermouth that she pales down with water or soda, or muddies with the sharp orange or red of a fruit juice.

But Robbie doesn't fire her because, like Toni says, he's got eyes for her. And one night, feeling no pain except the lack of a man in her life, Erica goes home with him. Home's not far, he says, they can walk it, he needs to be close to the club. "There's always some fuckin' crisis with a bar," he explains. Home is a deluxe high-rise with a doorman, wood-paneled elevator. Big one-bedroom apartment with a view, New Jersey, the Hudson between. Not much in the apartment. Big television, lavish electronics and bar. A couch. Unused-looking kitchen.

Robbie sets out some coke. Quickly, seriously, with none of the bonhomie of her Mexican days. He does two lines fast, then two more, before he lays out two for Erica and gets a bottle of Remy and thick bar glasses. "Or would you prefer champagne?" He leans back against the oatmeal-colored couch and lights a cigarette, crushes it halfway through. After a bit, they go in the bedroom.

"You're a beautiful bird," he tells her in the bedroom. King-size bed, satin sheets. Dresser, lamp. No books, photos, pictures on the wall.

The next morning, nearly noon, they get up and he makes good coffee in a Melitta, though there's nothing to eat. Erica can't wait to leave, she wants to gather up the threads of her own life. Yet she isn't that unhappy. She has a job, and now a lover.

Robbie is counting money at the bar and smacking a hand in

time to Clapton. Only he and Erica and the Mexican swabbing the floors are still at the Azure. Robbie looks at the Mexican guy and yells. "Not like that, you clod. Erica, you speak Spanish, you said, right? Tell Juano here to change the fuckin' rinse water when it turns black."

Erica sighs. She just wants to finish and get out of here. "His name's not Juan," she mutters. She slides a tray of sliced lemons and limes into the fridge under the bar.

"Ignacio, dice el patron que cambie el agua sucio de vez en cuando mientras estas limpiando el piso."

"*Si, señorita, ahorita,*" he responds, continuing to clean with the same dirty water.

"*No, ahora misma!*"

"OK." He lopes off with the heavy bucket; legs a little bowed, like so many of his countrymen, rickets, probably.

"Remind me to fire that idiot," Robbie growls.

Robbie can be a bit of a pain, but there are lots of tips stuffed in her pocket tonight, as she has ended up pulling a double shift when Donna couldn't make it. So that's good. The bad is she keeps making mistakes with the drinks. Tonight (Robbie's pointed out) she embarrassed him in front of a certain customer he wanted to impress.

"He said a *godmother,* for Chrissake."

"Yeah, Robbie, I know, but it was so loud, I thought he said 'godfather.'" She rolls her eyes. So one took scotch and amaretto, the other vodka and amaretto. How could he expect her to remember such arcane bullshit?

"I've counted on you, Erica, I had Toni give you a fucking *tutorial.* There was that Alexander thing and then, what was it? Yeah, you mixed up the amounts of grenadine and rum in that Cuban thing. Shit, Erica."

But by now Erica is used to Robbie's temper, a mixed drink of its own: a dash of curse words, a soupçon of sarcasm, a splash of Liverpudlian anger. It passes quickly, usually anyway. More to the point, she isn't afraid of Robbie because she sleeps with him.

"Robbie," she continues in her defense, "what am I, a fucking encyclopedia of obscure mixed drinks?"

She's aware that her pronunciation of "encyclopedia" and "obscure" are a bit slapdash. And she's bobbing as she speaks, also not a great sign of sobriety. She is what Robbie calls "a little pissed," sloshed or trashed in American, as she has the habit of helping herself to fingers of Remy from time to time; well, they all do. "And anyway, they drank the friggin' things anyway before they complained," she continues.

And she's tired, so very tired. If it wasn't for all the money she's making, Erica realizes suddenly, she'd quit the job. And Robbie too. What she wants is a shower. To get out of this damp skin-tight black t-shirt with "Azure" in blue letters across her chest. Take a shower and then fall into her own little bed. That's all she wants.

"Robbie, I'm beat."

"Yeah? Well, some blow will fix that." In his apartment, Robbie sets up the coke lines. Erica yawns and tries to stay awake. It's past the middle of the night; grey light is starting to seep in through the windows. But Robbie is energized, begins pacing, jabbing at the air like the bantam-weight boxer he says he'd been in Liverpool, and which he continues to practice at a gym. Tired as she is, she comes awake when the phone rings and Robbie starts shouting, then slams down the receiver and kicks the wall. He wheels around and stands over her.

"I can't fuckin' believe this guy!" He's shouting, pacing, a new level of the temper Erica has regarded as blowing off steam. She is suddenly alert.

"That bloody cunt," he says in his Liverpool accent which doesn't really sound like the Beatles. "They don't leave it alone. Fuckin' with me again."

"What, says Robbie? What is it?" Her eyes find her coat and bag, slung on the kitchen counter.

"Get me a drink," he said.

She pours him a Remy.

"The goddamn brother. Calling me again. I told them, you have piss-all against me, they ruled it misadventure. Or it was suicide. Didn't have nothing to do with me."

"What, Robbie?"

He's drunk now, he holds it well most of the time, but she's seen when it hits him—bam! And then she'd best stay out of his way. Instinctively, she stands up, as if she could race to the door and be gone.

"Stop hovering!" he shouts. "Sit down."

He gulps his drink, starts talking very fast. "This bird from Minnesota or some fuckin' northern place like that, she shows up at the Azure. OK, so she had this *look,* one of those white blondes. Swedish or Norwegian. Squeaky-clean look to her. Melanie, she tells me. Melanie. And she's celebrating with these actor friends, they're all actors is what she calls them, bunch of birds. She's got some bit part in this Off-Off Broadway play. Well, I don't tell her it's shit. And she's tall with this great bod." Robbie shakes his head. "I know what junkies look like, for fuck's sake, and she wasn't like that. Like a fuckin' Girl Guide, you know?

"Oh she fooled me. Happy with everything, pleased like it's Christmas morning. Glamorous, she calls it. It's glamorous being with you, Robbie. It's one big party. Her fooling me. She knew how to cover up the tracks, all that, very clever. Until I find some works. Of course she denies it but *I found her works.* And then I think about the money that's been going missing, a little here and there, from the bar. And I know: It's Melanie."

"Melanie worked at Azure?" Erica is perspiring. Tries to keep from looking at the door. Wishes she hadn't drunk so much at the bar. Snorted that coke. Her hands are shaking, she grits her teeth so her body won't shake. She knows it's going to be terrible, what he says. She just knows.

Robbie isn't listening to her; he doesn't seem to see her now. He's staring out at the grey of the city at dawn. "Then I come home one night when she's supposed to be here, I'm working at the club, and I catch her at it. I catch her with the belt tied around her arm and the works in, like that bloody junkie movie, *Panic in the Park, Panic in the Needle*. Whatever the fuck it's called. So I tell her to get her stuff and get the fuck out. We're done. She's crying and begging me. I tell her I'll call the cops and have her busted if she's not gone when I come back. And I go back to the club."

He looks at Erica suddenly. "Give me another." Erica feels like a rag doll, her hands are like big cotton mitts as she pours the booze, some of it on the counter. Fortunately, he doesn't notice. Nothing for her. Absolutely not. On second thought, she pours herself some too.

She manages to get it to him; Robbie grabs the cognac.

"I come back, she's still here. In the bed. But she's not moving. She's green. She's not moving. She's…"

"Oh, God!" Erica stands up, knocking over her drink. Neither of them notice. "Oh, God, shit, that poor girl." In that bed, his bed, the bed he and Erica screwed in.

"She'd ODed. I called the ambulance, then the fuckin' cops come. But I'd cleared out the stash. Then, *then,* they find out the next-of-kin, she had this little address book, and they call them. Here. Here!" he shouts. "They come here, the cops told them she lived here, they show up. One snowy afternoon, before I've gone to the club, these three Minnesotans are at my door. The brother, the parents. The parents are catatonic but the brother, he's like some Viking on a rampage. I won't let them in, he's pushing at the door, screaming that I was her drug dealer, I turned her on to smack, I killed her. And I'm trying to tell him no way, I never go near that shit, his little sister found it all on her own here in the Big Apple. And ever since, these phone calls, about suing me."

"When did she . . . it happen?" Erica says, her voice gravelly.

"January. January 5. I won't soon forget that day."

"Two months ago?" Erica begins to wheeze. Melanie's body, eight weeks ago, in Robbie's bed.

She doesn't realize she's crying. But she sees that he is, sort of.

When Robbie goes off to the bathroom to unload all that Remy, Erica grabs her bag and coat from the counter and runs out of the apartment, punches the elevator, praying that it comes right away, and it does. Outside, she forces her Raggedy-Ann limbs to move, *please don't let him get me,* and flags down a lucky cab blocks or miles away. Thank God he doesn't know where she lives. Well, he knows it's up near Spanish Harlem, that's all, though. "God have mercy, God have mercy," she mumbles, it doesn't seem to matter for whom.

THIRD WORLD REDUX

Money, that's what this piece of real estate is screaming, this dress shop for infants full of tiny thousand-dollar dresses, this toy store with works of art for infants, these wineries, French bakeries, perfumeries, antique shops, jewelers, little haute couture dress shops. Everything trimmed in gold and wrapped in jeweled tissue. Yet she's just five blocks west of the bedraggled bodegas trimmed in gang graffiti where she now lives. Erica wanders in and out of boutiques, astonished by the prices. At the very edge of this privileged zone, she comes upon the *Galerie Saint Soleil*, its windows blooming with strange paintings, door painted an intense tropical lime green.

Erica steps into a tall narrow room, every surface covered with paintings. Strange paintings. A tall, thin foreign-looking man with white hair sits behind a desk talking on the phone. She looks and looks at portraits of ebony figures, flying figures, great glittering eyes. Naïve but accomplished and full of power—she's not sure whether it's positive or negative power. It's unlike any art she has seen, a different plane, filled with a gorgeous, disturbing mysticism.

The white-haired man gets off the phone and comes around the desk. "I see you are enjoying the pictures. Pierre Picard," he says, extending his hand.

Erica mumbles her name. "They're amazing," she says. "Who does them? Where are they from?"

Picard's papery eyelids lift over piercing black eyes. "You have not seen Haitian art before? Ah." He has a French accent, or possibly Haitian French. "This is the Saint Soleil school, hence the name of my little gallery. Very dynamic, is it not? Stay for a coffee. Haitian, of course, extremely good. Or perhaps you would like a glass of wine? Things are a bit slow at present."

"Coffee would be lovely." No wine: She is in a "good" phase now, the regrettable *Azure* lapse and Robbie behind her. Now she is full of plans that do not include getting high. He draws a chair up to one side of the desk and pours thick, strong coffee and they talk. Erica tells him a bit about southern Mexico, the wonderful paintings, the light, even, hesitantly at first, about her own work.

Picard listens easily, like a tropical person, though interrupted several times by phone calls. Then a couple comes into the shop and asks about a large, forbidding work that hangs above the desk. He mentions *loas,* the gods of voodoo. Of course, as everyone has, Erica has heard of voodoo, from bad old Hollywood movies. The couple leaves eventually, promising to return.

"They will not return," Picard murmurs. "More coffee?" He smoothes back his thick hair, a constant gesture, she will learn; he also strokes papers, his linen shirts, and, very lightly, the paintings on his walls. "So you have come to New York to be famous?"

Erica takes the question seriously. "I don't think so, though I wonder sometimes. But it was time to move on, time to go to another place."

"Ah," he says. "Miss Mason . . . " (His French makes it sound like *Maison.*) "…This is sudden, I know, but I wonder if you might want a little job here at the *Galerie Saint Soleil*? My assistant has had to return to Haiti, a family emergency. There are always family emergencies in Haiti. Usually, I manage well enough on my own." This Erica doubts, seeing the mass of paperwork on his desk. "But I must go out to clients, dealers, exhibitions, more and more these days . . . at such times, I do not wish to close the shop. So I have the need for a new assistant. You have the eye, I can tell, and a *background,* you're an artist, you've lived in other places. You speak a foreign language—what a pity it isn't French."

He is not able to offer much of a salary but Erica can see for herself the pleasures of the atmosphere, the things to be learned... *this is perfect.* The next afternoon she begins the work, sorting and typing and taking messages. Picard also lends her a book about Haitian art. Soon he is seldom around during the afternoons she works. She brings along her portfolio to show him, along with the treasured *New York Times* article a freelancer wrote about the half-dozen American expat artists working in Mexico, herself included, but there is never the right moment to show them to Pierre Picard. Still, Erica doesn't mind the anonymity of the job; she likes being alone with these articulate, luminous, appealingly awkward paintings. Few people come into the shop, except when Picard has an appointment, and now and then, a stray like herself. She wraps paintings for shipping, opens the mail, takes messages. She reads the book about Haitian art and learns a bit about voodoo, the *loas* that traveled with the slaves in the African diaspora.

It is possible, she finds, to pass whole days and nights in New York without speaking to anyone except at her job. Well she is now recognized at the corner bodega near her apartment where she stops for milk or bread or beer, she says hello to her crazy neighbors in the building. But on the street, people hurry by never making eye contact, and she hesitates because of the *Azure* fiasco to go to the busy bar down the street, though she sees interesting-seeming people coming and going. She spends her free time stripping layers of paint off the shutters on her windows and visiting the secondhand stores that dot her neighborhood, where she finds several little treasures, an old crocheted tablecloth she turns into a bedspread on the futon she has bought for a mattress, a flapper's straw hat in perfect condition, a beautiful old silk flowered robe with a small tear in it. She draws and paints, listens to records, reads. Her mother calls, her sister Claire, Larry, her other college friend Sandra.

And Pierre Picard from time to time, when he needs her to be at a reception.

She has still made no new friends. At the receptions she meets brittle Manhattan women with tans and impressive jewelry, older gay men who collect and like to think they are getting bargains from Picard, who lets them think so. She meets wealthy Haitians, impeccably clothed, and artists, darker-skinned, all men, too thin. All the Haitians seem to like Pierre Picard, they talk volubly in French and Creole. Erica takes their coats and serves them wine and finds them catalogues.

Picard decides to throw a party in his apartment nearby on Park Avenue, a showing of works he's just acquired by the dean of the Saint Soleil School, Hector Hyppolite. Erica arrives early in a black skirt and white blouse, hair in a bun, wearing black stilettos she bought at Second Hand Rose. Picard's building is satisfyingly like one of those unreal sets from a lavish old movie in the depths of the Depression, everything gleaming, beautiful, white, perfectly white, with here and there an accent of red, a silk pillow and a collection of vases in carnelian, deep rose, scarlet, wine. The long butter-leather white couches back onto black walls, there is recessed lighting, old prints on the walls, one she thinks might be a Dürer. Not a Haitian painting in sight. Later, she discovers the Hyppolite paintings, discreetly priced, lining the walls of a small room.

Erica spends the evening on increasingly aching feet, she hands out brochures, fetches drinks, helps clear. When the party is in full swing, she manages to swipe a bottle of Pinot Noir from the sideboard, allowing herself a glass of this wine that is new and glorious to her. Later another, and another. She is feeling nicely buzzed when a gleaming-skinned ebony Haitian man, young, buoyantly enters the party in a white suit, perfectly cut, with a red satin tie; she sees Picard straighten and pass a hand over his hair and approach him, his hand lingering on the man's shoulder. So that explains why he has never made a pass at her.

Erica is introduced to him. Jean René. "You are an artist?"

He shakes his head, laughing. "No English."

"He's a marvelous artist," says Picard, his voice deep.

Many people are leaving now, there are several "sold" dots on the Hyppolite works, so Picard's party has been a success. Erica imagines these rich Americans and Haitians going on, sweeping in and out of legendary places, Le Perigord, glamorous night-clubs. But a fair number stay, all men, black and white, and at last the young red-haired pianist's renditions of Cole Porter can be clearly heard. It is late. The maid dozes on a kitchen chair, waiting to clean up. Picard, in a circle with Jean René at his side, waves her over. "Merci, Erica, you have been a marvelous help to me. Sleep in tomorrow, eh?" She goes to collect her bag and coat from the kitchen. Passing through the living room, a brown man with a round, owlish face and a bow tie—of which, she is to learn, he has a treasured collection—puts a hand on her arm.

"Ooh, cashmere," he says. "Stunning."

"From Secondhand Rose," she says. "Like everything I own."

"*You're* Pierre's new girl!"

"I work for him, if that's what you mean."

"Of course that's what I mean." He has a throaty laugh. "And are you mad for the Saint Soleil School also?"

"Yes, I'm fascinated by it. I'm Erica Mason, by the way. Pierre calls me *Maison*."

"Lovely name. *Per*fect," he adds obscurely. "Oh, I'm forgetting my manners. Scotty Jones." His hand is very warm, dry and small.

"I'm an artist myself," she says. *It's this Pinot Noir,* she thinks, *it's made me chatty.*

"How interesting." He does seem interested. "I'm an artist too—of a sort. Not a painter, alas. A designer. Interiors." He looks at her with his head to one side; it will be months before she understands the nature of that appraisal. "Would you," he asks, leaning forward, "care to accompany me to a little after-hours club, plenty of artists there?"

"I can't tonight, sorry."

But she agrees to meet him at Bradley's, the jazz piano bar in the West Village at ten on Saturday night.

Scotty Jones seems to know all the hangouts, good, bad, and underground. Scotty who never gets too drunk or stoned to help Erica into cabs, to prop her up when she stumbles, and crucially, to pay for the drinks and extras in the form of poppers and weed. Who never wants anything from her but her company. Bow-tied Scotty, equally at home at some Greek diner at four in the morning or the expensive brasserie in Midtown where rich nightlife ends up. Who seems delighted with her, calls her *sister*. "You sure there's no tarbrush in the Mason line?"

They meet Friday nights downtown at Bradley's, three weeks in a row. Scotty never goes to Erica's East Harlem tenement and Erica has no idea where he lives. She knows only that he comes from a large Trinidadian family, says he works as an interior designer, and, unspoken, that he is gay. About her, he knows more, that she is always scrambling to pay the bills and find time for her art. And, like the terrier he's named for, he has sniffed out the craziness, the better to dole out diversion and drugs. She needs both too much to ask her why he is doing so. Hey, this is crazy New York, right?

Scotty starts suggesting ways she can "update" her "look," suggesting a shop that sells cheap designer samples because he wants to show her some "superfine" spots where she needs to be "dressed." Erica fills a shopping bag full of lovely stuff from the discount hole-in-the-wall for a hundred bucks. "Now you need a fur," Scotty frets. Erica laughs. "Fur's not my style." Yet she enjoys this new dressing up, wearing heels, mixing with models and actresses and tanned businessmen—her form of "slumming." One night Scotty calls to tell her to put on her "best threads." As usual she meets him at Bradley's, as usual he wears a suit and bow tie. But instead of hailing a taxi when they leave, they climb into a stretch limo waiting on the corner.

"This is one of my running buddies, Orlando," he says, nodding at the man in the back. "This is Rica, the girl I told you about."

"Rica. That's like a Spanish name? You ain't Spanish. "

"It's Erica, actually. But I speak Spanish."

Orlando tilts his head, a large black man smelling of expensive men's cologne, dressed like a diplomat in a beautifully cut dark suit with a cornflower-blue handkerchief in the jacket pocket. He is smoking a thin black cigar that matches his skin tone. "You're looking sharp."

"Oh, this old thing?" Her dress is a long, shimmering black silk, Italian, which she'd picked up at the sample shop for twelve dollars, because it had a tear in it, easily mended.

Scotty passes her a joint. "Dynamite," he says. It is. Erica watches the streets fly by, glistening in the rain, the limo sailing uptown, across the park into Harlem, along 125th Street, Scotty and Orlando talking. Erica imagines herself as a movie star—yes, why not, Marlene Dietrich in *The Blue Angel*. The limo pulls up before an ordinary brownstone with well-dressed men and women, mostly black but white too, going in and out, like movie stars at a premiere, with the humble, even raggedy Harlemites looking on. Scotty and Orlando are on either side of Erica, like bodyguards, and then there are real bodyguards inside, who move aside for them. *Guarded like a speakeasy back in Prohibition*, Erica thinks, *a place where white folks went slumming. White folks like me.*

Scotty says, "Someone I need to talk to," and melts into the crowd of beautiful people.

"Welcome to my world, Rica." Orlando hands his cashmere overcoat and Erica's car coat to a stunning young black coat-check girl in a Playboy Bunny-like outfit. Black-and-white fur trim, black mesh stockings. "Thank you, Melody."

"Melody must be cold in that skimpy little outfit," Erica says.

Orlando's laugh has a hard edge. "You think she cares? The girl makes more money in a night on tips than you make in a week at your office." Hand on her elbow, he steers Erica into the room, who's thinking, *How do you know what I do for a living?* His tone softens. "Scotty says you like to party, get down. Dig jazz too. You know Roland Hanna? He falls by sometimes. Hank Jones, other brothers. They like the Steinway we have. And we keep it in tune."

"Yeah, I'm into jazz," she says.

"Good. Now, what you drinking?"

"Cognac, please." She has to tilt her head back to see this very tall man's face. He is not handsome. He's cold. He makes her feel cold. Where is Scotty? Nowhere in sight.

"Remy all right? Or Courvoisier? Good. Remy's my drink too. Come on."

She is introduced to a lot of people on the way to the bar. "How ya doin' Orlando, hey baby," that kind of thing. The women size her up, chilly. Smiling with their teeth. The men appraise.

On the second Remy, Orlando leans against a wall and says, "You not a fox, not slick, but you sexy for a hippie-dippie." He smiles, his teeth showing.

Erica has been trying to hear the piano, its waves of good music muffled in the din. She recognizes an old standard, "Fine and Mellow," which makes her think of Billie Holiday, who sang it perfectly. Now *there* was a different kind of chick. She's heard what Orlando said, though, and feeling cold, hugs her arms to her chest.

"What you do with yourself, Rica baby, besides have a ball?"

"I'm an artist. What about you, Orlando *baby?*"

"*An artist.* You know what? I'm a collector."

"Well that's handy, because I like to sell my work."

"And do you?"

"Sometimes."

"Enough to keep you in furs and diamonds?"

"Not my style."

"See, that's what I mean. You cute, but you're a hippie-dippie. Course, Scotty warned me. Special type. And it does take all kinds. Just brush up the attitude and you be fine." He points at a heavily made-up tall brunette in copper silk with a short man, blacker than Orlando. "How much you think that girl over there makes in one day?"

"I think you mean one night, don't you? I have no idea. A thousand?"

He laughs. "Better be more than that, that man is an African diplomat."

"Living it up while his people back home are starving. Very inspiring."

Orlando sets down his snifter and leans in close. She smells Paco Rabanne, cognac, clean sweat. "It's business. Like I say, you just need a little fine-tuning. Hair done, manicure."

There's a lull in the crowd noise; she hears the pianist, smooth figures sailing over a glassy sea: "Lush Life."

"Who's the piano player?" she asks, downing what's left in her snifter.

Orlando taps her arm. "But you got an attitude. Scotty didn't mention that."

"I knew this guy," Erica says, "back in the Midwest when I was in college. About your skin tone. He had a white Jaguar. What a beautiful car. He took me around to places like this, well not quite like this. We had fun. After a while, I met one of his 'ladies.' She probably had been beautiful once. Now she looked, not old, but used up, like she'd been waiting and waiting for something to happen, but she knew it never would. This guy tells me she owns several apartment buildings, blah blah, if I worked for him I could do even better."

Orlando looks at her.

Erica takes a step back. "You know what? When he got to know me better, he told me I'd make the worst whore in the world. Which I took as a compliment. And now I'm going to the ladies room."

Turning her back isn't an option. She's shivering as she picks her way sideways, clumsy and delicate, high and watching out for the minefield, aiming for the door, no, the coat check, because it's cold out there. She gives five dollars to the beautiful girl in the bunny suit and flies out the door, half-expecting Orlando or one of the bodyguards to wrestle her back in, but nobody does.

Somebody tells her there ain't no cabs up here in Harlem so she gives up and tries to walk like a normal person down 125th, to the subway, except there aren't any normal people out at this time of night on 125th Street, just drunks, junkies, street girls, and muggers. OK, Scotty had groomed her for Orlando's approval. OK, so she doesn't have any money to speak of. The gallery job pays shit and she's apparently permanently going to have to feed on 19 cents a pound chicken backs, pots of beans, spaghetti out the ears, with that doom-like mantra always in the back of her head: *You're gonna be out on the street any minute now.* She pulls her coat tight around her and visualizes that last drink she will pour herself when she arrives home.

"Home," she says aloud, and all the word conjures up is a blank. An empty glass. Waiting to be filled.

CLEANING IN THE DARK

Erica runs into Scotty eventually again at Bradley's, as she knew she would. It's been weeks since the Orlando thing. Scotty hadn't called again; she knew he wouldn't. Erica's loaded, nursing a new sorrow. Picard has given her a week's notice because he's closing the store. She's in blue jeans and a Mexican shirt, knocking back Remy's that she can't afford when she sees him farther up the bar with a blue-eyed girl with a cap of shiny black hair.

"Scotty Jones." She's given up her seat, almost sacred, to stand behind him. Scotty turns around.

"Hi there," Erica says to his companion. "You know this guy?"

"We're talking," the girl says, annoyed.

Scotty says, "Leave us be, girl."

"Scotty. Scotty! *Talking?* Let me tell you about Scotty." Erica leans in. "He pimps for a pimp." She smiles. "Well, I'll leave you alone to *talk* now. *Nice* to run into you, Scotty."

Anyway, it's time to go home.

On Monday morning, she puts on her work uniform, black skirt and checked jacket, and takes the train to 42nd Street, to a cramped office for an anonymous job that she'd found in the *Voice* advertising bilingual temp "positions." Her Spanish, typing skills, and the Pierre Picard reference get her a series of short-term jobs. The pay is more than she made at the gallery, the work simple, three weeks at a bank, a week at another bank, a month at a law firm translating commercial documents. The anonymity of being a temp is the best part of the deal, as she is like a being from another planet among the young women from Queens and Brooklyn who supply the offices of Manhattan with human labor. Clearly, the counterculture has not been a hit in the outer boroughs.

At the law firm gig, Erica has a desk with an electric typewriter and a bilingual legal dictionary smack in the middle of a sea of clerks. At lunchtime, when the other secretaries flee, she frugally eats her sandwich brought from home and drinks coffee from the office kitchenette, reading *ArtForum,* an old copy Picard had passed along to her. Then one day on a whim, she brings in a sketchpad and pens and pencils.

The attraction of this job is the overtime, and there is a lot of it, some big merger or something in Argentina. At five, the place is hers except for the partners in their offices who never notice her. And the cleaning staff. At first, they're as invisible to her as she is to the partners (no doubt she is invisible to them too, she realizes), these silent women and men pushing vacuum cleaners, hoisting trash baskets, wielding dusters and Windex. But gradually, Erica puts names to these people who are always moving, who look tired and sickly under the fluorescent lights—but then all of them look that way, Erica thinks.

She gets to know their names, potato-faced Galina with her strong peasant arms, emptying trash bins up and down the rows like a farm woman in the fields, whose eyes widen when Erica says hello. Hernán from Ecuador who polishes the brass fittings on the partners' doors and cleans all the windows every evening, and Jamaican Cassandra and Mexican Epifania, who dust and vacuum. And finally, Mr. Miles from Harlem in green coveralls, tending the bathrooms.

Erica begins to look forward to their arrival, the efficient way they spread out like a surgical team tending the body of Clarkston, Levine and Levine. Watching them relieves the monotony of looking up lifeless definitions of English and Spanish commercial terms and legalese, the tapping at her keys. She begins filling her sketchbook with what she comes to call her Cleaners in the

Dark, concentrating first on the figure of Epifania, her hands tensed and thin around her broom, though she has a doughboy figure. The countless decisions as she shades and strokes, shifting later at home to the act of painting, the tilting of the brushes, the olive-green of the whites of Epifania's eyes, the blood red-black of the tendons of her constantly working hands, this is Erica's pool of light in the darkness of Clarkson, Levine and Levine, of the tunneled, cracked streets of the bankrupting city, of her whole pinched life, and for as short or as long as she can stay with it, she is back in *her* game.

Asleep in her narrow bedroom, empty beer cans on the floor, Erica comes awake suddenly in the dark—cotton-mouthed, sour-stomached. There it is again—a scraping and rustling sound from the kitchen. She listens closely. That can't be a mouse. Shit, no, this is a bigger thing. *This is a rat.* Erica is pinned against the wall, hears simultaneously the strange, clotted hiss of an alien breathing—herself with instant asthma—and a crash in the kitchen. Holding her chest, she tries to think of a weapon at hand worthy of combat. This is the one time she is deeply in favor of gun ownership, would welcome a SWAT team or the NRA to her home. But the umbrella in the porta closet will have to do. That and pulling on her high yellow boots because she has a horror of rat scampering on her feet. More banging, rustling, and isn't that chewing? The garbage can has gone down, for sure.

She throws open the bedroom door and yells. The rat is rooting among the coffee grinds and chicken bones, though it's not the monster size she's seen twice, once scampering across posh Park Avenue boldly, the second time playing in the subway depths. Monsters twice the size of Maine coon cats. This one is a smaller fellow but it is hers.

Erica throws her umbrella at it, yelling. Nothing. It ignores her. She grabs the broom, hits out. The rat ambles behind the stove. She finds the spray can needed in every slum New York home for that other vile predator, the cockroach, and blasts the back of the stove, slightly worried as she does so that the gas appliance might ignite from the fumes. Or she might ignite. And why does no one come to her aid? Oh, that's right, this is New York; everybody remembers the story of poor Kitty Genovese in the 60s, left to scream as she was being stabbed to death on the street, while neighbors watched from the windows and did nothing.

This is one midnight hour when there really is a point to finishing off Larry Lopez's gift, the bottle of Bacardi she's been heroically saving for an occasion befitting something better than her staple of el cheapo Schaefer beer. There really is a point to getting *down*, having a good fucking cry while tabulating (over and over) all the reasons it is a mistake to be here, despite one of the cheapest rents in the history of her life and, probably in New York. The regularly broken lock on the front door of the building, the dimly-lit stairs up to her floor, the (realistic!) fear of some local junkie jumping out of the gloom with a knife glinting. Behind the closed door of her tiny bedroom, with broom in one hand, glass of Bacardi in the other and cigarette going, Erica listens for the rat, but he/she is quiet now, tummy full of kitchen garbage. Well into the bottle, Erica cheers up momentarily, thinks about doing a rat painting, though this jollity doesn't last long.

In the morning, before going to Clarkson, Levine and Levine, she finds the "super," that sour-smelling old man with a German accent in his lair on the ground floor, to complain about her "rodent problem." Exterminators come, he tells her, but . . . and here he inserts the universal New York Jewish-Italian shrug which means "fuck it, it's useless, fuggedaboutit." Buy steel wool, he suggests, and stuff it good into all the cracks so they eat it and their guts get mangled and they die.

SEEING RED

rica rarely goes out now after she comes home from the temp job. She shoves a chair under the front door and makes the rounds of the steel wool stations. But on weekends, she has to get out, go somewhere. Wandering around, she's found a neighborhood hamburger joint and bar in the 80s. Mojo's is a cheerful place with red-checked tablecloths, a singles place. She sits whenever possible at the end of the bar sketching, making a drink last. It is here she meets Red Nottingham. Tray of burgers aloft, he'd stopped one night to look at her drawing. For the Cleaners series.

"Don't go away," he says. A few minutes later, he's back. "That's good," he says. "Really good."

Erica looks up. He's probably in his forties, with thinning brown hair and a broken nose. "I'm glad you think so. I'm not so sure."

"Don't you trust that your work is good?"

She sets down her pencil. "Not for me to say." She shrugs. "But I keep doing it."

He extends a hand. "Red Nottingham. And it *is* good. I'm an artist myself—a writer."

"Erica Mason. And are *you* good?"

"Damn good. But it's a damn hard way to make a living. We live among philistines."

"You got that right."

Mojo's is always busy but Red finds time to talk to her whenever she drops in. Soon he is getting her free drinks, the occasional hamburger. They talk about art and books, nothing else. Quickly he feels like a friend. Red's clearly educated—it turns out he went to Princeton—and full of enthusiasms. Erica invites him over to her apartment on his night off for Mexican food. He brings wine and cocaine—a staple of his diet, she'll learn—also a signed copy of his first and to date only published novel, *Songs from the Night Before*. She ends up showing him all her work, the rolled-up Mexican paintings along with the sketchbooks, the painting for the book cover of *El Gran Temor* that was commissioned by the crazy Yucatecan novelist. "*The Great Fear*," Erica translates.

"Fabulous!" says Red, casually euphoric from his steady helper, rivulets of coke. This habit of his, Erica realizes, must explain the rundown state of his apartment when she visits him the next week. It's a better neighborhood than hers, he must make good money as a server and from the magazine assignments he tells her about. But his flat is shabbier than hers, if only slightly, and certainly messier. Dust balls in the corners, cracks in the walls. They dine on the metal cover over his bathtub in the kitchen.

But he is a kind man, she thinks. "I have got to introduce you to some art people," he tells her.

"But my stuff isn't, you know, avant-garde enough." She drinks the surprisingly mellow wine Red has produced along with fried pork chops and rice.

He waves a hand dismissively. "There you go again. I'll talk to Bruce and Larry, they know everybody," he explains, pacing, with difficulty, the tiny room, which lets onto his bedroom where she can just see a beautiful antique desk with a typewriter and stacks of paper.

The next time she sees him at Mojo's, though, he is full of his own news, an assignment from *Harper's* to interview Kingsley Amis, who has *not* won the Booker Prize this year. Red's pitch is that Amis is being punished. "He's politically incorrect, the feminists think he's poison. So they gave it to Nadine Gordimer." Erica, who thinks that Gordimer deserves the prize, says so. "She's a terrific writer," she says. Lies. She's only read reviews of this formidable-sounding author.

"And a bore," Red snaps, "all that political stuff. Amis has a sense of humor!"

Anyway, there's no point arguing; the female writer has, for once, won. Red is going to London immediately on his mission. "*Crushing* deadline. I'm cramming Amis like crazy," he says, which Erica assumes means cones of cocaine.

Right before she leaves, Red says, "When I get back, we'll find you a gallery." And Erica forgives his political incorrectness immediately.

Erica gets fired from the law office gig when some lawyer walks by when she's immersed in a drawing and complains about her "misuse of company time." She finds a new temp office. Ms. Weinstein, employment counselor at Top-End Temporary Services, tells her she has a "marvelous opportunity for you. You can stay as long as you want—if they like you," Weinstein adds in her longshoreman's voice, tapping her latest cigarette into a full ashtray. Everything about Ms. Weinstein is sharp: her spiked eyelashes, the lapels of her grey jacket, the points of her shoes, her long red nails. She answers the phone, smokes, shuffles papers, drinks coffee, yells questions at other Top-End employees and talks to Erica in a seamless staccato. Erica is fascinated. She has never met a dynamo like Ms. Weinstein before—she thinks she's in a class by herself. Actually, as Erica will find in time, the woman is a fairly common species in New York, a dynamo who if she hadn't had the bad luck to be born female would now be running a Fortune 500 company.

Erica nods eagerly at everything Ms. Weinstein proposes. She'd work anywhere right now, because she has to pile up money to get out of the rat hole. The work at the new office is, of course, boring, even insulting to her intelligence, but this is nothing new. There are five other noticeably attractive young women referred to as "my girls" by the one man in the place, the ancient Mr. Geiger, who favors suspenders and egg stains on his tie. Basically, they make phone calls from card files, Geiger's hordes of gold, contacts for the charity functions he runs. His girls are a cut above the ones she's known before, better dressed, with better accents. Also different is the welcome they give Erica to their little circle. Every Wednesday they take turns bringing in lunch for "the gang," as they call it. Cheery little parties.

One afternoon, Geiger emerges from his corner office, which has the only window, calling the girls to a meeting. They are to attend a gala for a big-name charity at the Plaza, he tells them. Buzz of excitement. "Cocktail dresses, ladies, and all the trimmings. And remember: You represent Geiger Associates."

That week's shared lunch is Mary Gorgonis's delicious spinach pie. Mary is a fresh-faced Greek beauty who can have no other fate in life than to become a good wife and mother; a little diamond chip engagement ring on her right hand attests to this. She is twenty-two. "Mr. Geiger has a closet full of cocktail dresses. Mrs. Geiger (she's gone now) got them wholesale in the garment district. The only thing you'll need are shoes." She takes Erica down the hall and opens the closet. "Aren't they gorgeous?" she demands. "You can try some on now if you want, we still have twenty minutes."

Erica stands before the colorful, awful gowns, which look to her like what a Mormon or someone from the fifties would wear to the prom. Nothing low-cut, nothing slinky. Some have sleeves, all have full skirts. She shuts the door. No way. She'll wear her black number, she thinks, the Italian silk. And her stilettos.

On Friday, the day of the Plaza event, Mr. Geiger doles out ten dollars for taxis to each of them, but Erica decides to save the money and walk over. In her low-cut, tight-waisted recycled designer number with a modified Veronica Lake hairdo and makeup Orlando would have been proud of, she teeters over to Fifth Avenue, aware that men are looking at her much more than usual. Well, OK, the dress is low-cut. In the glittering ballroom of the Plaza, she stands with her demurely dressed office sisters smiling at the suits and their wives or girlfriends and hands out programs. Geiger appears.

"Hello, Mr. Geiger!"

"Yes! It's . . . um . . .?" He doesn't remember her name.

"Erica Mason."

"Oh yes." He frowns slightly, moves on.

Now it's cocktail hour and the girls are supposed to be in the background, decorative, helpful if needed. Erica keeps getting hit on. Geiger passes by several times. Then the chicken dinner, the speeches.

Back at work on Monday, Erica is summoned to Geiger's office. He begins by extolling his "girls". "You girls are the backbone of my operation. Your work has been satisfactory, Miss, um Mason, but, ahem, now with summer coming, there's a slowdown and things won't really pick up until the fall. So I'm afraid I'll have to let you go."

"Miss Weinstein said the job is long term!"

"Of course, I'll pay you for the week," he adds.

At lunch, Erica confides in Mary over ham salad. "Geiger fired me."

Mary says, "Oh dear. He's very conservative, you see. I think, well personally, I loved your dress at the Plaza, but I think it didn't fit with the old-fashioned image he has of us. Anyway, you're an artist. So what does it matter?"

"The thing is, I've been trying to save up for a new apartment. Mine is the pits. I have to find a better place."

"Now, isn't that funny?" Mary's brown eyes widen. "My cousin Chris, he lives in Midtown? He was just telling me yesterday at dinner—all the family gets together every Sunday . . . "

"Of course," Erica murmurs.

" . . . that this apartment has opened up in the building next to his. An old man who lived there forever died. I think it was rent-controlled, so it can't be too much? Do you want me to call him about it?"

"Yes! Oh yes!" Erica says this so loudly that Geiger comes to the door of his office, frowning.

The next day, after Mary tells her it's a go from Chris the cousin, Erica heads from work to the bank, taking out all but twenty-two dollars, and walks over to a block in the 60s near First Avenue to meet the super of the building, a woman called Mrs. Desmond who looks like an old bulldog. The apartment is a railroad flat, in need of work, but it's clean and sunny and the neighborhood is safe, Mrs. Desmond says. And she can move in right away, having paid two months' rent and a security deposit.

Erica spends the rest of the week obsessing about money (she'll have to get another job right away) and making lists. On Friday at five, she gets her last paycheck. Geiger is interviewing a new girl for her job in his office. She says goodbye to the girls, hugs Mary and thanks her again and then she's gone, swept up in the river of Manhattan on a Friday afternoon. She moves her stuff in two taxi rides and spends the weekend cleaning the new apartment. She wishes she could tell Red, but he's not answering his phone.

TINY ITALY

Erica's new home is just another tenement for the hungry, tired, and poor a century before, but hers is only a block away from the elegant brownstones that march westward to Central Park. Second Avenue is the divide (the East River, that tarnished necklace of near-elegance, is the exception). From there, heading west, the streets become, as if by magic, full of leafy trees and skinny women in minks walking little dogs. Eastward are the tired old walk-ups, old people in old clothing, also some monotonous high rises and trendy hangouts along First Avenue for the office workers. Slowly, as the old people die off, younger people, straight and hip, are taking over their flats.

Like Erica. She thinks of her new block as Tiny Italy, just several buildings where old men in caps stand outside in all weather, an Italian dialect floating into her ground-floor apartment facing the street, and where stocky brisk women trudge up and down the stairs gripping heavy shopping bags and chat from windows while the aroma of tomato sauce and sausages floats over the little bastion of the old country. Across the street is an old pasta restaurant with a bocce court in the back. If you get your hands on one of these places to live in, safe and cheap, you never give it up.

Dear Claire,

Yes, of course you can stay with me while you're in New York! In fact, you'll be my first real visitor to my new and improved apartment. Just don't expect much beyond the basics. I'll have to go to work during the day, a boring office job at an import/export company that trades used auto parts to South America. At least I get to use my Spanish. The boss is an old Jewish guy from Poland and it's like an old movie there. He actually calls me "doll." Well, enough of that. I've started painting again on weekends. I turned part of the living room into a studio as it has fairly decent light. I have a sofa bed there for you to sleep on. (Got it free from a neighbor who moved away. As well as a lot of stuff off the street. Everybody furnishes their place that way here.) There's a Brazilian place we can go to that has samba on weekends; also there are jazz bars and a good little Indian restaurant. For starters. Can't wait to show my little sister around the city! It's tropically hot in July so be prepared.

Love ya,
    E

Erica thinks of Manhattan as a series of concentric circles, each a neighborhood or a bar; more truthfully, a place where people look for approximations of how they want to see themselves. Their vision of themselves. Places that prosper on dreams rather than reality. You can move easily in and out of these circles, too. Her first was the *Azure*, before it became Robbie's web. Then Bradley's and nightlife with Scotty. Awful Robbie, awful Scotty. And now, Benny's, a short walk from her apartment, a little jazz bar tucked in among the singles bars. By some miracle, Benjamin Masad, the owner, has business sense as well as good taste in music, hiring talent whose careers have burned out or fizzled, but who can't help but play well even so. Erica starts dropping by a couple of nights a week, the young woman at the end of the bar nursing her drink through a set, unless someone buys her another, which they almost always do. Part of the code of Manhattan circle-havens is anonymity unless you want to give it away. She doesn't, and soon nobody bothers her. But there is always someone new to buy her a drink.

One unusually suffocating hot July evening, the piano player is someone whose name she recognizes as having played with Bird: Charlie Parker, the Jimi Hendrix of the forties. (Both Bird and Hendrix were dead well before the age of forty from drugs.) Bo Craig is a white man, with hard little eyes and tough grey curls that spring up around his face. He looks only at the keys, plays fluently from the bebop repertoire and, occasionally, she thinks, brilliantly. At the break, Bo Craig gets a drink and stands at the bar with a jazzman's crusty ironic demeanor. Erica goes over and tells him she has several of his recordings. His face lightens for a moment. "Oh yeah? Who woulda thought, a groovy young chick digs my music," he says, but not rudely. She stays to hear the last set, and falters off her barstool at the finish. Outside in the post-midnight singles crowd ranging First Avenue, is Bo Craig.

"Let me help you get a cab."

"Oh, I'm just up the street." She weaves and Craig takes her arm. He walks her to her building and stands outside as she works to get the key in the lock. She turns to say thank you and darts inside, not before she notices the little puppy gleam in his tired old eyes.

Things, she thinks, *are looking up.* There's Benny's, and she's met two interesting people who might become friends: Philip Bookman, who is painfully plain and funny, and Mark Pellinelli, good-looking, rich, and (worse luck for her) sullen and with-drawn. She'd gone to hear the singer Dee Dee Bridgewater at the Vanguard, sitting at the bar, of course, to avoid the cover charge. These two were next to her and soon they were having a real conversation about the music. Mark Pellinelli argued that Bridgewater was Sarah Vaughan's heir—heiress, he amended—and Erica said they were two different singers and there was a reason Sarah was called The Divine One. Philip said yes, yes, she's right, Pellinelli, she's *right*. He said they had just started up a magazine called *Good Hip Music/G.H.M.* and were looking for contributors; they couldn't pay much, of course. Did she want to try doing something for the magazine? Erica asked why was it called *Good Hip Music?* Bookman pointed at Pellinelli. "He's the moneyman and what he says goes, to a certain extent," he added, with a little frown. Erica said maybe she could do some drawings? She always had her sketchpad with her now. She showed them some stuff she'd done in clubs, and then a few serious sketches, even a couple of watercolors: a tall thin woman with great shocks of hair sitting bolt upright on a bar stool listening, some black guys in caps bending with graceful angular body language, a little white singer putting on make-up backstage.

Philip likes her stuff, the idea of catching the atmosphere of a musician, of the fans, the scene, is good. Even Pellinelli seems to like her work; at least he doesn't say he doesn't. They make a date to go to the Tin Palace a few nights later; she sketches, Philip takes notes on the performance. Mark doesn't show. Philip says he can get her a press pass so she won't have to pay admission.

"You should come over to my neighborhood, to Benny's," she suggests.

"Benny's? What's at Benny's?"

"Right now, get this, *Bo Craig* is there. We've actually become friends, kinda."

"Does he still have his chops? I mean, he's been off the scene for a long time."

"Yeah, well, he still can be a monster."

"*Monster!* That's for sure. You know he *killed his wife?* Shit yes he did, how could I make this up?"

Philip Bookman has been steeped in the music from birth, his father was a record producer. Monk, Miles, Sonny, they all came to his house.

"Supposedly he strangled her, but they couldn't prove it, then he just disappeared. Moved somewhere way out in Jersey. Man, I have to go see Bo."

"He asked me out to dinner."

"What? He's like seventy."

"I didn't say I'd go. Just that he asked."

She takes Philip to Benny's, who reintroduces himself to Bo Craig at the break. Bo says, "Oh, right, I remember you. Bookman's kid. How ya doin'?" and splits.

"He knows I know," Philip says, brooding over coffee in her apartment later. "Hey, I got it!" He looks suddenly happy, a grin splitting his goofy face. "We'll do a 'Lost and Found' feature on him, you do a drawing of him at Benny's."

In a black felt Greta Garbo hat she's picked up at a thrift shop, Erica sits at Benny's at the end of the bar farthest from the piano. Not an ideal spot to see Bo from, but she's willing to sacrifice a clear view for anonymity. The piano player, who has been nothing but nice to her, now gives her the creeps. But she has a job to do and, as she admits to herself somewhere around the end of her second Remy, there's something perversely exciting about sitting here drawing his bent old back and splayed fingers playing all the old familiar stuff of twenty, thirty years ago in jazz, with a hard but occasionally also delicately filigreed touch. The touch of a sensitive soul who happens to have killed his wife. She gets the bones down in the sketchpad, will fill and frill in charcoal later, flees in the middle of a questing "All The Things You Are." She doesn't want to, well, interact with Bo Craig again.

"Well done!" says Philip of her drawing, which has turned Bo into an old bird of prey, his broken-veined big schnoz sniffing melodies, his talons extracting them from the black and whites. "We'll run it next month." "Lost and Found" is a big feature in the magazine, and the fragrance of the re-erected Bo Craig scandal brings the lovely vision of dollar signs to *Good Hip Music* money-man Pellinelli's eyes. But the whole thing—well, her drawing, her part in it—leaves Erica feeling slightly slimy, like she's deliberately stepped on an insect pursuing its rightful life. Or stolen a newspaper from a newsstand. Some slightly fetid kind of wrongdoing:

what the Catholics call a venal sin. Yes, she feels decidedly venal. Which calls for a nice clutch of Remy's, economically consumed in the privacy of her home, with someone battered and black singing the blues on the turntable—Joe Turner or Dinah Washington, pulling all the deep feelings, like rabbits out of a magician's empty hands, admitting everything in, too. Balm and wormwood together, for killer and for artist alike. Erica, who tries never to do so, almost starts crying, but instead, she passes out on her living room floor.

SISTA

Claire arrives, her little sister, who had always cried so easily. Like when Erica was four and Claire two and Erica managed to abscond with her in her stroller, hoping to leave her with a kind, loving family not her own, until their mother came rushing down the street. Scooping up Claire, she scolded Erica, who hung her head. But she refused to cry: That was Claire's turf. Later the two had become very close, finger painting and coloring together, usually happily. They'd both decided they'd be artists when they grew up.

Claire now works for a pharmaceutical company in Arizona, living in a nice condo (she's sent pictures) with Tim, her new, apparently well-off, boyfriend. She is model-thin and gorgeous. Leading the way into her new apartment, Erica takes one of Claire's bags from her new matched set of red luggage.

"Well, here it is. Your room. Well, where you'll sleep."

Claire sets down her other bag quietly. "Oh. Fine."

It's too early for a beer. Erica says, "I'll make tea." She puts crackers and cheese on a plate, while Claire wanders through the apartment, which takes about thirty seconds. At least it is clean; Erica had stayed up late scrubbing even the woodwork.

In the living room/studio/spare room, Claire settles into a wicker rocker Erica had lugged from the curb four blocks away, and repainted, though it is already chipping. Claire sets her mug down. "All these pictures and plants, the painted floor. It's very *cheerful.*"

"Of course, it's just a tenement," Erica says, feeling unaccountably cross. "Very cramped." (She thinks of the pictures of Claire's condo she'd sent: those commodious rooms, Mexican furniture, the little patio with lush potted plants, the pool and tennis courts down a landscaped path.) They haven't seen much of each other recently. Both moved away after college, are "home" only for the holidays, though Erica has missed many of those, traveling around. They write to each other occasionally or talk on the phone. But it's been some time since they've been together, just the two of them.

Erica feels a nervous twitch in her stomach.

"Oh what the hell—what's with the tea? We're not Mother. Let's have a beer!"

Claire looks surprised. "You go ahead. I'm fine."

Erica pours a beer into a glass, rebuked. But she's determined to be pleasant. "Well," she says, "tell me about Tim." All she knows about him is Claire met him through her job in pharmaceuticals.

"Tim is just great." She opens her wallet. He's a good-looking guy, the sun in his eyes, a wide salesman's smile. "He grew up on a farm. Really poor. With an *outhouse.*"

"Like a Mexican."

"He's incredibly hardworking, he's fun. It's good, Erica, it's really good."

"Well, I'm glad." Claire always lands on her feet.

"What about you?"

"Me? Nobody special." Erica drinks deeply, finishes her beer. Would like another. "Just dating around. You know me."

At one time, they had told each other everything, lying in the dark on their twin beds. That had changed when Erica left for college in the 60s and everybody seemed to be discovering drugs and sex.

"I'm sure you'll meet somebody here in New York," Claire says.

"Sure," says Erica. She stands up to get that second beer from the fridge.

They have dinner in the apartment with mediocre red wine, sitting at the kitchen table and chairs Erica got for twenty bucks from a guy who moved out next door. She's covered the table with a blue and white Mexican tablecloth and lit candles. Claire says the food is great. She has two glasses of wine. Erica polishes off the rest of the bottle.

"Coffee?" Erica offers, swaying a little at the sink.

"Good idea."

Erica feels that she's being invisibly reprimanded. They take their coffee into the living room in an awkward silence, broken when Claire sees the pile of sketchbooks. "Wow!" Claire pours through them. "I had no idea you'd done all of this. And you never mentioned this review in the *New York Times!*"

"Didn't I? Well, it's almost two years old. This reporter was traveling around Mexico on vacation and stumbled on a bunch of American artists and decided to write about us."

"Have Mom and Dad seen it? They never mentioned it to me." Claire is now going through the newer New York sketchbooks, the Cleaners series, the jazz club people.

"Mmm, probably not."

"Erica, you didn't tell them? They'd be so proud."

"It slipped my mind. Anyway, they think I'm living a bad bohemian life, their only wish is for me to settle down, blah blah."

"Oh, Erica, what do you expect, they're *parents.*" Claire's mood has shifted quickly, as is her way. "They just want you to be safe and secure. And you—you're like a mute when you're around them. And they don't know how to talk to you." Claire's eyes are shiny and she's sniffing. She starts unrolling a half dozen canvases Erica had handed her, the bright, fevered, light-drenched works she'd done in Mexico. "Oh, let's not talk about them."

"Fine with me. I've carried these babies halfway around the world, all the way by bus and train from southern Mexico to the Midwest and now, New York. God, I wish I was painting again." Erica stands up, stumbling a little. She goes for another beer.

Claire gives her a look. "Another one? Erica, sometimes I just don't understand you."

"Well, it's mutual. Sometimes I don't understand you either."

Erica feels them sliding into an old sisterly groove of arguments and reconciliations. Sounding to her own ears like a sullen teenager, she leaps in. "All this designer shit you wear now, that job working for the drug pushers—sorry, *pharmaceutical company*—my little sister who was going to do health care for Native Americans. I mean, what happened to you?"

Claire begins to cry. "You can be so mean." So after all, it is Erica who comforts Claire and then they both want to go to sleep. Lying in her little bedroom in the back of the apartment, Erica remembers when they were very young and Claire had been the one the teachers gave A's to in art class. Her work was always neat and colorful. Erica, on the other hand, was full of ideas, but didn't know how to execute them and was marked down for messiness. Things had improved when she got glasses in the fourth grade; the world became crisp and defined. Yet a part of her had not wanted to let go of her murky near-sightedness. It was the way, she knew, that she truly saw the world.

Claire is already up, all put-together in a crisp linen pants suit, when Erica shuffles into the kitchen.

"There's coffee and toast," Claire tells her. "Except the toast is cold by now."

Erica carries coffee into the living room and sinks into a chair. There is a neat little pile on the couch, running shorts, t-shirt, sneakers. "You going for a run?"

"Already did. Down by the East River. It was great."

Erica lights the first cigarette of her day.

"And I think now," Claire continues, "I'm going to walk over to MOMA, if it's not too far."

"It's not." Erica gives her directions. "Let me at least grab a shower."

"Well, that's OK. I called Anita. Anita Pallen, my friend from college? She's working at a bank on Park Avenue now . . . and we're going to meet at the museum and have lunch. That'll give you some time to yourself."

"Fine." Erica would like to go to MOMA, eat lunch, have a real New York day. In theory. She always intends to do these kinds of things, but somehow they don't happen. "So I'll go take that shower."

"But let's go to that Brazilian place tonight," Claire says.

"Sure."

It's a Saturday, the day when Erica usually cleans the apartment, does the laundry, and shops for food and booze. Clears the decks. But that's all been done before her sister came. After the shower, three more cups of coffee, and a couple of cigarettes, she feels better and decides to take a walk. It's a sunny, hot day as she heads up along the walkway by the East River to Carl Schurz Park next to Gracie Mansion, full on this bright weekend of families, couples, singles too. Everyone looks—not happy, exactly, but absorbed. And many do look happy. Chatting, kids running around. She sits with a book in her lap watching the churning river there. Even Claire, who's been in New York just one day, has a friend to meet and have lunch with.

Dear Claire,

I know saying I'm sorry doesn't cut it, but I am. Truly sorry about how your last night turned out. I wish I could have talked to you before you left for the airport. And I ask myself how I could have acted the way I did. "Mean," you called it. I had too much to drink, as you pointed out, and sometimes my frustrations overwhelm me then. All the . . . shit. But I didn't mean what I said to you. Claire, we both have every right to choose how we want to live and neither one of us should criticize the other for our choices. I know you get that artists struggle a lot. And I'm grateful for your encouragement and suggestions. I know you mean well. But, we live in different worlds. I'm not a career woman, but my art is my career, and there are big sacrifices that get me down and I get scared and fed up. That's why I need to unwind sometimes. And it does upset me when you criticize my choices. But I don't want to reignite that argument, there's no point to it. I am just trying to present my side. You certainly had your say and I get that you disapprove of me. Can we agree to disagree? I love you, Claire. I'm sorry if I hurt you. What I'm saying is I'm hurt too. I just want to do my sketches and paintings. It's been tougher than you can imagine adjusting to New York with no money. When I first got here, I was intimidated and overwhelmed. I've made mistakes.

    But I'm OK, Claire, I really am.

    Say hello to Tim. I hope to meet him some day.

Your loving, abashed, somewhat bruised sister,
    E

Erica drops the letter to Claire in the mailbox on the corner with a sense of nervous self-righteousness (when has she last stood up for herself, and to Claire, of all people?) that calls for a visit to the liquor store. It's become intensely hot, a swampy southern wet heat, and the air is fouled with the exhaust of endless cars turning onto the bridge ramp for Queens nearby. But there's a cold lump in her stomach, remembering the scene with Claire, or at least, a lot of it. Why had they fought? Why had she, *yes*, been mean to Claire? Claire who had brought her a beautiful bright pillow, Moroccan or Indian, from the MOMA store, who treated her to dinner, knowing she had so little. And ended up crying again—sobbing—on her awful last night.

Erica carries two bottles of Beaujolais up the street. There is the school playground where today kids droop in the heat on the swings, their parents immobile on benches. None of this is for her; how could it be? It is other people who fall in love, get married, raise a family. Erica can see only as far as the work at hand and, now, the two bottles of Beaujolais.

Claire is in her head again. How annoying she'd been, going on and on. Going way back: the drugs in college, the drinking now.

And smoking. She'd even gotten on her case about smoking. What did Claire say to her after that? Erica tries to remember, but she'd slid into a grey-out, where Claire's voice was off in the distance and the lights grew dim.

And now Erica's sitting on a bench in a playground, trying to remember. Oh yes, a bit comes back to her, she'd said "my turn now" and then told her sister the things that irritated her, then came Claire's weepiness, her wide-eyed, innocent, wounded face, as if she couldn't imagine how Erica could criticize *her.* And what else? The rest is a blur; she'd woken up in the morning on her bed, still in her clothes. And Claire was gone.

Erica walks back to her apartment along First, deserted in the mid-afternoon heat, and passes a little store, a boutique. Pretty summer dresses, sandals, jewelry. Why should it always be Claire with the nice clothes and the trips and the lovely condo and the rich boyfriend? Erica has two hundred dollars in her wallet, destined for landlady Mrs. Desmond. But the troll can wait. Erica goes into the boutique, comes out half an hour later with a large shopping bag and twenty-two dollars. Which will have to do until next week's paycheck.

MORE MIDDLE EAST

T o the beautiful New York woman."

"Thank you."

"It is good, this wine." He raises his glass and drinks. "I am in gratitude for your hospitality to an Iranian stranger for who you erase the loneliness in this new city. *Mamnoon*, Erica!"

He gives her a little Persian rug—a prayer rug, Farokh tells her, also enameled earrings in a beautiful little box. "Oh, Farokh, it's too much. I can't accept them."

"No, you must accept." He kisses her hand.

Really, Erica thinks, *Farokh is like a character out of* The Arabian Nights. Technically he isn't an Arab, of course, but as close as she is likely to come. Courtly like a Mexican but more exotic. And these gifts!

Later Farokh asks, "Mr. Simon, he is good boss to you?" He sits cross-legged on her bed with a sheet gathered primly around his slim waist; he is so slim, his skin all almond, his eyes too.

"Oh, he's all right." She doesn't want to talk about *that*. Mr. Simon pays her well enough, but he is creepy. Those glances, the hints. And, since Farokh's arrival at the office last week for some deal and her acceptance of a lunch invitation with him, it's as if Simon's smelled blood. He can't possibly know more—can he? Crude, that's what he is now. "Ach, what you do to me!" he'd exclaimed the other day as she was typing up the invoice for a pri-ority shipment of carburetors to Argentina. Erica hadn't stopped typing, but she heard him moan. Still, her work is not hard and the pay is good.

"He is a shrewd businessman," Farokh continues. "As are all Jews."

"I'm sure you are shrewd also."

Farokh smiles. "We understand each other, we have been in dealings for thousands of years, these Jews and Persians." He turns her hand over as if to read her palm. "I do not trust him, of course."

Erica laughs. "Of course. Neither do I. But I need the job so I can paint."

He looks at her deeply. "In Iran also, the artists have difficult life." His fingertips console her. "Tomorrow sadly I must leave for Tehran."

Erica nods, surprised by an old familiar sadness. They have not even had a full week together. Six days, and tomorrow it ends. She reaches for her dressing gown, aware of his eyes on her as she puts it on. She doesn't want to make love to him again, she realizes sadly.

It isn't late. From her open bedroom window float the always-excited voices of her old Italian neighbors, the pervasive perennial aroma of garlic, onions, peppers, and tomatoes.

"Another glass of wine, Farokh?"

"A little only."

She stands, looking at him, lovely on her bed. She had cooked him a meal earlier, savory Mayan *poc-chuc*, pork marinated in fruit and spices, with black beans and guacamole, and he had taken one bite and turned white. Shit, she had forgotten the Moslem thing! But then he laughed and filled up on beans and guac. And afterwards, she had shown him her sketchbooks and paintings. She had asked if she could sketch him, his fine foreign face, but instead they made love and then again.

The end is not to be hurried. "Would you like coffee? Tea?" And then it comes to her—she must give him a gift too. She chooses a sketch of a Mexican Indian peasant boy and his crazy mother in a beautiful *huipil* and sash, her hair in massive grey braids. "For you." She rolls it carefully inside a tube and tapes it.

At the door, they kiss as people do when they know they will never see each other again, to leave a blessing, a mark.

"*Bedrood,*" he tells her.

He has taught her this and several other simple phrases in Farsi; she has taught him a little Spanish. "*Vaya bien, Farokh.*"

The candles in the bedroom soften the ugly little room. She pops open a beer—there is nothing else left to drink but she has, she realizes, never once gotten drunk while with Farokh—and sits on the bed where he had sat, surprised by the strength of her sadness. Why? It isn't just the melancholy after making love, either. From the first moment she met Farokh at the office with Mr. Simon, it was clear—to her, at least—that they would have what she calls an interlude. Though maybe it hadn't seemed so to Farokh. She loved the intensity, the purity of these interludes, these interstices in real life. Farokh was an excellent choice, a romantic at heart—and married, she knew without asking. A wife, children: one of those large Middle Eastern families. To which he would always return.

Her eyes droop, she's not at all drunk tonight, but blurry. And her mind can't stop. *This is why I drink so much,* she thinks, *it's the over-and-over of it, I want to feel like I'm drowning in love; instead I have this.* She sees Farokh as he'd been only a little while ago, thin and brown and surrounded by the rumpled sheets, a man at rest after sex, smiling at her. This is how she will draw him tomorrow.

"The reason I love jazz," the man is saying at the loft, "is that you have to make it up as you go along."

"Half true," Erica responds, annoyed at being interrupted as she sketches, although she's used to it: A single young woman on her own at a club, it's inevitable. And especially when she is absorbed in her work.

"What's the other half of true?"

"Well, there are rules too, jazz is not all that made up. Riffs, ways to proceed. Even when they're broken, maybe especially then, because you really are aware of them then."

"Ah, a smart chick."

Erica reaches for the Red Zinger tea. The loft doesn't sell booze, though the aroma of weed is thick in the air. "First of all, I'm not a chick."

"Oh. A women's libber . . . "

"Oh, leave me alone, would you?"

"A hostile women's libber."

But he moves off. Erica lights a cigarette and stares at her sketch. It isn't going anywhere. She has no interest in "free" jazz really, it reminds her of the nasty icy crash from a coke binge or speed. However, *G.H.M.* is paying for this drawing and now that she is no longer working for Simon, she really needs the work.

Simon. The *fuck*. It happened after Farokh had been gone for two weeks. She was sitting at her desk with a stack of invoices, pumped up from the black beauty she'd taken in the morning, from a stash she'd bought off a guy in a bar after they were trading hangover woes. "Like coke, but cheaper, and I like the high better," he said. Erica didn't need a sales job, she knew street speed from back in her college days, people took it to knock off papers and pass exams. She had tried it back then, but it made her edgy. Well, that was then. She needed something to pump her up; she could barely drag herself out of bed in the morning, let alone face eight hours in an office. So she copped a couple dozen, "just in case." It seemed to do the job. She could sit at her desk near the smeared window overlooking the Garment District parade of black and brown men constantly moving crates from trucks and plump yarmulked and black-hatted Hasids doing furtive transactions out on the street. Office girls carrying coffee from the deli for their bosses. She lived eight hours in this ugly, energized corner of the city in a dingy office full of dented furniture and dust balls. A sleaze ball boss in an Italian silk suit and a Rolex, driving back and forth to Great Neck in an immaculate Lincoln Town Car. But on the beauties, it all had a manic shimmer.

Erica was racing through another invoice of car parts destined for loathsome Argentina, land of thousands of the "disappeared" by the ultra-right military dictatorship: 48 *carburadores,* 220 *almohadillas de freno,* she typed, and, as Simon appeared to stand beside her desk, 56 *radiadores.* She didn't like being interrupted but sometimes the boss man wanted to talk. Especially when his partner, Shlomo Meiner, was not in the office.

"What did you think of our Iranian friend? Well-placed in the government. I have big plans with Farokh."

"That's nice." Had he sniffed out the affair?

"Yes, very nice." He didn't move and Erica was aware of his eyes on her. She kept on banging the keys.

Simon moved around the desk. She felt his body heat. Kept typing. "And very nice to you. The Persian way. He give you presents?"

"Mr. Simon . . ."

"Look what you do to me! Look!"

She wouldn't look; she kept her eyes on the keyboard, on her hands. Then she did look at him, clutching and rubbing the bulging crotch of his designer suit pants. She shoved her chair back. "That's it, I'm leaving right now. You creep!"

"No, no, please," Simon said. He was abject, he was ashamed, he would never do it again, he said. "Here, a bonus," he said, pulling money out of his pocket—he carried around a big wad of cash like a drug dealer; she often wondered why he never got mugged. "Forget this, I beg you. A mistake."

Two hundred dollars. Nice, but nothing. A beautiful plan rammed into place and she smiled to herself. Don't walk out. Every job was crappy but you need a job. Correction: You need money. And Simon has pants full (ugh) of it. And much, much, more in the office safe. You can handle him. Demand a raise. "I need a raise."

"OK, OK, we'll talk."

"Now." And he agreed, added half again to her paycheck. Erica feeling like she could take on anything—could fling off her white blouse and black pants to reveal: Superwoman. Thank you, better living through chemistry.

Two days later, an unexpected opportunity came up. Simon's son Carl came to the office. A tall, athletic-looking boy of nineteen or twenty, home on a college break. Simon's only child, Erica knew. She watched Simon with him. A doting father. And she was the office "girl" he had continued, even after the incident with his pants, to try to get into the pants of.

Simon was taking him to lunch at Folcetti's, the pricey place where all the high rollers of the District took clients and showed off.

Seeing the boy formed a plan instantly in Erica's two-black-beauties-today head (if one was good, then two would be better). "Before you go, Mr. Simon, we need to look at this little problem with the GM order to Brazil." A good secretary, a whiz typist, trilingual. And fuckable!

"Let it wait, Miss Mason." He avoided her eyes, as if she were suddenly just a worker.

"It can't wait, it involves thousands of dollars. It won't take long, but we need to talk. Alone." Erica looked up at him and smiled, like a shark.

He sucked in his breath. "All right . . . Carl, can you wait in my office, just a couple of minutes."

The boy wandered off to his dad's enclosed office the other side of the room. Good. She didn't want him involved in this. Unless it was necessary.

Simon was standing near her desk again. Like he was in charge. Let him think so, Erica thought. Let him wait. Her hands were trembling a little as she moved papers around, picked up a pen. Repositioned the ashtray. Let him squirm. She looked at him and said sweetly, "I have your home phone number. Give me a thousand dollars severance and two weeks' pay—with the raise—or I will call your wife and tell her what you've been doing. And, I will tell your son." Now her entire body was trembling.

Simon took a step back.

"Look, we both know that it's peanuts for you. You carry around more than that in your *pants.*" She smiled, wondering if she looked crazy. She felt a little crazy.

"What is this?" he hissed. "You're trying to blackmail me?"

She rubbed her vibrating hands, damp with sweat. "What I am doing, Mr. Simon, is called payback. So give me the money now or I will tell your wife and Carl what a slime ball you are."

Sharp intake of breath. "*Shiksa* bitch!"

"If I were a Jewish bitch, I'd do the same thing, Mr. Simon."

And it was that simple. He turned away and counted out bills, then put them on her desk. "I could have you arrested."

She shoved the money in her purse. "And I could tell Carl what a shit he has for a father."

"Get out."

"With pleasure. Asshole."

Erica was trembling so much that she almost tripped as she made for the glazed door with "Simon-Meiner" adorned in gold leaf. As she left, she heard Carl ask, "Dad? Dad? Is everything OK?"

The musicians at the loft take a break, a conga player keeps tapping out a heartbeat, players in the downtown scene move in and out of the loft. A joint is passed around, Erica takes a hit. She is drawing a black woman in African cloth bending to serve tea, with a baby strapped to her back.

A guy eases onto the vacant cushion next to her. "Far out," he says, smiling at the sketch. Erica waits for him to start hitting on her. He doesn't. He's quiet and motionless. She is aware of him though, legs folded, hands at rest. She glances over; he's like a brown-skinned Cheshire cat. She works on the folds of the cloth, the curve of the back, the woman's Afro halo. The joint comes by again, she notices the guy declines it, passes it to her. The music starts again, an avalanche, no easing their way into it with these guys. She closes the sketchbook. The conga player has stepped it up; he's like a heavyweight boxer, how long can he keep this up? But he doesn't stop. The bass player appears to be trying to tear the strings off his huge instrument, the saxophone screams out the sounds of the city in trouble, ambulances, fire trucks, everyone on their horns, a riot in the ghetto. No one else seems bothered by the cacophony. White and black paying attention, serious. But Erica is in agony, praying for the end of these sounds, though it seems unlikely. Then, without warning, silence. Like a battle retreat, with bodies littering the ground. She can practically see them there. Herself among the wounded.

She's in no mood to work now. Standing up, she says to the quiet man with his flower-child vibe, "Well, goodbye. I have to split."

"I'll walk you outside. There are bad people around here at night."

They are almost out the door when a guy throws his arm around him. "Jimmy Loveness, man! Haven't seen you in I don't know how long. Damn man, where you been keepin' yoself? Archie, look who's here—*Loveness.*" Like he is some kind of celebrity, musicians immediately gather around him, treating him with a marked tenderness, almost like he is fragile, expensive china in danger of dropping. This would make a sketch. Their velvet caps, the snap of black physical punctuation, heads back, celebrating her strange knight.

"You got to sit in, man, Andrew will lend you his kit—Loveness, man, come on. Now is the *time.*"

But he says, "I can't, no, I am escorting this young lady."

"Jimmy! You hear that? Jimmy got to escort the young lady? Man, I hope she live close by since you don't take public transportation."

Erica wonders why the benign laughter from the cats at this. She says, "He's just walking me to the subway."

"That's right," Jimmy says. He licks his lips. He does that a lot but not nervously, more like he likes the taste of them. Who *is* this dude?

"Yeah well, you come back after, Jimmy, OK? The kit's always here, we been ready to play with you, my man."

They go down three flights of dingy steps to the garbage-strewn dark street below.

"So you're a drummer, Jimmy Loveness?"

"Was a drummer. I retired from all that. Of course, I still follow the music."

It is four dark blocks to the station. Erica is glad he insisted on walking with her. There are weary, hostile shadows around, night people probably needing a fix. But Jimmy walks along calmly, unperturbed.

"You are a talented artist," he tells her at the bottom of the subway steps. "It would be a groove to see some more of your work."

Without thinking, Erica says, "Well, come over to my place some afternoon and I'll show it to you."

"Day after tomorrow? Three o'clock?"

Erica pauses fractionally. She should be looking full-time for a day job again. "Fine."

She writes down her address and phone number—he doesn't have a pen or paper—and he waits until she is past the turnstile. He's smiling like a Buddha as Erica turns and mouths "thank you."

HOLY MAN

At three o'clock two days later, Jimmy Loveness presses the buzzer of Erica's building. Two of the elderly Italian men from the building passing by in the hall scowl as she greets him. The next day she finds a copy of *Playboy,* open to the centerfold, pushed under her door, to show what they think of her. *No big deal,* she thinks: She'd been considered a *puta* in Mexico by neighbors scandalized by a woman living on her own, entertaining male visitors.

Loveness is dressed in khakis, a faded work shirt, and Keds, also a red plaid bow tie and sky blue beret, sweating in the heat that stubbornly holds in autumn. He stands shyly smiling in the doorway, then immediately moves to the living room floor where he sinks into a lotus. Legs folded, hands loose at his sides, he doesn't move from this spot the entire time.

"I take no spirits," he says, waving away her offer of a beer.

So she makes iced tea. He looks at the sketchbooks, especially the Mexican ones. "These people are at *home,*" he says, pointing to a Mayan family she'd drawn at the Merida market. "Not, you know, uprooted. Vagabonds . . . "

"They fought a hundred-year civil war," Erica says. "They suffered under the Spanish. And they suffer now."

"But they didn't lose their place?"

"No."

"So it was worth it."

She tells him about the music, the liquid voices and guitars in the plazas, the dancehalls, the mariachi soul-men, the composer at a party, how everyone there cried and laughed when he played. Jimmy smiles his Cheshire cat smile.

"Jimmy," Erica says, "I'd like to sketch you. Now?"

"OK." She works silently, maybe a half hour, maybe an hour. His lips are liverish and fleshy, he has a broad African nose, tilted Asian hazel eyes. His skin tone is lightly-toasted sugar, entirely smooth; his multicultural face is like a child's, open and alert.

"It's not finished, but you can see it if you want," Erica says, closing the pad at last.

"No, no," he says quickly. "When you're done, if you still want to, show me then."

She gets them more iced tea and a plate of cheese, crackers, and apples and sets it down beside him. Jimmy eats delicately, happily.

"I want to know about you, Jimmy," she says, munching. "Tell me about yourself. You know, your face is like a little map of the world. What are your parents like?"

For a moment, his smile fades. He says, "It's not important. We all go back to Africa." He laughs. "OK, for you: I used to play drums. In Seattle. Where I came up. A hip scene and a lot of cats. I played with them, learned from them. Hendrix was there."

"Hendrix! Why is it I keep running into people who knew him. Like when I lived in Mexico, I was down in British Honduras—long story—and ended up staying at this commune where this old black cat claimed he'd been Jimi's manager. We actually got into an argument because he said he's the greatest guitar player ever and he didn't even who Charlie Christian was!"

"Shame on him," Jimmy says, smiling. "Charlie Christian was the guitar man."

Erica reaches for the box with her stash, starts rolling a joint.

Jimmy shakes his head no. "We did chemicals together, Jimi and me. But no chemicals now. Nothing. I gave it up since the revelation. Chemicals. Nightclubs. Money. Sex."

Erica chokes on the smoke. "But I met you at a club."

"No, a *loft*. The brothers get together there. I go there to feed the spirit. Like a church. I meditate."

"But . . . no money? No, uh . . . "

"I let the universe take care of me now. Sometimes I do play if the vibes are right."

"But . . . "

He taps a rhythm on the sketchbooks, which he's put in a neat pile. "You're on the path too, I can feel it. You're gonna find what you are looking for, Erica. If you let go. Cultivate patience."

Although she thinks he is probably crazy, another sixties dropout involved in weird shit, Erica finds herself leaning towards him, saying earnestly, "But life gets in the way all the time."

Jimmy beams. "That's OK. Trust and believe."

"But, believe what exactly?"

All those conversations, stoned usually (and Erica is high now, but not very), in college dorm rooms, apartments, bars, everybody playing, pretending that their thirst is to know what life is for, is just a game of semantics. An LSD poster, rock musicians as the new philosophers. She remembers then the first time she smoked hash, and somebody put on a new album: John Coltrane, *A Love Supreme*. "The Creator has a master plan."

"Loveness, it's like everybody else has a plan. They all seem to know . . . but all I know is I want to do my work."

"That's why you're here in New York," he nods. "People like us end up here. And it's why we met." Jimmy Loveness stands up, limber as a boy. "I have to go now. Can we go to Central Park sometime and look at the trees?"

"Sure, I guess."

He puts his hands together. "Peace."

After he's gone, Erica puts down the joint. She doesn't want it anymore. She sits on her couch, listening to the street sounds outside her ground-floor window and thinking about weird, sweet Jimmy Loveness. She falls asleep and doesn't dream. Then she works some more on her portrait of Jimmy Loveness.

In the evening, she gets a phone call from her mother. Erica immediately thinks of disaster. Her frugal mother rarely calls her, as she doesn't like to spend the money on long-distance calls.

"Granna's in the hospital, she fell down the stairs. I thought you should know."

"Again?"

"Well, you know how she is. It's those stairs! She insists she can manage that big house. I'm going out to be with her, and this time she has to move into the Gardens."

"She'll never agree to it, Mom." Her grandmother is a formidable pioneer-type woman.

Her mother says rather grimly, "This time she has to."

"Well . . . what can I do?" That, Erica assumes, is the reason for the call.

"Oh, dear, nothing, thank you. I just wanted to hear your voice."

This is unusual. Her mother has kept her distance since the difficulties of the sixties, what Erica once overheard her telling a friend was the "counterculture," from an article in *Time*. Everything is always "fine" with her mother, usually anyway.

"Well, it's great to hear your voice, too," Erica says, tardily. She's at a disadvantage here, she realizes, being semi-whacked on weed. "And I'm sorry about Granna. Maybe once she's in that Gardens place, she'll like it."

"Oh, she will! There's Aunt Lottie, a bridge club, a nice garden in the courtyard. And she'll still have her independence."

Her mother's voice changes suddenly, tenser. "And dear, one more thing, I know it irritates you when I mention it. But I *don't* hear from you. Are you doing well? How's your job?"

Erica stirs with guilt. "Well, I'm just very busy. I've got a new job, drawing sketches for a magazine."

"Oh! Does it pay enough?"

This is the thing, isn't it? Her art will only "count" in her parents' minds if it can support her. They feel it is a nice hobby, like sewing or joining a reading club. Not a profession.

"*Yes*. It does. And I pick up office work when I need to." Her mother makes artful use of a brief silence. "Well, dear," she resumes slowly, "to that point, I'm sending you a little check. Your father and I wish we could do more for all you children. Will you stay in touch more often?"

"Yes, Mom. And thank you for the check." *The little check,* she thinks, putting the receiver on the hook.

Erica flops back onto the couch again. The topic of money erases her good mood, the little oasis of peace she'd felt with Jimmy Loveness. It's all about money, and he's crazy. He should go to India and wear a loincloth and carry a begging bowl. They'd accept him there. But this is New York. Why can't she have been born into one of those families with trust funds? Just a little trust fund, enough to keep the world away. She's living off the blood money from Mr. Simon and that won't last long. Why does she have to work these stupid dreary jobs? Wasting her time, boring her, exposing her to slime balls. She's stuck. She isn't cut out for a life of crime.

The one time she shoplifted in college, a stupid little dress, she'd been caught, actually taken in a paddy wagon to jail, where her parents had to come bail her out. In college, she'd sold some pot, true, but everybody seemed to be doing that then, it was just a cottage industry. Here in New York, there's no way she could handle selling drugs. Which leaves, what? Being a call girl? Lots of women did it, dividing the sale of themselves from their real lives of going on auditions and so forth. But, as she had told Orlando, she would make a lousy whore. She's stuck with earning an honest living.

Her mom's call reminds her that her parents will be coming to Manhattan in a couple of months for that banking conference. At least she'll have time to prepare. *Clean up your act,* she thinks, but then, why bother? Her parents had been oblivious to her altered states of consciousness when she'd lived at Hotel Mom and Dad at various times during and after college. Her dad was always at work, or nursing a martini. Her mom, Mrs. "I'm Fine." Like the time Erica was sitting at the kitchen table at dawn, coming down from acid, her eyes pinholes. And, oh shit, her mother pads into the room in her fluffy robe and slippers, makes coffee, and asks if she wants some cornflakes. Jesus Christ, why couldn't she see?

Backdrop: The rain beats against the grimy sandstone of the building, plays a manic rhythm on the battered metal garbage cans arrayed so charmingly out on the pavement.

Loveness will be here soon, forging his moneyless way from lower Manhattan, unfazed by the torrents of rain that have canceled their Central Park plan. "It's just water," he'd said on the phone, laughing, in the background the din of what sounded like a rowdy school cafeteria, the men's shelter where he lives on the Bowery.

Erica has finished the picture of Jimmy, which Philip wants for *G.H.M.* along with an interview with the elusive drummer. He brushes aside Erica's protests that she isn't a writer. "Just tape it and type it up, I'll do the editing." Since it's double the money, she agrees; she still has the portable Olivetti from college. And she loves working for the magazine. It would be the perfect job except for the lack of steady money. Philip and Mike handle everything: the copy, typesetting, cover design. But getting advertising is the hard part. They haven't turned a profit yet, but as Philip likes to say, at least they're breaking even, and the backers have given them a year to get in the black.

So she's living on the edge again, what's new? And, suddenly, she's painting again. So it would a huge diversion, a betrayal even, Erica tells herself, to look for some day gig right now. Until she's done with the portrait of Edie Desmond, the "super" of the building who lives one floor above her, with two loutish teenagers and a black lover, having kicked out her classically brutish husband. Erica has gotten to know Desmond via the monthly rite of hand-delivering her rent check. She has persuaded her to sit for a portrait in her living room, bribing her with Entenmann's cakes. They've talked about her clothes. Desmond has chosen a dark green satin dress that cinches her waist like a string around a baked potato—wonderful. Erica has become typically feverish about this portrait, which was inspired by a visit to Scribner's bookstore where she came upon an art book with reproductions by Lucien Freud. From there it had been a straight line to the slatternly, proud super—impasto with acrylics—the flat steel-grey hair and suspicious small blue eyes, strong bulbous arms and legs, and of course, her militant chest (part of Desmond's job as super is to mop the five floors of hallways in the building). Yet Erica resists the easiness of seeing her as a caricature. Edie Desmond does have a proud air about her, of strength; she has triumphed in her way over large helpings of nastiness. Icing on the cake is the boyfriend, Lamont: big, silent, shambling, grey-black. But Erica discards the idea of painting them together. Edie Desmond, she decides, will fly solo.

When the buzzer sounds, Erica is just finishing Loveness's sketch, realizing that after all, he has probably eluded her. She turns the sketch facedown.

Loveness drips water onto the linoleum.

"You *walked* here in this storm from *Houston Street?*"

"Of course."

"Well, go towel off in the bathroom and take off those sneakers. They're soaked. You can put them on the radiator."

Obediently he goes to her little bathroom.

She has put Sonny Rollins on the box, very low; still, the music permeates the room.

"*The Bridge,* very cool," he says.

Erica hands him a glass of Red Zinger tea, no sugar. Some oatmeal cookies and an apple, a mother handing out a snack.

She has explained about the piece for *G.H.M.*, which Jimmy has agreed to only because she wants him to. She turns on the tape recorder and starts her questions but it's not good. All he will say is "cool" or "far out." Maybe he's scared of the past, he's clearly done a lot of psychedelics in his time. She says, "Let's do the blindfold test like in *Downbeat.*" In it, the musician guesses who's on an album. She plays cuts from albums featuring drummers. He knows them all immediately—Jo Jones, Elvin Jones, Roy Haynes, Art Blakey, Mickey Roker. Maybe his past is dead to him, but the music lives on.

Then she tries a few more questions. Like why, again, he gave up performing.

"No, no," he says patiently, "I gave up the scene. Clubs." He laughs. "I am always playing."

"Like I am always working on a picture?"

"Exactly. It's very simple. Money becomes a god and people lose their way. In giving it up, I found peace. I have a place to stay, food. I have my tapes. And I play; oh like when Leon Thomas came by the Mission to see me, and another time, Andy Bey. We played for the cats there."

OK, she thinks, *this works. Good.* "Um, what about the other stuff you gave up?"

"All the traps? The *encumbrances?* Sex?" He smiles. "Except when I met you, the Mother told me we are soul mates. That's why I come up here."

"The *Mother* told you? Who is this Mother?"

"The Mother is . . . who she says she is. You can't encompass her with words."

Oh boy. Not your standard jazz interview material, this. "Well, is she like your guru, or a therapist?"

She has no idea what the fuck this gentle and probably crazy man is talking about. She's pulled in two directions. The temptation to make him into a clown for the magazine and at the same time, a need to protect this gently lost soul. There is this—loveliness, yes, that's it—about him. Jimmy Loveness has thrown away the whole game—money and sex, competition in his profession. Yet she finds she envies him. She who slogs through lust and longing, who yearns for skin against skin. And this terrible need to make a living. And be seen.

"That isn't important. What is important is the path."

Later, she calls Philip. "Jimmy Loveness is beautiful and crazy."

"Yeah? Did you get the interview?"

"Yes and no. He did a blindfold test, got 'em all right. But the questions . . . man, he's too far out."

"But that's great! I mean, look at Sun Ra. Miles. Sonny. The Chicago dudes. Nut jobs but great musicians."

"Yeah, OK." She has the creepy feeling somehow that she's selling Jimmy Loveness for a few pieces of silver—next month's rent, to be exact.

SISTERHOOD II

Erica doesn't realize how much she's missed having a woman friend in New York until she meets Carmen Vasquez in early November while sketching dancers at Zamba's, a loud Latin club big as a barn. Wearing her brightest Mexican blouse, her tightest jeans, and more make-up than usual, she still pales in the exuberant, brown-skinned crowd. She finds a little table in a corner where she works, at first relatively undisturbed, sketching furiously, especially the older dancers who are ponderous yet graceful, more than holding their own in the young sinewy crowd. A waitress appears and she orders a Cuba Libre, and she begins to attract a little crowd of guys who come to ask her to dance then stay to watch her as she draws. Somebody buys her another drink, then another. It's not late, barely eleven, and Erica knows she should slow down and turns down the young men, smiling and shaking her head, who keep finding her in the corner. She needs to keep working and then split; Philip has warned her that Zamba's can get rough later on.

A couple sits in the empty seats at "her" table in the crowded room.

"Drink?" the man offers politely, the woman with him smiling in a friendly way. Erica knows she shouldn't; she wants to keep working, stay in the zone, finish this sketch of a white-haired man in a golden *guayabera* with a beatific look on his face as he guides his rail-thin ancient partner in a tight silver dress through an intricate meringue. Through the old dancers the rivers of the continents run. The couple at the table is looking curiously at her sketchpad, but say nothing.

Then Erica is done, closes the book, sits back, and lights a cigarette. "Thanks for the drink," she shouts into the cataclysmically loud music—a full orchestra. More *ron con cola. Ay ay ay.* The couple at the table are a picture of the rivers of race too, the woman with long straightened wavy hair, her skin like mother of pearl, glints of peach, pearl, coffee. Her mouth stained raspberry. The guy is—how does Erica know this? —not Latino, but American, a light-skinned man with a neat brown Afro. There is a final trumpet shriek and the band falls silent. They introduce themselves as Sonny Morse and Carmen Vasquez, nice to meet you.

"We're celebrating our engagement!" Carmen waves a diamond chip.

"Felicidades." Erica opens her sketchbook again. "How about a quick sketch as a gift? Yeah? OK, just ignore me and act natural."

"Act natural?" Carmen laughs. "That's hardly possible. And how can we ignore her, right, honey? She really stands out in this crowd. Blanca y rubia. And an *artist.*"

Her fiancé murmurs, "Let her do her work, Carmen."

"I can listen," Erica assures them, "tell me about yourselves."

Carmen Vasquez is the talker. She's a Nuyorican, working her way through City College, majoring in bilingual ed.; her parents from "the island" always speak Spanish to her. "Like we're still down there," she laughs. Sonny is a law student, she goes on, they met at City College, he turned her onto Malcolm.

"Among other things." He grins. "Her parents would faint if they knew what their little girl is involved in on campus—women's rights, gay rights, black rights, Latino rights. Everybody's rights!"

"Yeah, they wanted me to be a bilingual secretary. Baby, can you go get us some Cuba Libres?"

Erica buys the next round because she feels she must, and gives them the sketch. "It's not very good, just a quickie," she demurs, but they love it. She knows she should be going, but there's more rum, and now she's telling them about Yucatan, with the Cuban music and Cuban shirts and the Mayan women in their traditional dresses carrying great sacks of produce on their braided heads to market. "Once I met this Mayan farmer who told me his little corn plants were his children. I was a gringa in a strange land there too," she grins.

Nearby two guys start shoving each other, a chair crashes, and a woman screams.

"Time to split," says Sonny. They grab their stuff and head out. On the street, Erica and Carmen exchange phone numbers.

She's pleasantly surprised when Carmen calls her a couple days later. They make plans to meet at a little Puerto Rican restaurant Carmen knows uptown on the West Side. Erica notices the mole above Carmen's lip and the green flecks in her brown eyes, which she'd missed at dark Zamba's and which she'll add to the portrait she wants to start immediately. They drink Piña Coladas, order paella, and are soon trading intimate details of their lives, the way women do. Erica tells Carmen about Jimmy Loveness. "I'm not making it up!" she protests, laughing, when Carmen cracks up over "the Mother sent me." She thinks that Carmen's face is made for laughing. She lights up when she talks about Sonny; "we're best friends too," she says, "but we don't live together, my parents are very old school that way." In every other way, Carmen seems as independent as any white woman in New York.

After the meal, they take a walk down Broadway, then head west over to the Hudson. People out walking their dogs, jogging, night turning the light dusty, like a smoke-filled room. They lean over a railing, staring at the oily dark river and Carmen starts shrieking, "Did you see that? That . . . that?"

"Shit, it's a sheep!" Erica says.

The black-and-white carcass is whirling along, limbs to the sky, having drifted from God knows where.

"Around my neighborhood, sometimes you see dead chickens in the park—for *Santería,*" Carmen explains. "But a dead sheep? That's a new one."

They turn back towards Broadway and Carmen takes her arm companionably; Erica used to see girls in Mexico link their arms this way.

"Wanna stop for coffee?"

But Carmen can't, she has a paper due.

"I've got an assignment too. A new painting. Of you."

"Me?" Carmen looks entranced.

"I'll give it to you when it's done," Erica says, and in the darkness, she blushes.

Carmen invites Erica to dinner at her apartment on a Friday night. It's a big, shabby building not far from City College on Convent Avenue. The apartment makes Erica feel—once again—like she's back in Mexico: the faded pastel walls, the doilies on the plastic-covered furniture, the framed picture of the Virgin. Even the narrow dining room with its flowered tablecloth. Carmen's parents are surprisingly elderly, with the slightly bewildered look of displaced people. They are hospitable to her, even more so when Erica speaks Spanish with them. "This girl speaks a good Castilian!" Mrs. Vasquez exclaims, as if it is a miracle, a minor one anyway. In fact, Erica is—not surprisingly—more fluent than Carmen, who has never lived in a Latin American country. Mrs. Vasquez, wearing an apron, serves them all portions of flank steak, pureed potatoes, salad, and Coca-Cola. After the meal, she insists—in Spanish—that "you girls go enjoy yourselves, leave me to my kitchen," as "Papi" Vasquez, a man of few words, nods his head benignly. Carmen and Erica leave, heading for Carmen's neighborhood hangout. Sonny isn't going to meet them, she says, he has to study for his Law Boards.

They order beer but, as Carmen seems to know everyone, soon people are buying them drinks and Erica switches to rum. The jukebox is great: R&B, soul, Wes Montgomery.

"I met him once, in this bar I waitressed in in college," Erica tells Carmen, "a jazz hangout called Damian's. We had to wear these little black miniskirts with tight t-shirts with DAMIAN'S in red letters. So I get introduced to Montgomery and he doesn't say anything. Nothing. Just stares at my chest."

"Well you do have great tits," says Carmen.

Erica laughs uneasily and picks up her drink. Is she supposed to say, *You do too?* Then a guy comes up and puts a hand on Carmen's shoulder, how you doin', where's Sonny, that lucky son of a bitch. Erica, Ramon, Carmen introduces them; she's an artist. Oh yeah? He's a dark, Puerto Rican-looking guy in a suit, a lawyer, Carmen says. Erica thinks he looks like a thug. Carmen shows off her engagement ring, Ramon eventually suggests they go to this club a little farther uptown. He has a car, he says. It's, uh-oh, another *white Jaguar.* Isaac Hayes on the box, killer weed.

"What kind of lawyer is he?" Erica whispers in the back seat, Ramon alone in the front like a chauffeur.

"Defense attorney, does a lot of pro bono work for the community."

The club is way uptown, as it turns out, in a bad neighborhood, but, as Erica has learned, you never can tell: Inside is a kind of royal theme, red and gold. *Probably this is where Ramon gets his clients,* Erica thinks, then she is sure she spots Scotty. She moves into a crowd of dancers, finds her way to the other end of the bar. By this time Ramon is nowhere to be seen and she is seriously thinking about how she's going to get home. Carmen is partying hard, even harder than Erica, not exactly like a girl who just got engaged. She's throwing her arms around her partners, making deep Latin hip rolls. At last, spotting Erica, she comes to the bar and throws her arms around her. "I love this place!" As she laughs, her raspberry lips glisten; in fact, everything about her glistens.

Erica says yeah but she hates disco even with a Latin beat and she is determined to go home. "Carmen, I gotta split now," she tells Carmen.

"Oh come on, it'll be so much easier if you just crash at my place."

They end up in somebody's car, dropped off on the corner of the Vasquez apartment building. Carmen holds a finger to her lips when they enter the dark apartment; laughing into one hand, she pulls Erica down the hall past her sleeping parents' room to her bedroom, a small room—just a bit larger than Erica's—but a young girl's room, a single bed piled with stuffed animals. A dresser with a frilly skirt. And the room is spinning. All Erica wants to do is lie down on the fluffy rug and be still. She does and it feels good.

"Oh, you're shivering." Erica feels a warm blanket and a pillow slipped under head. "There." Yes, this is good, what she needs, but now, suddenly, there is movement, Carmen has slipped in beside her, her hands, warm and smooth, massaging Erica's forehead. "Better?" Gradually in the pale darkness, Erica can distinguish Carmen. She lies naked, toast-hued, her pointed raspberry nipples, her luxuriant bush (hinted at by the faint mustache that shades Carmen's lovely mouth), that lovely mouth on hers now. Erica lies still as Carmen begins to undress her, she raises her legs to get her jeans off and then . . . she remembers later thinking very briefly that the old people are just down the hall.

That's nearly all she remembers.

Mr. and Mrs. Vasquez seem unsurprised to see Erica the next morning when, sometime around eleven, she and Carmen shuffle into the kitchen. Mrs. Vasquez is doing her Latina thing, cooking a big casserole with onions, tomatoes, chicken, and yellow rice. She insists on serving "you girls" a big breakfast of toast and eggs and bacon and El Pico coffee. "Did you have a good time with your friends last night?" she asks Carmen tenderly in Spanish. Briefly, she strokes her daughter's hair. Erica is in an agony to leave. She eats as much as she can manage. The coffee does help.

Carmen wants to walk her outside when she is leaving. "Oh it's too much trouble, getting dressed, just for that. No, no, you stay here. Well . . . " Although she has never been in *this* situation before, it all feels familiar. Waking up the next day, running away. "Well. I'll see you later, then." Outside the air is gritty and grey, with the sense of a storm coming. The streets are full of poor people, Puerto Ricans, Dominicans, West Indians, white students—and trash. It flows out of wire baskets to line the pavement before all the little bodegas and botánicas and storefront churches. At a vacant lot filled with rubble, junkies in torn parkas, skinny and fat street girls, and idle old men stand around, not waiting for anything besides the next fix. On the next corner, customers stream in and out of an Orange Julius and as Erica continues to walk, she feels as if she is shriveling, drying up, her spirit fouled like her white jeans down where there is a large brown stain on one leg. She is frightened by how much she feels at home on these slum streets.

PINK SLIP

C hristmas of '75 comes and goes. Erica buys a tiny tree from the five-and-dime that twinkles plastically when plugged in. She sends a few cards and gets a package from home that she rightly suspects will contain stuff like potholders and kitchen towels— oh, and a check for a hundred bucks. She eats turkey breast and canned cranberries with John, a nice old sailor who has lived in the next building for decades. In that mysterious way of drinkers and druggies, they have unerringly found each other. They drink sherry, or rather she drinks most of it and John does most of the coke. He's an old, rugged, broken-down guy with traces of sex appeal, like Mickey Rourke or Nick Nolte and she likes listening to his tales about the neighborhood. Her favorite are those of a flirtatious Edie Desmond, who was actually good-looking twenty-five years ago and entertained boyfriends in her railroad flat while her husband drank during most of the twenty-four hours of each day in the nearby Blarney Stone. It's a farewell dinner, John says, he's moving to a retirement home for seamen in Brooklyn on New Year's Day as he can't cope with the stairs anymore. He's getting rid of a lot of stuff and Erica leaves that Christmas night with his gifts of pots and pans, coming back for a chair, a nice brass lamp, and a white fisherman's sweater still in its wrapper; also his plants. As a thank you, she invites him over to a dinner of tacos and salad and a cherry pie; John brings two six-packs and coke. Erica had had a short, mad love affair with coke in her early twenties, but had realized she's basically a downer person. Also, years before, her once-amiable neighborhood dealer, Frenchy, had turned into a gun-toting paranoiac on the stuff, confirming her fear of its powers. And her recent flirtation with black beauties only confirmed that her true love was the stuff that calms. She didn't bother running around for a new supply when the speed ran out. It had served its purpose—and then some. Really, she preferred booze.

Sometime during the second six-pack, John, who knows of her perennial money woes, mentions a job he's heard about from one of his many local contacts that he thinks will interest her. It's at this chichi wine store up on Madison: office work, off the books.

Erica goes there bright and early the next morning, the day before New Year's Eve, hangover and all, to apply. Several applicants have already beaten her to it, she sees. The little group sits in a de rigueur stuffily depressing room lined with empty wine boxes, carefully not making eye contact. Erica is about to bag it when her name is called by a saggy-looking man with bad skin, who also avoids eye contact, focusing on her (fudged) resume, in which she's worked for Philip as an "office assistant" for about a year.

"So why did you leave the job?" says the saggy man, poking a finger at the piece of paper.

"They're having a downturn," Erica responds, pulling that one out of a hat.

He nods glumly. "Hard times," he says.

Oh yeah, Erica thinks, *but rich people don't drink less expensive wine, ever.* She smiles. "As you may have noticed, my typing skills are excellent." This freakish ability of hers has landed her endless boring office jobs.

"Yeah," he says, and makes her take a typing test to prove it. Then she returns to the box-filled room, where now only one woman waits: a thin Italian girl in a cheap suit and tall, flesh-colored heels. Erica wishes she'd worn a suit, only she doesn't have one. She looks down at her black pants. What will happen if she doesn't get this job? She'll go back to a temp place, of course. It always seems to be drizzling when she's looking for a job. So far, no snow in Manhattan, just ice-cold January rain. But it's hot in this room; she's prickly with sweat.

The man is back. "Erica Mason?" She follows him, not hearing her sigh of relief. "Well," he says in his office, rocking back on his feet slightly, "You ain't kiddin'. 85 words a minute, no errors! The job is yours, sweetheart."

It seems there's a huge backlog getting invoices out because someone had quit during the holidays and meanwhile apparently most of the upscale Upper East Side winebibbing population has bought cases of vino at Madison Fine Wines.

That's just as well, Erica thinks. She won't have time to notice where she is, trapped again. The office is the usual glum set-up—grey metal desks with harsh fluorescent lighting, a nice contrast to the sleek, discreetly lit ground floor sales floor. The really good news is she gets 40% off selected wines. But it's a numbing routine job: a scanty lunch at her desk, more work. Uninteresting workmates. However, after a couple of weeks, there's a stunning new addition: a tall woman wearing a puce pantsuit, and is that a Cleopatra headdress and mask? Erica worries that she is having a major acid flashback, or else it is likely that this woman has escaped from a lockdown facility. In any case, it's way past Halloween.

"Listen to this, you're not going to believe it, not even in New York," Erica tells Philip that evening on the phone. "So, I'm sitting at my desk this morning at the wine store, bored as usual. And then suddenly there's this, this creature. Walking through the office, saying hello to people. This super-straight dude in accounts receivable says, 'Hi, Candace, welcome back, how was your trip?' OK, so, remember Liz Taylor in *Cleopatra*? I loved that movie, by the way. She's in this purplish pantsuit, normal-ugly, but oh my God, this make-up—like gouache, just layers of it, inches thick, I swear, Philip, and slabs of eyeliner and this pink foundation and false eyelashes and her lipstick! But—get this—she has on a

Cleopatra headdress, yes she does! With snakes curling around it and these black ridges of hair. Beyond Central Casting. But she *works* there! She's the boss's sister."

Philip chuckles. "You better be telling me the truth. Cause if I come over there to see this Liz babe and you lied to me . . . "

"Yeah, come tomorrow, so you'll know I'm not making this up."

"Ho-ly shit," he says, after he does come to the wine shop office. "You gotta paint this one, Erica."

Since the wine store is an easy walk from Erica's apartment, the theory is she has plenty of time to paint. And Philip is right, of course: She has to paint Candace/Cleopatra. But she's well into her portrait of Carmen now, a dreamscape prompted by all the Impressionists she's loved—with a sixties twist. A languid nude, a tropical wash of mangos, bananas, limes, the skin tone of milky coffee, but the face is all slashes of harsh psychedelic color. Like a militant modern Mona Lisa, this Carmen resists the viewer. Nightly, Erica stops painting suddenly, wrings out her brushes and grabs—at last!—the glass of wine she resists until she is done working. She flops onto her newest acquisition: an only slightly shabby velveteen chaise lounge she found in a secondhand shop. She calls it her fainting couch: an ideal seat from which to brood, to stare at the painting until she is sick of it and wants to—not destroy it, but throw it away. And resist calling Carmen. An ideal place to drink her lovely discounted wine and smoke and ignore the occasionally ringing phone.

On a Saturday afternoon, done battling the canvas and having her first glass of a good Pinot Noir, there's a knock at her door. "Just a minute!" She splashes water on her face and combs her fingers through her tangled hair, assuming it's Edie Desmond. Since doing her portrait, the super has become friendly in a slightly awed way, as if Erica has given her a touch of immortality. She and Edie had gone through her closet of awful clothes, settling on Edie's Christmas best: a shiny, tent-like red dress printed with holly leaves. Still, Erica is determined to force the long-buried glamour of Edie's younger days to the surface of the canvas, a tenement Sunset Boulevard *Norma* Desmond.

But it is Carmen, smiling, annoyed. "Finally! I've called and called but you're never there."

"Working." Erica steps aside slowly. "Wine?" She pours two glasses before Carmen can answer, her hands shaking so that she spills half a glass. Carmen doesn't see this; she has plopped down on the fainting couch.

Erica sets the glasses down carefully in the living room and leans against the wall, crossing her trembling hands across her abdomen. "So, how are you?"

"So, I am fine. And I am here because we're throwing the most amazing wedding party ever, at Roseland! *Every*body's going to be there. First Saturday in February, from one o'clock 'til five. And of course, Erica, I had to invite *you.*"

"Well, that's great, super," Erica fumbles. Suddenly her stomach heaves. She groans.

"Erica, what's the matter, you look *green.*"

"Something I ate." Erica mumbles, "I'll be right back," and heads for the bathroom. She heaves into the toilet twice, slowly feels better. Her face is unfamiliar to her in the mirror, this woman with shadowed eyes, almost gaunt. Yes, she has lost weight. She pulls herself together.

"OK now," she says, returning.

Carmen has been staring at her portrait on the easel. Usually Erica turns the easel to the wall when she's done working, but with the Carmen, she hasn't.

"That's *me*?"

"Yes."

"I look . . . distorted . . . "

The doorbell rings again before Erica can respond and Erica remembers suddenly, "Oh shit, that's Philip." They'd made plans to go check out this new Brazilian singer for the magazine, Erica sketching. Philip's immediately taken over by Carmen in the apartment, invited to the "best party ever" along with Erica.

"Sure," he says. Erica can't tell if he means it.

"Philip and I are going to check out this singer for the magazine," Erica explains. She looks down at her paint-covered jeans. "I'll just go change."

From the bedroom, she hears Carmen's bubbly laugh, Philip's raspy drawl. Erica sits down on the bed and shivers. She still doesn't feel great. What would Philip think if he knew what had gone down between her and Carmen that drunken night in her apartment, the so very *engaged* Carmen? Maybe Carmen had been too drunk to remember? Erica doesn't remember much— but enough. And for God's sake, what about Sonny? It's all fucked up, yet Carmen is fine and dandy. That's the way to play it, Erica tells herself, pulling off her jeans. All you did was get trashed and have sex with somebody you never intended to, that's all. OK, another woman. OK, and now you know for sure that's not for you. Dressed, she brushes her teeth and puts on a little makeup, cologne.

"Hi," she says, standing in the kitchen.

"Hey, you look good!" Carmen says smiling. "Doesn't she, Philip?" Carmen holds a glass of wine.

Philip's unfortunate complexion mottles further. "Yeah."

It's still light outside, the streets filled with early bar hoppers, people coming home from work. They drop Carmen off at the subway entrance.

"Call me," she says, looking at Erica.

"That's an interesting chick, where'd you meet her?"

"Oh, you know, just around. Tell me, what's this gig about?"

She half-listens. Follows Philip into a red-and-gold Chinese restaurant where they're led to a banquette with a good view of a tiny space with a piano. The place is more than half-filled.

"That party, with the salsa band, maybe we can do a piece on it," Philip says, digging into his Szechwan chicken. Always thinking about the magazine.

"Maybe." Erica doesn't want to think about Carmen anymore.

The new singer is doing Brazilian stuff, the usual great Jobim songs. She and Philip get busy with the notes and sketching between bites. The singer is striking in an ugly way, or ugly in a striking way, alabaster skin and long, bushy, blonde African hair. They are out on the street by ten-thirty.

"So?" Philip demands. He makes it a rule never to talk about the music while in the club.

"Nice, but . . . she ain't saying nothing new."

Philip laughs. "You're always tough."

"Just honest. And she's not the new bossa nova queen." Erica had inhaled a balloon glass of brandy at the end of the set and longs for another. She'll have it when she gets home; a bottle of Remy is stashed under the kitchen sink.

But Philip, who usually wants to rush off and finish his copy, lingers uncharacteristically, not only walking her home, but settling in on the couch, not the chaise. Erica makes coffee, adding a surreptitious, generous splash of Remy to her cup. It is not that she minds Philip's company. She enjoys his wry, world-weary New York wit. And now, the Remy leavens her mood. She feels horny. She's thought idly about what going to bed with Philip would be like, but only idly. Still, tonight he seems different, restless, glancing at her without saying anything. To her surprise—Philip's a temperate Jewish guy—he asks if she has something to drink in the house.

Erica laughs. "Remy Martin OK with you?" They abandon the coffee cups for cognac. She puts some smoldering Miles on the box, sits beside him on the couch. They end up in the bedroom, pulling off their clothes, rolling around on the single bed. But Erica can't get into it. Like Tinker Bell dancing on the ceiling, her other, sober self is looking down on the scene and asking what she has gotten herself into again. She's hoped they could delight in each other as lovers, but sex gets in the way of friendship or maybe it's the other way around. She knows this!

Afterwards, Erica reaches for her thrift shop robe and offers Philip a drink, needing one herself. He only wants water. Clothed again, he sits against the wall holding his glass, like a little boy, sheepish, maybe even a little afraid. He must have been teased a lot as a kid, Erica thinks, but she won't do that to him. She'll be kind to this homely man who makes her laugh—and who gives her paying work. He is about as sexy as a piece of fish but she kisses him goodbye. *Oh my God, I've done it again.*

When Philip calls a couple days later, Erica's relieved but a little hurt at his businesslike manner. He has a couple of assignments for the magazine, just sketches, no copy, and, oh, he's sorry, it turns out he's busy when Carmen is having the party at Roseland. Nothing is said about their night together.

Erica decides she'll be busy that day too. She spends the day cleaning the apartment, avoiding the easel with Carmen's unfinished portrait.

Something isn't right. Erica finds herself plodding home from work, picking at dinner, in bed at granny hours. And strangest of all is her relationship with booze. She and wine have separated, although she'd tried hard to keep things going. But wine, cognac, beer—even coffee—taste awful now, almost rancid. It's gotta be the flu. But for six weeks? *No*, she thinks. *No, it can't be!* It had been about six weeks ago that she and Philip . . . and she hadn't used her IUD.

It takes her two days to make it to the Duane Reade (the one out of her immediate neighborhood) for one of those home pregnancy kits. She feels nauseous the whole way, nothing new now, though oddly enough, once she has bought the kit and stowed it in her bag, she feels better, as if doing so has canceled out the chance that she might be—but she won't even think the word. That would be giving it too much power. It's a Saturday, cool but bright and she decides to head home down First Avenue, stopping at a grocery store to buy more breakfast cereal, eggs, bread, milk, and bananas. That's all she wants to eat lately.

After heading south for a few blocks, Erica realizes she has made a bad choice. She'd forgotten the school playground, which, as usual, is full of squealing, running kids, little kids in jeans and sweaters, some with knitted hats. She watches them like a mother, hungry, avid, in love. A little girl in pink with just one mitten, crying, and a woman, obviously her mother, flying towards her. A thin boy pushes past another kid at the top of the slide and whizzes down, yelling. And Erica turns away.

The kit confirms it, the fateful strip turned the dreaded pink, so on Monday Erica calls the Planned Parenthood clinic off Fifth Avenue and gets an appointment for later that week. It's easy to find the clinic among the posh doctors' offices in the former mansions. There is a small but noisy throng, people holding up signs with fuzzy, blown-up photos of fetuses and **STOP THE BABY KILLINGS, MURDER IS A SIN**. Erica is afraid they all know why she is pushing past them. And yes, they do. A young woman, about her age and mad as hell, points and shouts, "Don't kill your baby!" Erica reaches a cleared space in front of the granite building as several gum-chewing, overweight policemen keep the surging crowd back.

Inside is quiet and order. She rides alone up the elevator to the clinic, where there are the usual old magazines in the waiting room, people in plastic chairs, mostly women, also a few men, women who are young and middle-aged, mostly but not all white. There are the usual forms to fill out. Erica checks "no" next to alcohol and drug use, sits and waits with the rest until her first name is called. Then it's all routine on the clinic's part. An exam, confirming the results of her home pregnancy test, a conversation with a nurse practitioner who discusses the options. She nods her head vigorously. Yes, yes, this is what she wants.

The nurse explains what will "ensue." "*Out*sue," Erica feebly jokes. The nurse doesn't respond, just asks if she'd like something to calm her down? Yes, of course. Yes, yes, yes, she would indeed. Soon she's lying in a room without windows in the thick-walled building, imagining those people outside, the woman her age rushing in to save her from her decision. The room is very quiet and she's floating on some delicious unknown pharmaceutical that she would like to get up and rummage for in the cabinets for later, except she can't move. After the procedure, a kind of vacuuming of her innards that feels like intense cramps but is over quickly, she is helped to a cot in another tiny room. "Stay here as long as you want." *Well, that might be forever,* Erica thinks. She closes her eyes. Later, the clinic calls her a cab that is waiting at the end of the block, past the protestors.

At home Erica takes the Demerol she's been given and is asleep instantly. She's awakened at some point by hunger and the need to go to the bathroom, which is more of an ordeal than she'd thought it would be: Wasn't it supposed to be 1-2-3, this vacuum business? She heats a can of soup, eats a few spoonfuls. Back to bed. Her dreams are vivid. Carmen sitting next to her, pouring something—a sangria, apparently, not her first.

"It was all a mistake."

"Things just happen sometimes." Carmen pats her hand.

The dream swerves and Erica screams at Carmen. "How could you do that to me?" She smashes the pitcher of sangria against the wall, leaving a huge red stain and Erica jolts awake. An hour later, coffeed-up, she sets up the neglected Carmen painting, revenge flowing through her paintbrush. Her Carmen is cracked down the middle.

PASSINGS

Dear Mom and Dad,
Great news about your trip next fall! It's been way too long. Fall can still be very warm here, so pack appropriately. We can definitely go to Central Park—the leaves change much later than in Wisconsin, you'll be amazed. As for my apartment, it's small but cheap and safe. That's the important thing in this city. Work is OK, a paycheck. My Spanish and my typing have been "marketable skills." But I'm not really an office-type person, as you know! I'm still doing my art. There are about a million artists in New York—literally—so needless to say, the competition is tough. But of course it's a very stimulating city. I'm sorry I haven't been that great about staying in touch, but we'll catch up next month. See you then!

Love,
Erica

"Sonny Rollins?"

"The one and only great tenor sax."

She has avoided Philip and he has avoided her, but eventually work brings them together. When he calls her to go hear—and draw—this great musician, she says only, "When?"

Erica is feeling better. There are days she almost persuades herself that the whole Planned Parenthood business didn't happen, but she's surprised how long it has taken. And she's cleaned up her act, avoided buying the discounted wine ever since the procedure. All winter and spring she's been painting, allotting herself only a modest beer or two with her evening meal, the occasional joint. Workin' on the chain gang at the wine shop. She's nearly done with the Carmen painting at last. She's decided to send it to Carmen as a belated wedding gift.

She's wearing a new skirt of pretty Greek cotton, for once not bought secondhand, which swirls around her as she walks and walks through the park. As dilapidated as it is, and sometimes dangerous (she always stays on the main paths), neglected like everything else in this era of budget slashes, union fights, and the din of a more dire fate to come if New York does go officially bankrupt, Erica craves grass and trees and the sound of birds. The heat on this late June afternoon is heavy, the green-grey trees in the park droop as listlessly as the people. Most are sitting on benches, the usual crew of old people, office workers, and the homeless. Children sullenly lap ice cream or drink soft drinks, mothers or nannies motionless beside them. *Outcasts,* Erica thinks, *we're all the outcasts. Stuck in the heat. Everybody who can afford it flees to beaches, mountains, somewhere else. And we're what remains.* The park itself seems depressed, like a play with a sparse, indifferent audience. She's used to heat from her Mexico years, but not this thick, foul air. By the time she reaches Philip's rent-controlled apartment (inherited from his parents when they moved away—the most coveted of prizes for a New Yorker), she almost falls into his arms when he opens the door of his capacious, ramshackle place.

She always pretends nothing happened between them that unfortunately memorable night months ago, and has promised herself never, ever to tell him about Planned Parenthood. But now she feels Philip tense against her and she steps back. Before he looks away, she sees his haunted expression and understands that he is in love with her.

"I'm just a little overheated. I walked here."

Recovering quickly, he says, "You walked in this heat? What are you, insane? It's a furnace out there."

"Yeah, I'm probably insane."

They head for the living room, which is filled with shabby, comfortable chairs—his parents', obviously—and Philip's hundreds, no thousands, of records. The air conditioner hums. Philip brings her a Coke with ice.

"This is the life," she says, trying not to be awkward. Fortunately, there are the photos to go through, Sonny Rollins on the record jackets Philip has pulled from his vast collection. He is almost too striking, so tall and planed, kinglike. Erica decides she'll draw him when he's not playing, but listening. Work for the body language. *Sonny,* she thinks suddenly, *Carmen's fiancé. Or husband now. Carmen, shit.*

She watches Philip's lumpy body in the baggy chinos and short-sleeved shirt that constitute being dressed up for him, and remembers him nuzzling into her. His chalk-white body. "God, you're beautiful," he'd said. Standard-issue pillow talk, but from him it meant something.

The doorbell trills and he goes to get the Chinese food he'd ordered. They spread it on the coffee table, pushing the piles of papers to one side. There are dumplings and spicy chicken with snow peas, rice, fortune cookies: "The night life is for you," Erica reads aloud and they crack up.

Philip reads his: "You are magnetic in your bearing. Yeah, that's why I get all the chicks."

Erica says quickly, "Tell me more about Rollins." Philip Bookman is a walking encyclopedia of the players and the music.

"OK, the weirdest gig I ever saw him at. When he had the Mohawk? The Blue Note, packed of course. The whole first set, all he does is run scales. Brilliant, but only *scales.* The sidemen are playing their brains out, no expression. And he doesn't stop. Even his fans couldn't take it, a lot of them walked out. He finishes and there's this silence. Some tentative claps. Sonny bows and walks off. And then the next set, when the place is half empty, he's on fire again." Philip shrugs. "You never know what you're gonna get with Rollins."

"That should make tonight interesting."

They walk down Broadway slowly, not touching, yet she can feel his desire. She chatters about the sea of people they pass, all these Columbia students, these tiny old Jewish people with shopping bags, these junkies in the medians on broken park benches, these hookers on the corners. "You're trashing my neighborhood!" Philip objects, pointing out the bookstores, Zabar's, the little Ethiopian and Chinese restaurants. Erica sings, "New York, New York, it's a helluva town!" and takes his arm suddenly. She wishes in that moment that she could feel the way he does about her, all the way into the Blue Note, and then their familiar roles, Philip writing furiously, Erica sketching, Rollins blowing West Indian musical breezes this night, so strong she thinks she can almost feel the fire burning in the great musician's belly. But there is this secret sadness, this shame, that Philip doesn't know is between them.

Deep South heat holds all the way to the end of September. On the way home from her lousy job (which has the terrific perk of strong air conditioning, unlike her apartment), Erica often lingers at the rundown playground next to the yellow-brick school with metal grates on all its windows like prison bars. Erica stands outside the fence with a coffee. She accepts the sad swelling of her heart. It's fitting, she deserves it. It may never be for her, to be part of the magic circle of parents who contentedly watch their children. There are afternoons when she walks right by, ignoring the playground, the shrill whoops and cries. On those days she is a New York woman with things to do, shopping, books to read, bottles of wine to open, the painting of course, maybe an assignment at a club.

She is working on the Cleopatra painting. Cleopatra, the accountant queen of a wine shop. The challenge, the necessity, is to go beyond the bizarre in Candace and find her there. Otherwise she will have a caricature. Erica fears that this is happening. She watches Candace obsessively at work, this woman who is never without the hallucinatory headdress, the over-the-top makeup, but is also a whiz at the calculator. In fact, Candace has the flat eyes of an accountant or a judge.

One morning, Erica finds the crack, the vulnerability, literally, in Candace's inches-thick pancake makeup. A crack has formed down her cheek. *So this is it,* Erica thinks. She rushes home from the wine store and works late into the night on the painting, drinking strong coffee, nothing else, and calls in sick the next morning, and again the next. "Cleo in New York," a scrum of accountants and office "girls" in the background, nicely grey, in charcoal. As a joke, Erica paints herself among them. She stops, pours (at last!) a glass of cadged Pinot Noir, regards the puce pantsuit, the death mask, the long crack along the cheek that becomes an open wound oozing blood and pus. *Not a pretty picture!* she thinks. *Definitely not.* Before she lays into the Pinot Noir seriously, she calls Philip. "It's done! Cleo is done, man." He suggests she bring it to the office next week, they'll have lunch and celebrate.

Erica carries the wrapped painting to work in a large shopping bag on the following Monday. There are mounds of invoices on her desk, stacked up during the days she called in sick to work on Cleo. She has a headache, a hangover that presses harder on her forehead as she removes the first invoice and begins typing. Minutes later, she types "Chardonnay," and then stops.

"Going to the ladies room," she says to the room at large. She gathers up her coat, her bag, the shopping bag with the painting, and leaves the office, finds a pay phone on the corner and calls Philip. Fortunately, he's in. "Don't come to the office," she tells him. "Come over to my apartment. We'll have sandwiches. I just quit my job."

She celebrates her liberation that night, taking the subway downtown to the loft where she'd met Jimmy Loveness. She hasn't seen him in months, putting him off, tunneled between labor and painting. Maybe he'll be at the loft tonight. In any event, she has that periodic need to bust out and have an adventure.

A tall, slim brown woman in a caftan, one of the musicians' wives or girlfriends, looks at her suspiciously when she asks about Jimmy, who's not there.

"Jimmy Loveness?" She draws out his last name so it sounds like four syllables instead of two. "Why you asking?"

"Well, he's a friend of mine." Erica is suddenly acutely aware she's one of the very few white people in the loft. The woman says nothing, looks at her. "I thought I'd come by to say hello," Erica adds, "I haven't seen him in a while."

The woman suddenly inhales sharply. "Come over here and sit down."

In the corner of the loft farthest from the musicians, who have taken a break, she points to a cushion on the floor. Erica sits awkwardly, her bag with the sketchpad banging on her knees.

The woman lowers herself more gracefully. "So you haven't heard about Jimmy." She closes her eyes and her head moves, back and forth. "Jimmy Loveness. Lord have mercy. He was cut, near that flophouse he lived at, some crazy wino did it. That most peaceful soul."

Erica feels a vein drumming in her forehead. "Will he be all right?"

"Honey, Jimmy Loveness *passed*. Bled to death on a rotten wino street where he didn't have no business being."

"Oh, God." Her head pounds.

"Not seven days ago. Havin' a memorial here for him tomorrow, raisin' money to help his family."

Family? Jimmy? Erica sees his face, that last time he'd visited her, his big gentle smile, his strange words, his long hands smoothing the pages of her sketchpad. "This is dynamite," he'd said; he talked a combination of hippie and hip. That darling man. Erica wants to cry, to scream, but most of all, to get out of there.

She says, "I can't believe it."

The woman stands up. "Believe it," she says. She touches Erica's shoulder.

Erica finds her way to the subway. The people on the train are menacing, in black-and-white like an old film noir. She stops at the liquor store that stays open late for a bottle of Remy. She sits at home in the dark, listening to all of the saddest jazz she can find. Mostly Billie Holiday. At some point, she calls up Philip.

"Shit, Erica, it's the middle of the night."

"Do you know about Jimmy Loveness? He's been murdered."

"What?"

"Jimmy. Loveness." She tells him what the woman at the loft said. "Who could have done this to Jimmy, he was—he was like a puppy. He was in love with me, too." She's crying now.

"What? Erica, are you drinking? Pull yourself together."

"You know what he said? He said the Mother sent him to me. I thought it was *funny*. The Mother. But really he was like this— like a holy man in India who gave up everything: playing music, money, sex."

"Erica, look. This is horrible news. But I have a meeting in the morning with Mark about the magazine that's real important. Try to get some sleep, OK? We'll talk tomorrow. Get some sleep."

Philip joins her at the loft the next evening for the memorial. African robes, herb in the air. A Buddhist monk in a corner chanting. All kinds of people, including guys from the Mission. Erica cradles her sketchbook during the music. Archie Shepp towers on the saxophone, Leon Thomas's huge voice. No drummer today, Jimmy's sticks are crossed above the kit. When the music stops, she goes to the wall behind the drums.

"I'd like this to be up on the wall."

The portrait of Jimmy she's worked on had dictated itself in pastels, Jimmy in three-quarter profile, looking beyond the picture, smiling as always. Wearing a pure white robe, African. Behind him, craggy mountains, mist, a high lone bird. She affixes it with masking tape she's brought.

A man holding a flute tells her it's beautiful. "I knew Jimmy. Not for long, but . . . "

"Yeah, Jimmy got to everybody. He was a pure soul," says the flutist. More people are coming by to look at her picture, black, white, Asian. Shepp takes up his horn again, unleashing a riot, a fierce lament that has Erica in tears. Philip sits writing fast, flipping pages. Roy Haynes comes by, the master drummer there to pay his respects. Sam Rivers steps in, more singers. Joints are passed and Erica inhales, still crying. She thinks about how she had fought to keep her laughter from exploding that afternoon when Jimmy declared himself. How she'd been *entertained* by him, someone to add to her collection. Like Cleopatra. She feels unclean. It had been so easy not to take him seriously.

Philip looks sad too. Everyone is sad. Black men cut down so often, jazz musicians among them. But there is, thank God, another element here. The flutist whose name she doesn't know plays sweetly, a bittersweet Japanese-sounding refrain.

At last, as the room is beginning to empty out, Philip says, "I think we should go now. Don't forget the picture—I want it for next month's cover."

CAN'T GO HOME

F all of 1976 is late, too warm and dry, the leaves hanging burnt on the trees. Erica's parents are coming soon. She prepares for their visit, scrubbing the apartment, hanging Indian fabrics at the windows, buying a cotton rug. Knowing they'll still see it as a hippie crash pad. She hasn't looked for a new job yet, even though money is tight. She just can't, she can't face those dingy offices, those sharp-nailed temp "associates" who rifle through her fudged resume, who see her as a typing whizz without face or form or feelings. So for the moment, Erica cuts back on groceries and buys cheap wine.

Marjorie and Ken call from the Sheraton when they get in from the airport. Erica walks over for a late lunch with them, wearing her most conservative skirt and blouse as a sop, thinking as she dresses of the time—she had been 18? 19?—and she'd showed up with a new pair of jeans and turned around to show them the American flag sewn across the butt. Dad, World War II vet and POW, turned white and her mother actually yelled at her, a rare show of emotion. Yes, she had put them through it . . .

When Erica enters the lobby of the Sheraton, she spots them immediately, a middle-aged couple, a little greyer and heavier than the last time they'd been together. They could be anybody's parents, her mother smoking a Marlboro, her father looking at the *Times*. So obviously a couple, always presenting a united front. Always taking the other's side: "Your mother thinks . . . ", "Your father is upset that you . . . " She feels a rush of love and anger and sadness, opposing currents in a rough river.

"Hi there," she says, standing before them.

Her father gets up immediately. "Hi there, honey!"

"Hello, dear," her mother adds. She remains seated.

Hugs all around, Erica bending over her mother to kiss her. It feels unnatural to Erica.

"We thought we'd have a nice meal here, then take a little walk if you'd like. Your father has a dinner meeting so he'll need a little rest after that and I know you have to work tomorrow too, but we have tomorrow evening free."

"We'd like to take you out to dinner then," Ken adds.

It is so like Marjorie to suggest having a "nice meal" at the hotel, the last place Erica would have suggested in a city that teems with good restaurants. Insipid chicken salad, soup, conventioneers.

"Fine."

Afterwards they walk down to the park a few blocks away. Marjorie and Ken exclaim how warm it is here in New York, how the trees still haven't shed their leaves; back home in Milwaukee, there'd been hard frost weeks before. They both unzip their jackets. They stroll over to the little lake. "Those people! They're feeding the ducks, right under the sign that says not to." When a beat cop ambles by soon after, Marjorie says, "I'm going to inform that policeman."

"Mom, he has other things to do," Erica murmurs. *Like catching rapists and muggers,* she thinks.

Her mother pouts minutely. "Well, fine." It all comes back to Erica, perfectly preserved: Marjorie's abrupt withdrawals into hurt silence, her mouth set, her bedroom door closing. Erica, the cause of so many of them.

Ken buys them pretzels from a cart near the Plaza Hotel, which they all pretend to enjoy. They stand on the corner breathing the nasty sweat of the drooping carriage horses waiting for fares. A homeless guy stops nearby to root through a trash can, dislodging and eating a discarded hot dog. Marjorie murmurs, "I think it's time we headed back to the Sheraton, Ken."

"Honey, you know the restaurants here, pick out someplace special for tomorrow," Ken says. Erica feels petty and mean-spirited. He'll buy her a fancy dinner, after all, while she clings to her ancient adolescent resentments.

She says, "Arturo's across the street from my apartment is supposed to be really good." She's heard about the food, the bocce court in the back, also the made guys who hang out there sometimes, but she's never eaten there, of course. For her, a big splash is a Sabretto's hot dog from a cart.

Her parents come over in the late afternoon the next day, Marjorie over-perfumed and scarved, Ken in a sports jacket and tie. Erica shows them around her apartment, thinking how shabby this little old railroad flat must look to them. They make polite murmurs, sit on her freebie couch with more cheap Indian cotton covering its stains and rips, accept a glass of wine, look at her art. With a sudden urge to please them, grimly aware that it's another holdover from childhood, Erica turns a casual suggestion Philip has made about submitting her stuff to *The New Yorker* into a firm possibility that the magazine is going to publish it.

"Why, isn't that terrific!" Ken enthuses, "all those great cartoons!"

"And you love the Updike stories," Marjorie reminds him.

"And what about your job, how is that?" Ken prods, on a roll. *Job* to him of course means forty hours a week, while her art— even in *The New Yorker*—is a hobby, much like crocheting or beadwork. She knows he worries about her future.

"Oh Dad, it's just a gig to pay the rent. Just boring typing and stuff."

"But you're so talented, dear," Marjorie inserts, coloring. "You speak two foreign languages, and you always got good grades. Can't you find something that utilizes your talents?"

Erica is feeling that Alice in Wonderland shrinking sensation that her parents always invoke in her at some point in their company. *One pill makes you larger and one pill makes you small.* Now her voice takes on the edge of the chronically misunderstood teenager. "Mom. My art *is* my job."

Her mother, easily rebuked as usual, twists the handles of her black handbag.

"No need to snap at your mother, she just wants you—*we* want you—to live a fulfilling life and not have to worry about the bills." *And find a husband,* Erica adds silently.

Her mother adds valiantly, "Well, anyway, this seems like a very safe neighborhood. And your art work is very impressive, dear." She looks at her watch. "Well. I'll just go to the powder room before dinner."

Ken drains his wine glass and stares at a peculiar mask from Mexico she's mounted on the opposite wall, a wolf face complete with whiskers, carved in wood and painted. The Indian tribe — she can't remember which—that made it got totally ripped on mescal, then danced around all night. Wolves, eagles, jaguars . . .

"Honey," he says suddenly, "are you happy here?"

Well, this came out of the blue, Erica thinks. She shrugs. "Are you?"

"Yes. Because I have you and Claire, and your mother, of course." Ken lets out a long sigh, a whooshing sound. "One day, when you have children, you'll understand."

"I don't think so, Dad." She doesn't know if she means she'll never have children. Or just that she'll never understand.

At Arturo's, they perk up in the festive setting, candles on the tables, checked tablecloths, Al Martino on a tape, a basket of garlic bread, pasta, and red wine in a straw basket. Her parents tell her about their visit to the Museum of Modern Art that morning, the thrill of seeing Monet's *Water Lilies,* her mother's favorite painting. (Claire had loved it, too, Erica remembered. Ironic that she, a New York artist, is the one who hasn't seen the painting. There's really no excuse, is there?)

They've bought a print, which they'll have framed for the living room. "And this is for you, an early Christmas gift," Marjorie says, slipping a wrapped book out of a shopping bag while they're drinking their coffee (American for them, espresso for Erica).

Erica pages through the reproductions of 19th-century American art. She would have preferred a book on *modern* American art.

"It's beautiful," she says and smiles at them. These are her very nice parents, trying once again to bridge the gap with their difficult daughter, their wayward child.

"How about a nightcap at my place?" They're leaving tomorrow afternoon, back to the Midwest.

Her father looks at his watch. "I don't think we can. Up at the crack tomorrow for the airport," he says.

"Dad, it's nine o'clock."

"And all that wine with dinner," her mother adds. "We're pooped, dear."

They stand outside Arturo's, the wind blowing, waiting to hail a taxi.

"It was so lovely to see you, dear." Her mother kisses her rather formally on the cheek.

"You'll let us know about *The New Yorker.*" Her father hugs her briefly.

Erica waves them off. As he got into the taxi, Ken had slipped her a check. She opens it in the apartment. Five hundred dollars! There's the rent taken care of, groceries, Con Ed. She pours a brimming glass of cognac and sits back on the fainting couch, smiling about the unexpected freedom the check brings but perversely blinking away tears. The liquor doesn't take the weight off her heart. But it does an efficient job of diverting her.

LOVER MAN

A party full of clean-cut people with dazzling teeth, guys in suits and girls in suits with blouses with bows. Erica is there too, in her embroidered Guatemalan poncho, black turtleneck, and jeans. Toni, fresh out of college in her first job as a receptionist, who's recently moved in across the hall from Erica, has persuaded her to come along to the apartment of a rising young banker-type she knows. In one of those ugly box buildings. There are cases of inoffensive wine, tapes of soft rock playing, windows that overlook a concrete garden below. It's a mild Friday night in late January. Erica takes off her poncho and folds it over her arm. She doesn't want to lose track of it; she has lost plenty of things that way at parties. People are eyeing her, not hostile, more like, *who's the freak?* This is understandable, she's the only artistic-type in view. But, she thinks, *I'm not the freak here; you are.* She is sitting alone, munching cheese and crackers, topping off her wine glass, when Toni beckons, and Erica sees her in paint, a red-cheeked wholesome cherub. In five years, she'll be a mommy.

"Erica, here's another Tony. He's a riot."

Oh yeah, Erica gets it: Tony is a riot of cocaine-induced mania, the high of choice of ambitious New York, the sizzle to the steak of making it. Well, well, a little magic carpet ride. (She does, occasionally, break her no-coke rule.) Before long, she's got Tony in the bathroom, laying out lines on top of the toilet tank. Oh, he's a riot, coming on to her in the cramped space with a faint *eau de mildew.* As he claws at her, Erica says, "You're not funny anymore, Tony," and wrenches away. Back to the suits. She finds another empty chair by a coffee table covered with bottles of wine, some of them not yet empty, bottles of beer in a bucket of melting ice. At a moment like this, Erica realizes, she can make her choice: up or down? She could eat something, there's a mangled birthday cake on the other end of the table, to slow this hurtling through space. Or stay on the roller coaster. But she finds, drinking more wine, that this isn't such a good decision. The room is overheated, too loud. And these people who are not her tribe. They are disgorged from subways, buses, go-and-fro five days a week, thousands and thousands of them. *All the lonely people, where do they all come from? How do they stand it?* Erica's rush makes her feel passionately that she wants to know. There is only one thing to do, so Erica does it, she pours another glass of wine, some of it splashing on the table.

Erica is woken up on a feeble February dawn by pain. She runs her hands over her aching face and arms. There's a soft, squishy spot on her cheekbone. She's pressed against a wall, a man's shape next to her in an unfamiliar room. Snoring. She lies as if frozen, brain like a book whose pages are stuck together and won't open. OK, she's woken up with a stranger before, someone she met in a bar usually, no need to freak out. But she *hurts.* The shape stirs. She closes her eyes and whimpers. Hadn't she dreamt of something— or someone?—falling on her, tall, dark? Shouts. It was her making noise as he hurt her. And his name comes too, and the bar. Brian. Bartender. Somewhere farther up, another East Side saloon.

Erica climbs very slowly over the shape and out of the bed. All she can see is his head of thick black hair. The room is an attic with a sloping ceiling. Messy, pants and shirts heaped on the floor, empty pizza boxes, beer cans. She eventually locates her clothes, her bag and her poncho. In the tiny bathroom, she sluices water over her face and toothpaste into her mouth. Then she looks in the mirror. Her right eye is swollen and is turning yellow and purple; there are bruises on her arms. She goes to the bathroom, has dry heaves. And it clicks: She'd gone to a bar with Tony the cokehead and a few others from that party to some bar up in the 80s, and there she'd made a friend of the big jolly bartender Brian, a Remy friend. Pouring her refills, gold in her goblet. Little slices of the night keep coming up in her head like a Cubist painting, random slices. Holding each other up and singing on some street, stopping to laugh at the outrageousness of being hammered, and then . . . here. Where they started fighting because she didn't want to fuck him. She just wanted to sleep. So the big guy got pissed off and pushed and slapped her around.

Erica rakes her hair with her fingers. She opens the bathroom door softly, softly; what if he were awake, waiting for her? But he is an unmoving shape in the bed. Erica tiptoes to the apartment door, leaving it wide open: *fuck you, Brian,* and goes down six flights down to freedom. She leans against a wall outside, trembling. She finds her sunglasses but of course there are no cigarettes left, she always smokes them up when she's drinking. At a corner newsstand, she buys a pack and sucks down the smoke like life itself. The headlines of the papers at the newsstand say Sunday. Sunday! She's lost an entire twenty-four hours. It's not the first time she's lost chunks of time, but never this long. And she's never been beaten up before.

Late that day, the phone rings. "Hey, babe, it's Brian! You free tonight?"

Erica says, "Wrong number," and hangs up. She hopes to God she didn't give him her address during her lunacy. She lies under a blanket on the fainting couch with a cold compress on her face. She's taken some Tylenol, wishes she had something stronger, but she's in no shape to go drug hunting. A cold beer would be the thing, but getting up is too much of an effort. After a while, though, it isn't.

Philip calls with a gig a few days later, when the bruises have faded enough to conceal. "Sam Rivers, free jazz. At a loft—not, you know, the one Loveness went to."

"Oh, man," Erica protests. "Rivers is tough on the nerves, like listening to a chainsaw playing, I don't know, Negro spirituals. But OK." A gig is a gig. And she needs to get out of the apartment.

Philip gives her the address. "Tomorrow night at ten." He pauses. "I'll be covering Phil Woods at Fat Tuesday's, so you're on your own."

Maybe she'll meet somebody sane. A reasonable man. Wouldn't that be something. She has no clean clothes left so she bundles her laundry over to the basement of the building next door, where the tenants in her building have use of the washer and dryer. She is reading a paperback and smoking a cigarette, waiting, when a very dark, muscular man comes in whistling with a load of wash.

He sticks out his hand. "Thomas Thomas, I'm the new super here!"

He sounds so proud that she smiles. And Thomas Thomas?

He laughs. "Everybody look that way at my name. Blame my mama."

"I'm Erica Mason. I live next door." Thomas Thomas, besides being a friendly, garrulous guy, is also a restless one, she notices. He keeps getting up and down and looking around him. *Not a cokehead again,* she thinks. But when he invites her to stop by his place (first apartment on the right, ground floor, any time, come by and have a drink), somehow Erica knows it isn't a come-on, so she thinks, *Why not?* She has no other plans.

The dryer cycle ends and she heaps her clothes into the basket. "Nice meeting you, Thomas Thomas."

He chuckles, a little too long. Yeah, he's on something.

Erica decides to go downtown a little early and check out SoHo where the loft is. She's been there two or three times and wants to know it better. She's wearing a shirt from Chiapas, jeans, her old Frye boots. She reminds herself sternly that she is going out to work, not blow money in a bar.

She walks around SoHo, this once-crumbling area of dead or dying factories now being turned into lofts for artists, often with no heat, water, or plumbing. She's wishing she had new boots; the

Fryes have lasted since college, but there are cracks now beyond repair. It's a cold night and people hurry past. She comes upon an old cafeteria, likely a holdover for the factory workers of old. She drinks bad coffee, has a muffin, and smokes two cigarettes. The cafeteria, its fluorescent lights, cheap Formica tables, the sweating man in a stained apron rearranging steam trays and the elderly waitress with clotted lipstick, make her feel like she is in some old and not very good movie. *The place should be all black-and-white*, Erica thinks; automatically, she gets out her sketchpad to draw the waitress who leans against the counter, the porky cook, the Puerto Rican busboy with slicked-back hair and the old couple silently eating grey meat with grey string beans—perfect! She is happy again. Nobody bothers her.

Eventually the waitress approaches.

Erica slides her hand over the page. "More coffee?"

The waitress pours more of the bile-colored liquid into Erica's mug. Erica watches her closely: the pancake makeup, piggy nose, circles of blusher on her cheeks. A group comes in, talking loudly, they don't notice Erica.

They're talking about a friend's show.

" . . . Twelve percent, that's what he offered him! Can you fucking believe that?"

"Shit. He's desperate though."

"Only sold one, he's practically slitting his wrists."

"Getting fucked up for sure right now."

They laugh, edgily.

Erica drinks the glass of water she's had to ask for twice—why do New York restaurants hate to give patrons water, maybe because it's free?—and wishes she could spit it out on the floor to get rid of the nasty coffee taste. Or better still, a drink. Rum. She's gone through phases: gin, then vodka, even ouzo and tequila. That's all in the past. Now the rhythm is: wine, beer, beer and wine, wine and brandy, brandy, or rum. She packs up her stuff, leaves a dollar and a half, which includes a quarter tip, and goes over to the rowdy artists' table for directions to the loft.

Yeah, they know it. Someone points to the end of the street: three up, take a right one block, right again, middle of the block. No sign on it, but you'll hear the music. Is there, she wants to know, a reasonable bar on the way? "Reasonable?" someone says. She says, "Not a dive." They laugh. "They're all dives. Try Maxie's, it's the best. Corner of the third block up before you turn . . . you dig Rivers, huh?" Two of the guys are a lot older than her, one is a butch woman who ignores her, and another guy looks to be in his thirties. With the most alluring ice-blue eyes. It's not really my thing, Erica says about Sam Rivers' music, but it's money. She tells them about the magazine and the sketches and the guy with the intense ice-blue eyes, says suddenly, "I'll go over to Max's with you. If it's all right."

They introduce themselves as they walk.

"Anders Andersen," he says.

"Hey, that's almost as good as this guy I met today in the laundry room of my building—Thomas Thomas."

"Yeah, well," he says, "it's Icelandic."

"Wow," Erica says, "that's really exotic. Like being a Hottentot."

He shoots a look at her. They both laugh.

It's still early at Maxie's, with the regulation old guys, and one old woman, planted as if forever at one end of the bar. Erica and Anders go to a little table, Formica again, which looks out on to the dark, deserted street. It's nine-thirty. An hour later, they go over to the loft, where the music wails and thunders. Erica works fast. Anders leans back with his eyes closed. "I dig Blind Lemon Jefferson myself," he says, when they leave. They go to another bar and talk. Hours pass. Erica has only one drink; she's deep into his eyes already. Anders tells her he's an academic who hates academia, he's writing his doctoral thesis, it's almost done after seemingly forever. She doesn't understand it, something about philosophy linking schizophrenia and art, or the creativity of crazy people, maybe. Even though she's probably a crazy artist, he knows much more about art and insanity than she does, she can tell right off the bat. She doesn't care. She watches him: long, lean hands; lean, sensual mouth; those eyes.

"I'm just your garden-variety neurotic painter," she tells him at one point. But he wants to know more. So she explains the way she works, how she has to fall in love with something about a person, how she imagines people's lives, in her head, on paper or canvas. "It's not something I can *plan*. When I want to paint something, I just do it, the right medium presents itself. I'm just one step up from primitive," she says.

"You're selling yourself short," Anders tells her, laughing.

"No, I'm not. I'm fine with it."

They meet at Maxie's three days later. Then they meet in a café in Little Italy. Another on the Upper West Side. They walk and talk and listen to records. She's desperate to go to bed with him. As if he can give her what she's desperate for and never knew she needed before she met him. Every touch is liquid fire, cool and hot, honey and lava. How much she has needed this, needed him. She is amazed by her gratitude to him. They lie peacefully together, like spoons, until the fire builds again. It happens again and again. Every time for her. She has never understood women who give up their lives to be with a lover. Now she does but senses that it has to be her secret, her precious, burning, secret need.

It's only a month, in windy March, before Erica packs a suitcase and some art supplies and takes them to Anders' good-sized apartment on the Upper *Upper* West Side, in an old building where most of the tenants are Dominican. She stays there every weekend; Mondays to Fridays they have their own spaces. That's how Anders wants it. He also often has to work on his thesis on Saturdays, even some Sundays. After he emerges from his study, he unwinds, lying on the floor in his sparsely-furnished living room listening to his cherished blues records: Muddy Waters, Robert Johnson, Lightnin' Hopkins, Blind Lemon, and others Erica's never heard of. She wouldn't care if he loved polka or Muzak or punk. She is careful about the booze, sipping when she is with him. There is a bottle at the back of "her" part of his closet, behind some shoes.

In bed one Saturday night, Anders suddenly starts to tell her about his closest friend Adrian, who was also a painter. He dropped out of Harvard suddenly when he was twenty and moved to an unheated garage, where he made huge science-fiction murals on all the walls, then the floor. Anders was the only person allowed to see them. Then, abruptly, Adrian painted everything over in black, including himself, and was found on a Cambridge street painting over mailbox numbers. His parents managed to get him into McLean's, where Anders had what he calls a "surreally painful visit with him." But after Adrian left the psych ward, larded with Thorazine, he went back to the garage. "I saw him one last time there," Anders says, hugging his knees and rocking slightly but speaking in an even, matter-of-fact way. "He was off his meds, of course. Adrian would never tolerate anything fucking with who he was. He talked about how he needed to save the world by painting everything black because colors, including white, emitted pernicious . . . I don't know—vibes or chemicals—that got into people's brains and took them over. And a few days later he hanged himself."

Anders is staring at the rumpled bedclothes. "That day they found him in the garage was the worst day of my life, but it gave me my life's work. Those murals he did were like doors into the mental processes of a schizophrenic. I switched majors, went into psychology, philosophy, then art history."

Erica wants to say something to console him, but Anders gets out of bed and dresses. He'll be in his study, he says.

Sometimes he's sociable, taking her to friends' apartments and bars around Columbia, or down to little galleries where his friends have shows in heroin-soaked Alphabet City. They go up to the Village to this new little club they call CB's, which some artists tell them has "these fuckin' great bands, man." CBGB's is a grungy, post-hippie stoner bar with speed-skinny kids in skin-tight ripped jeans and leather jackets. They get some beer, find a table. Some scruffy-looking dudes get on the stage and start blasting.

The club kids love it, but Erica drains her glass and leans in to Anders. "Let's split."

"No baby, it's kind of fun to see what they're doing. It's *ironic-post-modernist*, Erica," he adds, as if she were "slow." "Wait until the set is over, OK?"

Out on Bowery and Bleecker, Erica lets out a huge sigh. "Shit," she says, "I need a drink."

Anders laughs. "Aw, come on, it wasn't that bad. The Ramones are the new big thing. And what about that Blondie? Punk rock, baby."

Erica feels a stab of rote jealousy. Blondie, some chick called Deborah something, is an enticing mix of sexy blonde and grunge, waving her great little butt in tight pants at the audience. "I call it retarded rock."

"Don't be so elitist, Erica."

"I'm not. I dig the blues. But this is like burnout music. I don't see any great irony here. It's posturing, it's hard-core junkieism, it's . . . "

Anders takes her arm and suggests they walk over to SoHo to Maxie's where he introduces her to a large, bearded sculptor called Wally. "A fellow artist," he says, and cuts off Wally's probably just-being-polite questions about Erica's work, saying, "No good talking theory to Erica, she claims she's a primitive, but she's really an elitist." After a tiny silence, Wally laughs and shows them a new piece he's done, stashed in a beat-up briefcase. It's a tiny black figure with outstretched arms, in one of them a gun. "Still doing Vietnam," he says, "but I've almost got it out of me system, I think." Erica ends up sitting on a chair drinking wine with Wally, pretending not to watch Anders, who's with a group of people she doesn't know, including a large-busted woman with damp black eyes and a lot of raven hair that she shakes and smoothes a lot.

When they get back to his apartment, Anders immediately makes love to Erica on the living room floor, then puts on a robe and sits reading intently. Erica, on the couch nearby with a blanket pulled around her, says, not able to remain silent any longer, "So Anders, what's the book you're so into there?"

He looks up unsmiling. "What? Oh, it's Prinzhorn, Hans Prinzhorn's *Bildnerei der Geisteskranken*."

"Ah."

"*Artistry of the Mentally Ill* in English. I'm going over a few points for the thesis."

Dismissed, Erica thinks. *It's like the tide, being with him. He rushes in, he rushes away.* She goes to the bedroom and gets a bottle of wine from "her" wedge of the closet, drinks quickly, then recorks it. This, of course, he must not know about.

On a bright and cold Saturday afternoon, she and Anders are coming back to his apartment with groceries, a rare domestic event as, skittishly undomesticated, Anders cedes the homey arena to Erica. They've discussed this and agreed it's not out of male chauvinism but deep indifference. Also, despite his physical beauty, he is a slob who seldom cleans his apartment. His idea of groceries is a loaf of French bread, cheese, olives, and a six-pack. On this afternoon, as he opens the front door of the apartment, which lets directly into the living room, he drops the bags, shouting, "What the fuck?" He rushes over to the closed windows, where a man's head is bobbing up and down outside, his hands scrabbling for a hold on the minute edge of the window outside. Throwing open a window, Anders grabs the man's arms, yelling for Erica to hold *his* legs. "It's the window washer guy, Jorge. Jorge?" The man outside screams "Help me!" thrashing, cursing, praying in Spanish. Down below on the street, a crowd has gathered and is screaming too. How long this goes on Erica will have no idea. Anders can't heave the man into the room so all they can do is hold on so he won't fall. Erica is about to lose her grip on Anders when firefighters come rushing in, grab the man, and pull him into Anders' living room. As he'd been washing the windows, the scaffold Jorge was on broke at one end; it dangles still, slapping against the building. Jorge is put on a stretcher and the firefighters depart.

"Jesus!" Anders says at last. He gets beers from the fridge.

The bizarre near-death experience for some reason casts a pall on the rest of their day. Anders buries himself in the Prinzhorn. Erica tries reading too, a darkly gorgeous novel by the West Indian-born Jean Rhys, but she can't focus for long. She cooks some spaghetti sauce, makes a salad, but Anders says he doesn't have an appetite.

"Look, I just need to get out of here for a while, maybe go down to Maxie's." He doesn't ask her to come along.

Erica finishes off the six-pack after she eats, takes a bath, tries to read again. He's not back by the time she falls to sleep at last, and she dreams that she and Anders are lost in a snowstorm.

It isn't many days later that Anders calls her and says he's sorry, "it's" just not working for him. They meet at Maxie's, where he has a few drinks and she has a few more, and he tells her about his mother. She fell down some stairs on a New Year's Eve while drunk and broke her neck. He was fifteen.

"You didn't—see it happen?" Erica feels breathless. Why is he telling her such a private, intimate, horrible, precious thing now, when he doesn't want her in his life? She doesn't wonder long.

"No. I did not. But I . . . but you see, you remind me of her," Anders says. "At first, I didn't get it. Yes, she was beautiful, and artistic . . . she designed textiles. And you are. But then I saw what it was. She . . . she was a drunk. And you get drunk a lot. I know about your bottles in the closet, Erica."

In April, Erica tells the window washer story to her old college friend Sandra, who is in New York for some teachers' conference and has come to her apartment for dinner. "That's the moment when I knew things weren't going to work out," she finishes.

"Oh, come on. How could you?"

"I just did," Erica insists. "We'd been talking about living together, me moving in with him, of course, since he has the good apartment. Then this—gargoyle—right outside the window, ready to fall to his death. It was very ominous. It was a sign.

Anders changed right away. It was like I heard a door slam. He just withdrew more and more. Of course, when he told me about his mother, I realized he's still fucked up from that." Also, he'd found her empties stashed in the closet. But she doesn't want to talk about that.

"But you rescued that man together," Sandra points out.

"No, but he was like a messenger, all the negative stuff between us." Erica takes a healthy hit off the joint Sandra hands her. Clean-cut and clear-eyed, a model of middle-class success, Sandra always has a stash with her and it's usually dynamite. "And everything did go to shit."

"Well, at least it happened *before* you moved in with him."

Erica has thought about this too, of course. What if she had given up her cheap, hard-to-find apartment? Where would she have gone after Anders had cut her down at Maxie's? Back to the awful Y? But she'd known it was over even before he canceled their next weekend with some bullshit story about having to go visit a sick friend in New Hampshire or somewhere north. She'd said, "Have a great time," put down the phone, and cried.

Still, the night they drank at Maxie's together had been a shock to her. It didn't matter that she'd felt it coming. After he said those mean things about her being like his mother, Erica was very quiet. At last, she started talking about "somebody else." Anders said no, there wasn't anybody else. It wasn't that. Didn't she get it?

"Lying through his teeth," says Sandra.

Erica had had to go to his apartment one last time to get her stuff. When he wasn't there, of course. She wandered through the rooms, stuffing her bits and pieces in plastic bags saved from the grocery store. Three months' worth of stuff, including her new sketchbook with ink drawings of Anders at his desk, lying on the couch with a beer on his stomach listening to T-Bone Walker, and the last one, of Anders nude on the bed. As she was getting ready to leave, she heard his key at the door. Walking in like everything was normal—well, it was, wasn't it, back to normal for him. They

sat in his kitchen drinking some fresh-ground coffee from the Melitta—the one culinary thing he cared about—and having an offhand conversation that made her feel crazy.

Leaving his building stoned only on caffeine, Erica stumbled and reeled as if she were drunk. She caught a bus, transferred to another, sat with her eyes tightly shut and willed herself not to think of him. And to her surprise, she was successful. For some reason, she was able to picture herself back in grade school. Her best years. Anyway, she'd always loved the beginning of a new school year, the smell of new textbooks, the new skirts and blouses, and especially, the stiff, shiny loafers. The era when she believed that being good would get her good things. Erica didn't realize that she'd begun crying on the bus, but they were quiet tears. When she finally got to her apartment (she couldn't think of it as home), she dropped the loads of bags and fell, sobbing, to her knees.

"Then—you'll never guess what, Sandra—but three days later . . . "

"He called you."

"Yes!"

"And he wanted to see you again."

"Yes!"

"Well, they always do. And of course, you gave in." Sandra speaks with authority: Her free-living, Harley-riding boyfriend has been in and out of her life for years.

"Yes, I did. And when he came over, I kind of turned into my mother—serving him coffee and cookies. I actually made the cookies the night before. Oatmeal chocolate chip."

"Erica, for that bum?"

"Yeah. He ate *four* of them. And drank two cups of coffee. Then he put his head in his hands and started telling me how he felt so bad about us. Like I was supposed to comfort him after he pushes me out of his life?" It was his haunted, open expression that did it, that led them on a not-very-circuitous path to the bedroom. And now she hurts even more than before.

Erica grabs more beers from the fridge. She should be getting through the pain now; it's been almost two months. But talking about Anders has made it raw. She remembers Anders wiping his face on his shirt after he'd fucked her that last time and said, again, that he was so sorry. *How he wished things were different.*

"All those corny love songs. That was me with Anders. I was so happy! Even living on that crappy block with the Dominicans throwing garbage out of the windows, turning their boom boxes on full blast in the middle of the night to party."

"He's not worth it."

"So I slept with him again."

"Classic mistake."

"It was the last time, Sandra. And you know, it was *strange.* Because it was still *good.* The last thing he said was he hoped we could be friends."

"That really works," Sandra says bitterly. "Men." Her whatever-you-call-it is currently separated from his wife again, living in Key West on a boat he's fixing up. Sandra suspects he's running kilos over from the islands. But she's going to fly down to Florida to see him after the conference.

They meet the next day on the West Side for a goodbye lunch, then walk over to Central Park, Erica subdued, wishing Sandra could stay for a while longer. She's leaving for the airport in a couple of hours. Sandra produces a joint—naturally—which they share on a bench right in the park, taking in the skateboarders, the rollerbladers, the normies, the hustlers. A couple with arms linked passes; the girl looks up at the guy and laughs.

Erica sighs.

"Yeah, I know," Sandra says, "love is a bitch. For me too." She sighs. "Even if Don never does get a divorce, I can't let go."

They finish the joint and hug. Erica decides to walk home through Central Park. She's wearing a jacket and gloves, because there's some freaky late spring blast from the north. But it's a bright blue day.

THE PARK THING

Fuzzy-headed from Sandra's weed, Erica ambles crosstown on the winding paths with the grand old trees with their baby-green fluff of leaves, still magnificent in the unkemptness that has become Central Parl. She's almost forgetting Anders and everything but the beauty of the day for moments at a time. A kid's ball rolls to her feet. She looks around and sees a tiny boy in a too-warm parka, round eyes staring at her, and she rolls his ball back to him. He gives her a shy smile. She stuffs her hands in her jacket pockets and feels some change, which reminds her to go through the apartment when she's home for any stray quarters, even dimes and yeah, nickels. Money! Damn! It's that tight. She's overdue on the electric and the phone, though the rent is paid. She kicks some half-frozen leaves. Shit! It's always about the money when you don't have it, it rules everything, no matter what you do to escape it, get high, go out and have a good time like she's done with Sandra, blowing her modest wad on restaurants, that club. No way could she have let Sandra know the depth of her—say it!—poverty. Sandra with her good job, the perks and the pension, had no idea the strain a couple of nights out made on her budget. Sandra's never been in need of money. Even when she was a bare-bones college student like everybody else, her skills at shoplifting had provided her with all the amenities, from steaks to good-quality clothing.

As Erica fumes on, she hears tennis balls being whacked.

Which means that somehow she's taken a wrong turn because she shouldn't be over here by the tennis courts. She must have veered north instead of going east. She looks around for somebody to ask which way she should go to get to Fifth at the fork just ahead, but the area is, abruptly, deserted. She makes a guess and continues. Almost immediately, the path becomes overgrown, with high weeds on either side. Finally she sees someone, a tall guy, coming towards her and asks him if she's on the path going east? He nods yes, and she goes on, but the brambles get thicker now, blocking out the light. She stops when she can barely push through them.

Later, she'll replay the afternoon over and over in her mind, the series of mistakes she made: her stoned inattention, her blithe assumption of safety in the park, her stupidity in taking a stranger's word and walking into a deserted thicket. It is so very quiet. Erica feels completely alone all of a sudden. And then, the man reappears.

Everything happens very fast, but her movements feel slowed down. He's lunging at her and she wants to run but she can't, he covers her mouth with his hand so she's unable to scream. She thinks, *Bite him,* but things move past that, he's pulling her into the weeds, past the weeds to a sort of clearing. He slams her onto the ground. She doesn't feel the sharp prickles of the brambles tearing lines in her face, her arms; she doesn't smell his moldy animal scent; she doesn't hear herself finally manage to yell. All she can think is: survive. She barely registers the sharp thud of a rock against her head as she thrashes under him, the rock leaving a bloody gash under her hair. She doesn't know what he looks like; all that's in her vision is the jagged edge of a bottle he's holding. For some reason, she notices it's a *Coke bottle.* That distinctive shape and milky green color. *Where did that come from?* she thinks. What she will remember, besides the Coke bottle, are his next words:

I'm gonna fuck you, then kill you.

The jagged glass glints. In a garden-variety nightmare she often had as a child, Erica would dream she was being followed.

The nightmare part was the struggle to scream for help. Pinned to the earth now, she doesn't hear her own voice crying **HELP**.

There is nothing left but what is between them and a strange, floating sense of surprise that this is it, the pointless end of her. Then very gradually, she realizes that others have arrived. She lies facedown in the dirt, pinned by the man; then the pressure is gone and she just lies there with noises around her, feet running, yelling. She pulls herself into the brambles, where someone, an angel—but she doesn't believe in such things—finds her and coaxes her out, then holds her up and takes her to a grassy spot. A policeman is there, shoving the monster into handcuffs and away. There are two angels, a stocky American Indian guy, and a lean, good-looking black man in tennis whites. They tell her they heard her scream. Each came from a different place. They chased her attacker and pinned him down, tied him with a belt, and the jogger ran and found a cop. "I beat him with my racket," says the tennis player.

She goes with them to the police car with the monster sitting in the back. The cop flips open a notebook, asks questions. "Lady, we gotta go to the station nearby," he says, closing his notebook.

Erica starts to shudder. She can't get in a car with the monster. The jogger gets this. "You can't make her get in there with that son of a bitch. Look at her! Get another car for her." The cop rolls his eyes, but calls for another car. Erica gets in. The tennis player wishes her luck and leaves, the jogger gives her his business card. "We'll nail that bastard in court. Call me anytime you want to, you know, talk."

Another cop is nicer to Erica at the little station, gets her a glass of water, explains what's going to happen. He asks her if she wants a taxi to get home and she bursts out crying. He says, "Oh what the hell," and drives her there. She showers for a long time and goes straight to bed with a bottle of wine. She keeps the lights on all night, doesn't remember falling asleep. In the morning she can't eat anything, even though she's hungry and her last meal had been lunch with Sandra in a different lifetime. Erica is wired, like she's done a lot of coke. She pulls out her easel, puts it away, decides to take a walk. Thank God she lives in a crowded area. After a few blocks, she turns around, breathing raggedly, needing to get behind closed doors.

She calls the jogger, whose name is Aaron Hill. They talk a little, mostly about the court date. He asks if she feels like having a meal. Maybe another time, she says. She wants to talk to Anders. She doesn't call him.

A week later, she meets Aaron Hill in a pub not far from his office near Times Square, hamburgers and a pitcher of beer. Erica says yes, she's doing OK. For the moment, she is, enjoying the packed, noisy atmosphere. She only feels safe in crowds. Aaron, a broad, coppery-skinned Mohawk who works as a television producer, tells her about the documentary he's doing on the beautiful Chrysler Building, which his "forefathers"—his word—had constructed along with the Empire State Building and the Brooklyn Bridge.

"Men of steel," he said. "Not afraid of heights. My people helped build all the great skyscrapers in New York."

"Your family must be proud of you," she says. "My family . . . "

Suddenly her eyes fill up; this happens routinely now. "You know, I can't ever thank you enough. You and Dean, you saved my life."

Aaron puts a large, man-of-steel hand over hers. "Let's not talk about that." But she sees he's pleased. He pays for the burgers, puts her in a cab. "You'll be all right?" he asks.

"Thanks, Aaron. For *everything*."

Erica sits staring out at another New York night, pressed against the side of the taxi with her hand on the door handle the entire ride. She's ready to jump out if the driver seems the least bit suspect.

Larry Lopez is coming back to New York, this time for a job interview in the burgeoning field of Hispanic academia. "NYU," he says over the phone, "they're paying for the flight and shit, putting me up in an apartment in Washington Square."

Larry always lands on his feet, or rather the foot he keeps in the straight world of job hustles in Gringoland. The other foot is on a barstool at some Tex-Mex joint, drinking beer and listening to *rancheras*. Through his endless connections, he's heard of another great Tex-Mex bar in the East Village, which is where they end up after a meal in Little Italy. Larry's still in his interview clothes, tweed jacket and pressed khakis, exhilarated about the NYU plum. He orders two Dos Equis and checks out the bar. "Hey, Rica, you're the only gringa here," he points out, unnecessarily.

"I'm practically a *cuate,* man," she retorts. "I actually *lived* in Mexico, remember. And I speak better Spanish than you do. In fact, Larry, maybe you can get me a job over at NYU too?"

Larry grins. "You don't qualify, baby."

"Well, fuck you, Lopez, there's plenty of gringos who are Mexican too. Germans, Brits, Russians, Jews. Even *norteamericanos.*"

"Hey, it's brown folks' turn now."

"Yeah, yeah."

Soon they're back reliving the past as they always do, the protests, the marches, the underground newspaper that lasted four issues, the crazy people in the movement—Theo, Chacon, Fudge, Guadalupe, Betty Ramirez. Larry loves talking about the insane 60s, and the last time he was here she did too. But she's not there with him tonight. The court date is coming up; she's chewed down her fingernails, lost weight. And she's back to drinking too much.

"Let's order tequila," Erica says, "get good and wasted." Since what she now refers to as "the park thing"—which she hasn't told Larry about yet—she craves tequila again. The week before, she'd thrown a glass of it at the mirror behind the bar at Benny's and was 86ed.

"Jesus, Rica, take it easy," Larry says at some point.

She doesn't remember getting home, and the next morning she discovers she had forgotten to lock her door. *Jesus, after everything that's happened,* she thinks. She can't go out for days after that.

Larry calls a week later from Chicago. "I didn't get it," he says.

"Jeez, I'm sorry."

"Fuck NYU, man, there's plenty of jobs around. Anyhow, Flora wants to go back to Texas, her parents are getting old and need some help. They're waiting to kiss my highly-credentialed Chicano ass at the college in San Anton. "

"You always land on your feet, compadre."

"Yeah, thanks. Listen, Rica . . . you were really wrecked that night in New York, you know? Gotta slow it down, you know?"

"Yeah?" *Fuck you,* she thinks.

"Stick to beer. My drink. Corona, Bohemia, Dos Equis, even fuckin' Schlitz, not that crazy shit you go for."

"OK, OK, but it's tough times here in the Apple, Larry."

She hadn't told him about the attack. Didn't feel comfortable.

May. She's standing in a cacophonous hallway of the courtroom in lower Manhattan (no benches here), victims, criminals, relatives, and lawyers jammed together, everybody waiting for something. Only the lawyers are easily distinguishable (briefcases and suits), the others could be interchangeable—which Erica is to find out soon enough in the courtroom.

She is wedged between a man with a runny nose, either a junkie or a guy with a common cold, and an elderly black woman with a felt hat jammed over her forehead saying "Lord Jesus, no," over and over. Erica is rigid with what she doesn't know is a panic attack. All she knows is that she's entered another rung of hell. Nowhere to sit, the air fuggy with sweat and the misery of the criminal class and their human collateral damage and the vultures who serve the system. After a long wait, a fat guard flings her name into the hall and Erica pushes her way into the courtroom.

Scarred walls, a ceiling fan stirring soupy air, a judge on a platform above the hoi polloi, his balding head bent, maybe grabbing a quick nap. *Sensible,* she thinks, breathing thinly through her nose. She wishes she could pass out and sleep the whole thing off. Next to her appears a young Assistant D.A. who clearly hasn't seen her case until this moment. He speed-reads through the police report. The only positive thing is the sudden appearance of the nicer policeman who didn't make her ride in the same car as Marco Reidoff, which she has learned is the name of her attacker.

"Name? Address?" The judge is awake.

Erica's agitation increases. "I can't say it, *he's* here!" She has recognized Reidoff instantly in the second row, staring at her, his mousy hair, scraggly beard.

"Young lady, answer the questions." The judge looks annoyed and toys with his gavel.

The Assistant D.A. whispers to her. "You have to, Miss Mason."

Next a pudgy Legal Aid attorney representing "the defendant" gets to ask her questions. Again, the Assistant D.A. whispers that she has to respond.

"So, isn't it true you habitually went to the park soliciting clients?"

Erica repeats slowly, "Clients? I was walking through the park in the middle of the day! That's a crime?"

Somebody in the courtroom laughs. "Answer the question." The judge again.

"I was walking. Through the park. I lost my way, and then that *monster* grabbed me. He told me he was going to . . . "

"Isn't it true that you were a prostitute looking for clients in a part of the park known for such activities?"

"I'd just had lunch, I was walking home!"

"Move on, counselor."

"Why were you walking in an area known for crime that day?"And a bunch of other crap like that until even the Legal Aid lawyer seems bored. Then the Assistant D.A. reads the witnesses' sworn testimony; the nice policeman confirms it. The judge dismisses her. A ruling will take place within the month.

"He'll be convicted," the Assistant D.A. tells her. "He'll serve time."

"I don't want Reidoff to just go to jail! I want him to get help, women need to be protected, he'll do it again!"

"Look, that's not how it works." The Assistant D.A. is polite but clearly anxious to go. He has a thick stack of cases cradled in his arms. He touches her arm. "If it's any help, there're people lobbying for a victims' rights department, so someday . . . " He shrugs. "Things may be different for people like you."

On the subway back uptown, Erica has to transfer at Union Square. Graffitied signs point down a flight of stairs where, suddenly, she is alone in a tunnel that connects to the other line. Erica thinks *people like me* and has an acute premonition that the tunnel is about to collapse. She bolts, as if running for her life, stumbles with relief onto the platform where bored New Yorkers wait in the dim filth for the next train. She wants to hug the first person she sees, a burly woman in an awful mint green and magenta knitted cap and then everyone else, one by one, these people who are her salvation: She is no longer alone in the dark tunnel, waiting to be hunted down. Home at last twenty minutes later, Erica breathes in the safety of her little railroad flat. She wishes she'd never have to leave it again.

Except that she has to get a job. And she does. She catches a break; a friend of Aaron Hill's friend is compiling something called *The Food Bible* and needs an illustrator. Her assignment is Cheeses of the World, pen-and-ink sketches. She goes down to Murray's Cheese Shop in the Village, but on buses now. They are much slower but she can't handle subways anymore. Her pay is . . . cheesy, too, and *The Food Bible* boss is manic. Still, she enjoys the work. Especially the section on odd cheeses. *Yarg* and *moose milk,* which she finds with difficulty. *Stinking bishop* she can't find, and finesses. When she brings in the sketches, the manic editor throws a fit. Who would have thought that anyone knows what a stinking bishop actually looks like? But he does. And he fires her.

So Erica's back to square one, again. She'll have to type in some dreary office again. But when a letter arrives informing her she has to be in court in five days, she tables everything. Except wine at home. For the sentencing, she wears black pants and a black turtleneck, a woman in mourning; Reidoff has killed the vestiges of joy in her. She stands motionless as the judge pronounces his sentence: eighteen months in jail.

The nice policeman leads her away.

"That's it? He tried to kill me! He did it before, you heard! He attacked two other women, that they know of. How can they, how can they! He'll just get out and do it again. He needs psychiatric treatment."

"Yeah, see, he didn't hurt you, that's the thing. Don't take it so hard. At least he's serving time."

Erica whispers raggedly, "He didn't *hurt* me? How can you say that? You have no idea."

"OK, I know it was rough. Look, there's a nice little Chinese place people around here go to, just around the corner, why don't we go eat something."

"Oh sure, like this is a celebration."

"Look. Think about it. You got rescued—and he got caught. That's a lot more than a lot of people get. Believe me, I seen a lot."

Erica doesn't see how sad he looks because it's fast, then the neutral cop expression is back. She can't hear that she got rescued; she doesn't feel lucky, she can only think about her own nightmare. Because she is reluctant to be alone now, she follows him through the crowded masses without noticing anything or anyone, like the other cops twigging their eyebrows at him as they pass. But the Chinese place is a good idea. Tea. Noodles. Chicken something, hot, with peppers. And he lets her talk.

"The worst was that piggy little Legal Aid guy accusing me of being a prostitute!" She sort of wants a drink, but she'll wait until she can do it the way she wants. Alone, or rather, with a soul sister on the box. *They* get her pain.

"They just throw shit around to see if something will stick, those guys, they're like Neanderthals—usually, nobody pays much attention. Look," he goes on, "my advice to you is forget this. Move on with your life. You're young, you got a whole future ahead of you."

Future? She sips her tea. What a joke. If he got to know me, he'd realize it was my fault that it happened. Because it would never have happened if I wasn't high.

"Look, ah, Erica, would you like to go out to dinner some time? No pressure," he says hurriedly. "I know some good places, perk of being a police officer."

"You've been great, just great to me," she says hurriedly. "I'll never forget it. But I can't, I'm sorry." Erica realizes she doesn't remember his name, it has not seemed important.

"Of course, you got a boyfriend," the cop says, clearing his throat. He doesn't insist on picking up the check when she offers to pay her share.

AFTERSHOCK

Erica starts meeting Aaron Hill once a week at Millie's, a pub near his office, where they always sit at a table in the back, away from the bar populated by media guys. They meet early, have a few drinks, sometimes food, and afterwards Erica walks home, or in bad weather, takes the bus. She always avoids the subway now and she can't afford cabs. She sees nobody else.

One evening, Aaron invites her to tour the Chrysler Building, the site of that documentary he's just finished. She meets him there on a rainy Saturday afternoon. He's brought binoculars for her to check out the famous gargoyles—eagles and radiator caps from Chrysler cars of the twenties that decorate the façade. They ride up an elevator paneled in beautiful wood mosaics to what had been the public viewing gallery, now closed, to which Aaron has a key. He takes her arm as he points out the terraced crown with its silver sunburst cladding.

"Fantastic, right?" He gives her a tiny hug.

"Beautiful." Erica edges away. She wonders why she is not more moved by all this gorgeous Art Deco ornamentation, why even lovely things bounce off her now as if she's wearing armor. Why does Aaron's presence—it's the first time they've met anywhere but Millie's—provoke only indifference? Her lack of emotion preoccupies her, even frightens her a little. Not long ago, she had enthusiasms and appetites, the sketches, the paintings. Had been in love. She wishes she could mourn these losses. But she can't.

She makes an effort with Aaron, pretending to be interested in what he is telling her, nods and smiles as he talks about the men— two of his uncles who had worked right here, high above the city. They hoisted heavy steel, dangling high in the sky. The fitful sun vanishes behind pewter clouds. Rain begins to plop, slow and thick, then fast and hard, outside the magnificent windows.

"Erica." Aaron says. He turns from the obscured view and looks at her. "I think of you all the time. I . . . "

"Aaron. Please." She is terrified. Alone in this high, empty room with him. She begins to cry. "Please. I can't sleep without the lights on, I can't take the subway, I can't breathe sometimes."

"Let me help you. I want to be there for you. Hold you." He's almost groaning.

"You can't help me, Aaron. Plus you're married, remember?"

Back down in the great golden temple that is the lobby of the Chrysler Building, a kaleidoscope of exotic marble on every surface, Aaron asks in a flat tone if she has an umbrella with her.

She pulls up the hood of her raincoat. "No. But I'll be all right." *When?* she thinks.

"Can we meet at Millie's Thursday?"

A man bursts past them, streaming, heads for the elevator. She and Aaron step back. "I don't think that's a good idea."

"Why?"

"Aaron?" Here it goes, first the cop, now the Mohawk. "You've been wonderful. Really. And I'll never forget what you did, never. But . . . "

"Well, fuck," he says. "Goodbye, then." He leaves. In a moment, Erica is out in the rain, the downpour, welcoming the wet, her feet instantly soaked. Water seeps into the raincoat, into her hair, and as she splashes through dirty puddles she sees ahead in a doorway an ashy, dark-skinned woman wearing a large trash bag. Just a trash bag! Like a shivering statue, with her palm outstretched. People are hurrying wetly past, anxious to get out of the rain; maybe they don't even see her. But Erica stops. Of all the dire, often heart-breaking scenes of the homeless in this broken, Dickensian layer of New York life, this is the heartbreaker for her. She takes out of her wallet one, no two, no five, of her precious few dollars. "Here," she says, and the woman's sandpaper hand snatches it.

"I can't seem to get started again," Erica tells Sandra on the phone. "I try to go out, I try to paint, but . . . " Somehow, she ends up wandering around instead, walking around the Upper East Side, this alien patch she inhabits. She's been 86ed from Benny's, she no longer meets Aaron at Millie's, she doesn't have any money and worries about it all the time during her wanderings, which end with cheap beer at night on the fainting couch. Which is progress, in a way.

Sandra was appalled, of course, to learn about the attack. "Oh my God!" she'd said, "I must have been on my way to the airport when that happened! Oh, how awful for you." But now she seems impatient when Erica brings it up again and again. "You can't let the fear get to you," she says, "you have to fight it."

Claire has urged her to see a therapist.

Nobody understands. Then too, her real problem is money. "I have to get a job," Erica tells her.

"Well, call up that agency you worked for."

"God," says Erica. She's past that.

She calls Philip next. They haven't talked in a long while. Work for *Good Hip Music* has dried up, but still, he's her best bet. "I'm kinda having a hard time financially," she says.

"Me, too," he says gloomily.

Neither can afford to go out to dinner right now, so she invites him over for enchiladas. He brings a bottle of wine (*thank God,* she thinks, *no Schlitz tonight*) and she puts on a Bill Evans album, low, and they talk. Erica tells him about the attack, about the panic that can overtake her at any time, how she has a hard time concentrating. She omits the weird, dark things that have been happening more often now when she drinks. Blackouts. Getting angry—thrown out of Benny's. The night she found it irresistible to meet a wrong number at a diner, then brought him home, drunk, of course.

"Why didn't you call me?" Philip asks, pale, shocked.

"It was too painful to talk about before," she says.

"God, it's so *awful*." To her dismay, Philip puts his head in his hands. Surely he isn't going to start crying.

"Well, there was a happy ending, I guess, because I was rescued." For the first time since it happened, she realizes this is true and feels a flicker of good energy.

"Right," he says, lifting his head. "Of *course*." His eyes are dull. "I wondered what was up— I called a bunch of times but there was never any answer. And well, I've had my own shit to deal with." He takes a long drink from his wine glass, unusual for Philip. He never gets loaded.

"Pellinelli's closing the magazine," he goes on, flushing. "OK, so it hasn't made a profit yet, but we were building it. We were given a year to make it work. It takes at least a year. But he's decided to pull it. Wants to take what's left of his money and move to New Orleans."

"Asshole! What are you going to do?" *G.H.M.* is his life.

"Look for another job, what else? I have a couple of prospects."

"I'm so sorry, Philip." *And for me,* she thinks.

"Yeah, well, it's a drag for all of us, but we'll figure something out."

"Sure we will."

They eat the enchiladas and salad in her kitchen, which has defied her efforts to make it look cheerful. It remains stubbornly gloomy with its one useless window looking out onto the dank courtyard. But the food is good.

"Delicious," Philip says over coffee in the living room.

He leaves soon after; he has a job interview the next morning. And the next morning, Erica surprises herself, gets out the easel and a blank canvas. She paints a watercolor, all greens and browns, of a field and children running among wildflowers. It's nothing special, a memory lifted from childhood, when she was very young. And happy.

BROWNSTONE
BROTHEL GIG

Thomas Thomas gets Erica her next job after she runs into him in the laundry room again and starts hanging out at his place. Booze, weed often, conveniently delivered pizzas solving the problem at least of food, and yes, human contact. Always at Thomas Thomas's place—he's called T.T.—never hers. Because, he explains, he has to be home and near the phone, "in case a tenant need something." His phone rings frequently and he's always leaving, always says, "Be right back." Fine with Erica. There's everything she needs here in his small apartment crammed with a big TV, the stereo alternating between Marvin Gaye, Isaac Hayes, Aretha. Zebra-striped couch, red velveteen drapes, glass-topped coffee table. Very clean, the coffee table frequently windexed, the shag rug vacuumed. The "goodies" in the baggies in a locked drawer.

Erica finds it restful to be with T.T. because he never makes a move and is always welcoming, plus he's crashingly dumb, which is relaxing. Her head just stays on cruise control while she gets high. He reminds her of hippies who took too much acid. But in fact, as she learns, T.T. had been a boxer, lightweight semi-pro. So that explains the spaciness. And now, here he is, tending to this five-story walk-up on the East Side. Plus whatever else he is into.

One evening when she drops by, T.T. says, with his wide grin, "Heard about a job if you're still interested."

Sick of the stage she is at, scrounging for change in purses, drawers, and coat pockets, two weeks behind on the rent, she says, "Man, yes! What is it?"

"Ah, you know, though, maybe it ain't your thing."

"A job is a job, T.T. I really need one."

"OK, then, listen up: It pays real good, three hundred a week *off the books*. And easy too, all you got to do is answer some phones, stuff like that. Like a, um . . . "

"Receptionist? That's OK. "

"Just, I gotta tell you 'cause I know you went to college. It's a place where ladies turn tricks."

"Shit, T.T., a whorehouse?" Erica starts laughing. What would Marjorie and Ken think? Claire? Sandra? Philip? Anyone she knew?

"It's a class place though," T.T. adds reassuringly. "In one of them good brownstones. Working girls there are like . . . uh . . . housewives and students. Actresses."

"Fuck it, am I that broke?"

"Ain't you?"

Suddenly they both are laughing helplessly, T.T. doing his teeth sucking, sway-jerking black thing, Erica reduced to yelps. She knows she will do this. And it's not just the money: It's irresistible, the idea of going underground, so to speak, in a brothel. Painters throughout history have gotten good material in brothels.

And it wasn't the first time she'd been introduced to the world of "working girls." While in college she'd met Larry Bond, a.k.a. Zilma, in the lobby at a Four Tops show she went to with Sandra. Larry was a handsome dark-skinned man with a gold front tooth and a beautifully cut suit who invited them to an after-hours club after the show. Sandra had blown it off. Erica, driving the old station wagon her father had given her, wanted to go. Larry took one look at her car in the parking lot and started laughing. "Ride with me, girl, and ride in style."

She had to admit his immaculate white Jaguar was a superior ride. She started meeting up with Larry on weekends after work, entranced by the shadowy black world of little clubs with organists and saxophonists testifying, and haughty black women in furs propped at the bar who made a point of ignoring her and throwing verbal knives at the men.

One night, Larry said he had to meet somebody at a hotel downtown. That's where she spent time with her first live working girl. Dawn wasn't really a girl anymore, she was a fleshy woman, white, in a tight pantsuit. She sat silently in a chair in the suite while Larry made phone calls. Hair teased, heavily made-up and not particularly attractive, Dawn looked like she had a slow leak, that there was not much anybody could say or do to move her anymore. Unhurriedly, she drank bourbon and smoked Newports. When Larry said he had to go somewhere for a little while, Erica moved over to sit next to Dawn, who had the television on, no sound. "Do you mind if I . . . ?" Erica held up a joint. Dawn waved as if a fly was bothering her. While Erica got high, Dawn buffed her nails, had another drink, smoked, flipped through a movie magazine. About as exciting as being at a bingo game in a nursing home, Erica thought.

"How you know Larry?" Dawn suddenly asked.

Erica stirred. She'd been far away. "Oh, just around. Do you call him Larry all the time?"

"Yeah."

"I think it's so funny his real name is Zilma."

Dawn sniffed and went back to her magazine.

Larry returned with some Chinese takeout and handed it to Dawn. "Come on, let's go," he told Erica.

"Bye," Erica said.

"Later," Larry said.

"Sure, baby," Dawn drawled.

In the car, Erica wanted to know about Dawn because she had recently started sleeping with Larry.

"She ain't nothin' to you," he said.

143

"She's your main whore, right?"

"Where you get this shit? Main whore." He laughed. Larry was always shaking his head or laughing at her. Occasionally, though, he wasn't in such a jolly mood and then she felt his anger like a cold wind. Like when he drove through part of the ghetto, down row after row of shabby streets whose sole signs of affluence were occasional beautiful cars like his. He slowed the car before a rickety house needing paint. "That's my mama's house," he told her, then drove off. "Black man can work at the bottom in a plant or be a janitor or some other little shit. Or make real money managin' bitches. So then I can take my fine little white girl out wherever she wants to go."

A few nights after she'd met Dawn, Larry took her to the house of a friend who wasn't at home. In bed, he started trying to fuck her from behind. Erica struggled and slapped him. Lightly, though. "Don't!"

"Bitch, don't ever strike Larry Bond."

"You scared me, Larry." Erica heaved herself out of bed. "I have to go to the bathroom." She scooped up her clothes and got dressed there. She had to get away. All she knew was they were somewhere in the vastness of the ghetto. Thank God she'd followed him this evening in her car, which she sometimes did.

Larry loomed in the doorway, in his underpants. "Where you think you're goin'?"

She was praying as she said, "Home."

"Just like that, huh?"

"I need to, I have a lot of studying to do."

His head back, his gold tooth gleamed as he laughed and laughed. "College girl, you a rotten liar. And you would make the worst whore I know."

"I take that as a compliment," Erica said.

For some reason, Larry relented. "Get the fuck outta here then." He turned his back. She was history now.

Erica is thinking about this while pondering working at the

brownstone whorehouse. "So who do I talk to about the job?" she asks T.T.

A fifteen minute walk from her apartment takes Erica to the brownstone in the East 50s where she has been hired to work from three p.m. to ten, when the night receptionist comes on. Erica can get up reasonably late, get some art done, and it's still not late when she leaves work at the brownstone. She goes in early the first day to check it out: The building is just like all the others on the block from the front. Several women go in while she's watching, young mostly. They look like students or waitresses. Men, she'll soon find out, come and go through a side entrance in the narrow alley next to the building.

At three o'clock, she climbs the stairs and pushes the buzzer, saying "Margot," her nom de guerre for this gig. There's a foyer beyond a small waiting room—never used by clients, she learns—and two small offices on either side. Helen, the brown-skinned, brown-eyed, brown-suited woman who manages the office and gave her the job, greets her, gesturing toward one of the rooms. "This is where you're gonna work, Margot." A drab little space with a metal desk with a swivel chair, a black phone, a black appointment book, and the Script, a page and a half of which she is to read over the phone to what Helen calls "our prospective clients."

"Each of our ladies has a column for each day in fifteen-minute intervals," Helen explains. "Of course it's vital that you record the time, date, and above all, exactly what the client orders for his visit." She pauses to stare at Erica. "I don't want no screw-ups, understand me, Margot? Now, look over the Script carefully, I'll be back in a few minutes."

Five minutes later, Helen returns. "Any questions?"

Erica fingers the Script. "Just one—what if they, uh, ask for something that's not in here?"

"Good question. Just repeat what's there. If they get funny with you, hang up. That's it. Simple, right?" She massages her hair, a large woman, attractive despite all the brown. "There's a coffeemaker across the hall, a small fridge, water, and a bathroom next to it. The ladies sometimes use the kitchenette too. But do not fraternize with them."

Fraternize? "You mean talk to them?"

"Correct. Don't. You have your business, they have theirs. That's a rule we stick to." She pauses. "And if a client—this should definitely not happen—but, if a client ever comes into this part of the building by accident, do *not* engage him in conversation, call me right away. Now, what else? You have a half-hour for your dinner break at seven—I'll take over then—and of course, if you need to freshen up. Any other questions?"

Her first phone call, she fumbles the Script:

"It's twenty dollars for twenty minutes, ten dollars for each additional minute. Ten dollars additional for BJ, BL, BLS, twenty dollars additional for CIM, GS."

And a paragraph more of inscrutable acronyms, followed by directions to the side door to the brownstone. She knows what a few of the acronyms stand for and can only imagine others —GS: *goat sex?* BLS: *bacon and lettuce sandwich?* Explanations are not part of the Script. Just as well, because she doesn't want to know. After a few times, the phrases come smoothly and mechanically. The phone gets busy as the evening progresses. Erica has brought a sandwich and takes her half-hour break in the dentist office–like waiting room, reading a newspaper.

The only interesting interruption to her work comes right after that, when Helen has stepped out (her phrase), for her break and one of the "girls," a woman who looks to be in her thirties, somewhere between plain and attractive, comes into Erica's office.

"Mary? Where's Mary?"

"I don't know. I'm the new receptionist, Margot."

"Oh." She doesn't bother introducing herself, which Erica feels is natural enough under the circumstances.

"Look, Mary lets us use the phone for emergencies. Can I, just for a sec? Brownie's out, she won't know."

Brownie, that would be Helen. "Well . . . " Helen has said

nothing about whether or not the "girls" may use the phone. Just then it rings. As Erica rushes through the acronyms, the caller hangs up. She shrugs. "OK."

"Thanks." She bends over the desk, nervously dialing. "Hannah? It's Jane. How is she—oh she still does? Poor baby. Well remember, Tylenol, only two, and lots of water, juice if she wants. Yes, I'm still at school, but class will be over shortly, then I'll come right home. OK. Hannah, you're an angel."

Hanging up, she throws a quick "thanks!" at Erica and rushes out.

Erica thinks about her limited knowledge of working girls. Dawn is it, really. Neither Dawn nor this Mary jibes with the way they're depicted in paintings—lush in French, tubercular in German, porcelain dolls in Asian art. Dawn was like a tired saleslady, Jane is a harried mother. She starts drawing on a piece of paper—she's forgotten her sketchbook—imagining Jane at work, wearily removing her clothes in a dimly-lit room, the john a shadow on the bed. As her first day at the brownstone ends, she's drawing a sketch of Jane between reading the script and writing in the appointment book. The other "girls" are still only names, eerily like the "temp" girls from Queens: Connie, Lara, Keisha, Maria . . . Maybe they *are* the temp girls, moonlighting or even having switched "careers." There's certainly a lot more bread to be made in the brownstone than anywhere else she's worked.

Her day ends drearily. More and more of the men who call are now slurring their words and she has to repeat the Script. The rules say twice is her limit, then she hangs up.

The next day, Erica leaves the brownstone for her half-hour dinner break to spy on the johns' entrance she's found out about from the Script. By now, many people are home from work in their apartments, but there are still plenty of people out shopping, dining. She stands across the street from the brownstone, looking at her watch from time to time, as if she's waiting for someone. But of course no one pays her any attention. Mostly ordinary-looking guys go into the narrow alleyway, tapping at the johns' door, guys in suits, guys in jeans, mostly white, some black, a few Asian. Then the grand prize: a head-dressed Arab. She wishes she could see their expressions. Do they look excited, bored, just blank? She'll paint a conga line, an ant line of johns in Egyptian relief: "Brownstone Brothel Johns," what else?

By Wednesday, all she can think about is the paycheck on Friday night. She gives up being "good," bringing a bottle of rum and a can of Coke in a bag along with her sandwiches. Getting a slow buzz on helps with the loathsome Script, the crude remarks on the other end of the phone. On Thursday, she lands another prize during her stakeout across the street at seven p.m., a Hasid in a trademark nineteenth-century black suit, hat, and side-curls who hurries into the tiny alley and disappears inside. She has met a couple more of the girls, as hers is the only telephone in the place. One is a college student (she makes a point of telling Erica this) who would be anonymous on any campus, and the other a coffee-skinned Latina.

"I need to use the phone, could you leave for a couple minutes?"

"You must be Maria? I can't do that," Erica tells her.

"It's a private conversation!"

"Well, there's a pay phone on the corner."

"*Chinga tu madre,*" Maria tells her. She draws the phone protectively close, speaking in Mexican Spanish in a low voice. "Baby, you have to get it for me . . . I swear I will . . . just this one time, I promise."

"Where you from in Mexico?" Erica asks her in Spanish. "And by the way, don't curse at me again, you understand?"

Maria glares at her and flounces out, yes, flounces: She's the only one Erica has met who looks the part in a tight black skirt and shiny red low-cut blouse. Erica can't decide whether to put Maria in the painting or not, she's such a cliché. But yes, because she's for real too. Splashes of red in the dark.

On Friday night at ten, Helen hands Erica an envelope, six new fifties inside. "See you on Monday, Margot."

Erica hesitates. "Right," she said. "Well, good night."

"Good night."

She walks up the quiet street to the brighter avenue with lots of people around. She has not brought any booze with her to work on Friday except for a can of beer. She plans to go home and have a long shower to shed the atmosphere of the job, have a little wine, and go out and party. Instead, she falls asleep in her robe on the fainting couch, thinking about the new painting.

"Hit the road, jack, and doncha come back no mo, no mo, no more, no more . . . " Erica sings loudly along with Ray Charles, an album Anders had coveted. Perversely happy, or as happy as she can remember being in a long time. High on wine but not too high. The apartment has been thoroughly cleaned, down to the kitchen shelves and the individually dusted books in crates. There's a new plant hanging in the living room window, her refrigerator is filled with food, she's bought good coffee, a case of beer, three bottles of acceptable wine, and a carton of cigarettes. She has taken the back rent up to Edie Desmond. She is doing sketches for the brownstone painting. And she has blown off the brownstone gig.

All set. She might have decided not to quit if she hadn't run into the "student" on her way home Friday night. The young woman was leaning against a wall on First Avenue near a rowdy singles bar with her backpack and a bloody nose. She clutched at Erica's sleeve. "I know you, right? From the job, right?" Erica hoped she wasn't hooking there on the street where she'd get busted in no time. Keep it in the brownstone, where it was tolerated.

"Uh, right," Erica said, reluctantly acknowledging a kind of solidarity. Yes, they were all in it together at the brownstone. "Is there something I can do? You're *bleeding.*"

The girl removed a handkerchief, which had partially covered her face. She looked bad, as if she'd fallen on her face into a pile of gravel. Her right eye was swelling and bloody. "Motherfucker hit me five minutes ago. Accused me of holding back on him. Said he'd fix my face so I can't work. Then some guys going in the bar scared him off."

Erica took a step back. "Who was this guy?"

"My boyfriend, what you think?" The girl looked at Erica like she was crazy.

"Your boyfriend did this?"

"Shit yes, and for no good reason this time. He knows I do him right, greedy motherfucker."

"Listen, you've got to go to a hospital, that eye looks bad."

"Nah, I'll just clean it up later."

Erica took another step back. "But your eye . . . Listen, I'll get you a cab, you go to the E.R., you really should." She dug a ten-dollar bill out of her bag. "Here, for the fare."

The young woman laughed. "What you think, I don't have any bread? Like I'm really gonna let him have all of it?" She reached into a back pocket of her jeans. "I got a stash. Um, like, will you ride with me? It's just, I don't really want to be alone right now."

"I would but I have a date (mental grimace) but you go there, OK? Look, I have to go, so, well, good luck." As Erica hurried away, she knew she wasn't going back to the brownstone. She had to find a less hazardous line of work.

With cash in her pocket, she's fixed up the crib, stocked it, and paid the rent. She'll get some *real* work done now, damn it! For a week or two. When the phone rings, she doesn't answer it. When Thomas Thomas knocks on the door, she ignores it. The new painting requires silence, pacing, coffee, cigarettes, curses, muttering, wine at the end of the workday *only*. She's been off her stride but now she can feel she's back. She's used to being surprised by what wants to come out in a painting, but never more than this one. She has thought she'll focus equally on the johns in the alley and the "girls," but the charcoals, acrylics, and brushes say otherwise. At first she doesn't get it, but she stays with it. A room begins to take shape: It's her little office, the black telephone. A woman gets in the picture, she's bending over the phone in her bra and panties, holding the mouthpiece, her hair in pigtails, a long, red scar down her face. The room fills up with "girls," a housewife in glasses, naked except for a frilly apron around her waist, her breasts two flat, horizontal scars, mastectomized. The student with a broken face, wearing only a backpack. A Latina in high-heeled black boots; *her* breasts are as sharp as the knife she holds.

The painter is suspended in the technique of the picture, not trusting it but aware of sudden, rare successes in the maddening decisions of color, light, texture, form. She is in despair, she watches the painting get away from her, she hadn't wanted all this decadence. And she is exhilarated. This narrow, stubborn, wracked reality closing the door on everything but its own world.

Erica knows all this is possible because she is able to do what she has done before—hold off the booze until the work is done. But some days she has to leave the canvas and walk around the peopled, traffic-congested streets of her little piece of New York. On one of these walks in an autumn that has just arrived, she stops at the playground next to the school as she has so often in the past. But the sight of children at play doesn't call to her now. She just needs to give her head a rest, and looking at children is as good a way as any. Another time, she notices a small store with a Going Out of Business sign, goes in and buys strange, beautiful earrings and a bracelet. She is buoyed by a blissful sense of possibility; her constant, chronic fear of running out of money seems to have vanished. What she will do when the last bit of brownstone pay runs out, she has no idea. It doesn't seem to matter.

The night Erica finishes the painting she puts on some get-down New Orleans music, uncorks a bottle of red, and celebrates to the sounds of funky Professor Longhair. Then she goes over to T. T.'s, explaining she's been working her ass off (she doesn't talk about the week-long brownstone gig) and she's done now. Her reward is lines of white on the table, T.T.'s booze. T.T. is especially restless, though, and soon says he has to split, so she walks up First to Benny's, boldly goes inside—luckily there is a new bartender who doesn't know her checkered history—and sits at the bar in a bright Mexican blouse and the new dangling earrings, accepting drinks from some advertising guy called Jud, and his mates. She grooves on the guitar player in the corner, she is queen of this night.

She ends up in Jud's fantastic apartment on Central Park West, sublet from Burl Ives, of all things. She stares out at the fantastic view and tries to keep up with Jud, who seems to have pyramids of coke, one in every room, but she'd rather drink good old Remy. She wakes up the next day on his bed, fully clothed. Jud, in his boxers, starts haggling for what he'd missed the night before, both of them sour of breath and body. Erica says first she needs coffee, orange juice, and toast, although she can only drink the coffee. Jud goes off optimistically to take a shower. Erica finds her bag and leaves.

This minor escapade does nothing to deflate her mood. At home, she showers, has scrambled eggs, more coffee. She's thinking: *This is it.* She is going to look upon her creation for the first time in the daylight. She turns around the easel, ritually facing the wall as always when she's not working on it, and she sees the flaws immediately, an awkward curve of a foot and too much shadow on a face and yes, that aquamarine doesn't quite work, it detracts from the figures. So, more work.

Erica sits perfectly still. Staring at the title in pen and ink across the bottom of the painting, tall, irregular, old-fashioned lettering:

The Brownstone Girls

Ever since she crash-landed in Manhattan, she's felt small, shadowy, easily passed over. Overwhelmed by the size, the movement, and especially by the talent she runs into everywhere in this city, the Haitians and then Anders' friends, the downtown crowd. But this picture shows her power, she knows this. She has channeled pain and rage into these battle-scarred women. And she wants people to see it. What is she waiting for? She wants to have a show.

MOJO WORKING

The trees in Central Park, statuesque, a school of wintry, bare, marbled limbs, ripple as the icy winds blow, but Erica doesn't notice their magnificence. For her, even walking outside the park along Fifth Avenue is almost too close to danger. She turns away as she marches on, hunched in her Army-Navy wool with a scarf bunched at her throat, and observes the stone mansions across the street, the women in chignons and wrapped in long sleek furs, the important men in impressive overcoats, the West Indian nannies pushing covered baby carriages and wheelchairs, the brass-buttoned doormen shivering minutely, the laborers eternally tearing up the streets, jackhammers like machine guns, the flow of delivery men. And on her side, under those bare-boned trees, bench after bench of homeless people of all colors and afflictions, camping out on this prime real estate. One of them, hard to tell if man or woman, lifts a can of beer and says, "How ya doin', comrade?" *Comrade?* Erica flinches. She has a place to live; this person has a park bench. So why is she flinching?

The wind picks up and Erica pulls her coat closer. She is walking for miles in order not to drink, in order to think of a plan to make money. She supposes she'll have to call Ken and Marjorie again. They're used to her appeals, and in the end, they'll come through. Payment will be their unspoken disappointment in her, and her shame.

The memory of her last job interview plays through her head

as she walks, a scene from a bad movie. A really bad movie. When she hooked up at Benny's with Jud at the fabulous Burl Ives sublet, she'd told him about her job woes. Jud had said, "Seriously? Cause I know this guy, he's kinda out there, but he actually *pays artists*. You know that woman who paints like sexual flowers? Funny name, Irish maybe? Lorna O'Keeffe?"

"Georgia," says Erica.

He writes down a name and phone number and she tucks it in her bag. At the time Jud suggests this she's on her fourth or fifth Remy, so it all makes sense that someone would pay for variations on Georgia O'Keeffe.

Erica calls the guy about the job. Mr. Wulff, he's called, fittingly. He has some kind of accent, German she thinks.

Mr. Wulff asks her a few questions about her background as an artist, then says, "Fine, good, why don't you bring your portfolio to my office today and we'll talk further."

Now: this very day. In a little more than an hour. Erica puts on a clean blouse, black slacks, polishes her loafers, tidies her portfolio. She would take a bus but there isn't enough time as it's all the way down in the Village. She'll have to take the subway. Solution: smoke a joint, half a joint. But it doesn't make it easier. The grime, the trash that litters the train, the screeching of the brakes, the passengers who sit as if they are condemned, the graffiti on every surface of the cars, like a tattooed freak at the circus. Then she must find Mr. Wulff's office, which is at the end of Christopher Street, where she's never been. Gay men rule here, gay energy, gay anger at straights, too: A guy screams "breeder!" at her. She remembers the faces of the protestors in front of Planned Parenthood, the shouts of "baby killer!" and thinks, *I can't fucking win.*

Wulff's office is in a small brownstone (brownstone!) with crumbling steps. She presses the buzzer.

"You are . . . ?" a man asks, edging open the door.

"Erica. Mason."

"Ah . . . yes. Wulff!" he calls. She follows him inside, where a young woman leans against a chair, mouth open in sleep, a baby on her lap. Another woman, tall and lean with springy black hair, passes with a sheaf of papers and climbs the stairs. Wulff appears, a thin, watery-looking man dressed in grey shirt and pants. "Come," he says. She climbs a narrow staircase behind her.

Up to an attic, obviously remodeled, now an open space, modern, with a skylight. Photography equipment everywhere and in a corner, a bed. Where's the art? Erica wonders.

"You're a photographer?" she asks.

"Yes, yes. Now, let us see what you have done." At a long table, he flips through her portfolio, pursing his lips.

"Not very much nature here," Mr. Wulff says. Erica feels as if she's being graded down.

"There's a field of wildflowers," she points out.

"Yes, that is fine. Well . . . " He closes the book with a snap and peers at her. "Have you before transmuted a photograph to a painting?"

"No."

"Ah." He sighs. "But it should not be a problem as it simply requires a certain level of draftsmanship, which you have demonstrated. Also, how can I say? A certain flair. That is the important thing here. By the way, the pay is three hundred dollars for an eight by twelve rendering, usually in oils but each client has his preferences, of course—and so on, commensurate with the size the client orders."

"Well. Yes I suppose . . . "

"As I believe my friend Jud has told you, I encourage my artists to think in the mode of Georgia O'Keeffe, you know her, yes? Good. So. Now I show you some examples, some photographs and then when they are recreated as art."

Afterwards, when she has left (fled!) Wulff's and is walking what feels like the plank of hostile Christopher Street, Erica tries to empty her head of everything except for the progress of her feet to the subway. Otherwise, the panic that was seeded near the tennis courts in Central Park will have its way with her.

At the gate to the train, she fumbles with her token and a boy darts in for it. But Erica elbows him away, hard, and scoops it up. She doesn't have enough money to buy another.

"Mothafuckin' honky."

Erica slides onto a seat on the train, pushes trash away from her feet, and closes her eyes. Maybe someday the Mr. Wulff event will become another funny New York story, but not now. Behind her eyelids, she helplessly relives the last part of her interview, when Wulff handed her the book of what she thought would be art. She hadn't wanted to understand what she was seeing, resisted it. Wulff was saying, "You know, have you thought about being a model for us, also? The pay is *quite* good for that." She finds she can't move, yet she keeps turning the pages. OK, yes, flowers are sexual—she remembers the botany class she squeaked through in college— stamens and pistils, right? And feminists love O'Keeffe's female flower sexuality. So this is a variation of that. Except it's not. It's picture after picture of real women's vaginas, clitorises, gaping or filled with an amazing assortment of objects. She's afraid to look up, because the grey Wulff is there. In slow-mo, head down, Erica pushes her chair back with a tremendous effort and reaches for her portfolio.

"I guess there could be worse shit than this." Her knees are actually knocking together. "Like maybe snuff films." She has managed to get to the door of this awful room.

As she clatters down the stairs, she meets the brisk clacking of a typewriter by the bushy-haired woman—typing invoices?—and the baby is yelling "Fucking perverts!" she yells. The woman with the baby looks at her wide-eyed.

She's safe on the train, even though she's terrified of them, and that thought makes her laugh, and then she can't stop. She doesn't care. How does she get in these situations? She's known a string of strange people in her life, but it's like everywhere else was the bush leagues, and New York is the Majors, when it comes to weirdness. She hunches over on her seat, moaning. When she straightens up, an older black man with a heavily-pitted face, in some kind of uniform, lifts his eyebrows and very slightly shakes his head. But no one else seems to notice her; certainly no one cares.

That night, exhausted after her long walk all the way up Fifth Avenue to the nineties and back, she calls her dad, explains how hard it is to find a job right now, there's a mini-recession in New York, and of course she'll find something eventually . . . he asks only how much she needs.

Her frugal father surprises Erica, again, with a check that will cover several months' living expenses, if she is careful. Another surprise is a phone call at last from Red Nottingham. Back from London, he sounds exhausted, but he's high on his Kingsley Amis piece, which will come out soon in *Harper's*. And he's about to hear the fate of the new novel his agent shopped when he left for London. Meanwhile, he's back waiting tables at Mojo's.

Erica goes in to see him the next day, before it gets busy. Without the young Upper East Side crowd she's used to seeing at night, Mojo's has a neglected, tatty look. She and Red take a table near the kitchen and have burgers and beer, on the house.

He's in a rotten mood. *The Lingering Melody* has been turned down by five houses. "People in England respect writers, they don't expect them to write blockbusters, for Chrissake. We're not producing widgets for some factory, and they understand that. But here? Philistines." Red steaming with indignation is something Erica's used to, but this is a blow. And speaking of blow, he's more off-kilter than she's remembered, a little too edgy. This rejection has really gotten to him.

"So, Red, let me tell you a funny story to cheer you up? Erica's Latest Adventure. You've heard about the boss who walked around with a hard-on in the office, blaming me. You've heard about the manic cheese editor who tore up my drawing of stinking bishop. Now let me tell you about the vagina salesman."

They both end up screaming with laughter. Red jumps up, shouting, "New York, New York! You gotta love New York!"

The waitress comes over and says, "Red, we got work to do."

"So," Erica concludes, "I'm still looking for a job."

Red looks thoughtful. "Hold on." He disappears into the noisy kitchen, comes back minutes later, grinning.

"It's all about timing, me girl," he says. "The early-shift hostess just quit. So, you got a job."

A job! And thank God it's not waitressing. Erica lasted three days when she tried that, a ditzy comedian who spilled water on kindly old folks, mixed up orders, scooped up, more than once, nickel tips as a result; once, nothing.

Red introduces her to the weaselly-looking manager, Mr. Mortis (no first-name basis here), who is distractedly yelling at a Mexican line cook who stoically chops onions while he's berated. Erica presses against the steel refrigerator in the crowded and amazingly hot kitchen. Abruptly, Mortis stops yelling. "Red says you got experience, and I need someone right away. Tuesday, the wait staff will show you what to do, come in at four Tuesday."

Erica asks him about the pay—that minor detail. "Minimum wage, and good tips." Red explains after that the tips are pooled "and usually good."

He finds her a polo shirt with MOJO'S in red across the chest. "And get a black skirt, Mortis likes them to be tight, black tights, and black shoes." They both make a face.

"I got a job," she tells T.T. later, handing him a bottle of his favorite Johnny Walker Red. Her first gift to him.

"Whoa," he says. "You look like you ready to party, girl!"

Erica smiles. "No, this is for you." She hates whiskey. She tells him about the hostess gig and has a beer. As usual, T.T. is moving around restlessly, peeking around the drawn Venetian blind on his front window, hopping to answer the phone. On the third call, Erica stands up. "Got to go, T.T." In fact, she does. Red is taking her to Lenora's, that salon of the bohemian famous of the literary, movie, and theatre firmament, basking in Big Mama's gruff approval. "She can be a real bitch though," Red warns her, "to everybody else." Erica has sworn herself to coolness, no tipsy entrance, no throwing glasses.

It's too early when they get there for the real action at Lenora's, but Red's pal Theo Friedlander is already there at what is "his" table, Red tells Erica. Friedlander is drinking champagne with a golden black girl with extremely long arms and legs.

"Nottingham, back from the other side of the pond!" Friedlander is a handsome, grizzled man in his forties who speaks with invisible quotation marks around everything he says and an expression to match. Red hunches in beside him, Erica next to the golden girl, who ignores her.

"Theo, Erica Mason, a very talented young painter who lived in Mexico with the natives."

"Buenas noches." Friedlander extends a lazy hand. "This is Marlena Dixon, a talented young model who hasn't lived in Mexico but *is* one of the natives."

Marlena smiles very briefly, as if she can barely be bothered.

Despite a slowness of speech and movement, Theo Friedlander, who's escaped a lucrative career in Hollywood as a script doctor to become the hailed author of several Philip Roth–like novels—*Girlfriends of Forty* and above all, *Slam,* which somebody huge like Robert Altman has optioned—is clearly a cokehead. Nose like a collapsing bridge. He and Red take frequent bathroom breaks; meanwhile, Erica, fortunately with a view of the room, drinks the luscious champagne with silent Marlena. The restaurant, with its insignificant bar near the entrance—Lenora encourages *her* people to drink at the tables—is a mix of French bistro and bohemian/hippie, as evidenced by the floor-length tie-dyed curtains. Erica longs to study the wall crowded with paintings and drawings that Red has told her are for sale.

Back from the men's room, beaming, Red urges Erica to come meet Lenora. But she is currently conversing with Mia Farrow. "Theo"—he pronounces it *TheO*—"you gotta have Lenora meet her, she's a terrific artist."

Theo, finding this amusing, laughs with his shoulders hunched, teeth showing, like a very intelligent squirrel. "So you say, Nottingham, my fine fellow. So you say. But not with Mia in her sights. Maybe later."

It's clear to Erica on champagne that the whole thing is a stage, including her. The writer crowd that convenes at Theo's table as the night goes on wears gravitas like a cape. They also stare intently at Erica's cleavage in her new low-cut green dress (Secondhand Rose) as if evaluating a new bauble before indulging Red—clearly in his most cherished element—in journalism gossip. The actors are, well, actors, the artists play artists, the producers . . . and Lenora, a mound of a woman with Gertrude Stein features, directs this whole, nightly show with gusto.

Erica has avoided coke runs with Marlena, but the number of champagne bottles accumulating at the table tell their own story. Red's coked-up energy makes him walk around and talk, introducing Erica and her art to all kinds of people. Unknown attractive females are common at Lenora's and Erica is easily taken in stride by shouting, witty drinking-types who display no further curiosity about her. And there is the monarch of the joint, Lenora, heavily everywhere, all but extending her ring to be kissed by her subjects.

At last Erica slips away to look at the art on the wall: There is a Judy Chicago, a David Smith drawing, but mostly work by artists she hasn't heard of, even those with impressive price tags. And she feels the bud of an idea for a painting opening.

Back at Theo's table, Red throws an arm around her shoulders as Lenora approaches and explains, "This is a terrific young artist!"

Lenora has acute, tiny eyes behind ugly spectacles. "Well then, lemme look at what she does. Afternoons around three are best." Then with a fast waddle, she's gone: Tony Bennett and company have just walked in.

"What did I tell you? Lenora is a patroness, like those grand dames in Europe, once she sees your stuff, she'll want some plastered on that wall."

"You should be her publicist, old man." Theo hunches into

silent squirrel laughter. *All he needs is a nut between his paws,* thinks Erica. But she's hardly paying attention to them; the bud has sprouted into flower while she watches Lenora, who is so like some impressive, cumbersome animal. There's a picture to paint. Rhino? Hippo? No, a bulldog, queen among her subjects. The restaurant will be a forest floor, the journalists prowling jackals, Theo a squirrel, his model a tigress, Red a laughing hyena . . . and Erica a Little Red Riding Hood almost hidden in the background.

"Red. Red. RED, I've got to leave now."

"What? Not now! The party's just getting good, I hear De Niro is coming."

Like she is going to be hanging out with superstars? She kisses him on the cheek. Her savior. Champagne sours so quickly, it is wafting from his skin and, she is sure, from her own. "No, I must, really. Thanks so much for introducing me to Lenora." (The thought of laying out her wares under her gimlet eye brings on an ancient longing, one she has thought had been permanently quelled, for a quaalude or two. But she *will* do it; going through hellfire is part of the game in New York.)

"And Mia is coming over here," Theo murmurs, actually consuming nuts from a bowl now.

No one notices her leave in the excitement of the actress's approach. Erica skims down the streets, exhilarated. She wants to get home to start a sketch of the vision lest it start to dissipate. She *will* do the painting—if for no other reason than to watch Lenora's reaction when she sees herself portrayed as a bulldog, a bulldog with a tiara.

Erica can never completely get the odor of grease and a thousand cigarettes out of her hair and skin after a shift at Mojo's. Nor the rude customers, the horny customers, the drunk customers, the cursing kitchen help, Mortis barking at everyone. But now there is money, and not only can bills get paid, but she has enough to buy clothes, art supplies. Better wine.

To her surprise, the Lenora painting insists on being a tribute to a great Mexican artist she'd been turned on to while living there: the deeply satirical pen and ink master Jose Guadalupe Posada. For several nights she goes to Lenora's to sketch from the Siberia of the bar, where nobodies congregate.

Meanwhile there is Mojo's. She sees another side of Red, who has a knack, which surprises her, of calming down customers and staff. And he works double shifts without complaint when somebody doesn't show. Also, once the curtain has gone down and they sit together in the suddenly quiet restaurant, having a drink or two before going home, she comes to see how much the world has hurt him. He rages at a review of his Amis piece which dismisses it as "essentially a rehash of what we already know about the great misogynist author," but it is the implication that Red Nottingham is a hack that cuts him deep. He has been writing seriously for twenty years, has one published novel and a bunch of articles to his credit, is chronically broke, is a coke fiend. Yet he bounces back, sends out query after query to magazine editors, badgers his agent about the new novel. One night, depressed, Red tells her he's writing porn. "Until something sells. It's actually pretty boring stuff. I mean, just how many ways can you describe fucking?"

"Well, there's always the Kama Sutra," Erica murmurs, "if you run out of ideas."

Jardín Zoológico de Lenora is propped against a wall, settling, waiting for its fate. Erica hardly knows what to think of the new painting. This is the blindness that always sets in after an extended effort, along with the usual let down. What, after all, has she wanted to achieve? Whatever it is has been lost in the process and something else has asserted itself. More, this painting has prompted her old restlessness. She wishes she were on the road again, in some Amazonian village or the mountains of Nepal. Instead, she goes to Mojo's, changes into her work black, helps set up, checks supplies, takes reservations, sometimes helps serve when absolutely necessary. Mortis is everywhere, cursing and yelling in a hoarse whisper so customers don't hear, the staff cursing back in low tones too. She is used to it now: Restaurant people are far more artistically temperamental than artists.

The most wearying part of her job is presenting that consistently friendly face to the customers. When a princess type starts screaming that a mouse has run over her foot and Mortis is nowhere in sight, Erica gets down on her hands and knees and looks under the table.

"There's nothing there," she lies soothingly. She orders a bottle of good wine for the table and makes a mental note to tell Mortis they need more traps. There are always mice in restaurants! There are always, too, customers disgruntled with a meal, drunks hitting on her, people trying to leave without paying. Her job is to keep smiling, scheduling, seating, appeasing until Flo, a redhead from Astoria, comes on at ten, Flo who's used to dealing with greater aggravation, and bigger tips. Erica, stuffing her tip take into her bag, can at last breathe free, but there are hazards ahead, the challenge of getting home without stopping at the other pubs and bars that call to her along the avenues. If she stops at one, she'll probably wake up the next morning with most or all of her money gone. Also she's developed a fresh source of humiliation, a new propensity to lose her balance. She wakes up one morning to discover her good coat is ruined, soaked with blood. Her nose will retain a scar.

Occasionally on a night off, Erica visits Red at his apartment, Red at ease in his broken-down armchair, full of Lenora gossip and complaints about the writer's life, the "table" over the kitchen bathtub full of beer cans, takeout, and sometimes, lines of coke. But he's also her cheerleader. Now he's urging her to take the painting to Lenora.

"I will, I will."

"She won't *do* anything to you, Erica. She'll either love it or not. What do you have to lose?" He knows she's terrified of Lenora. "You have everything to gain," he adds.

"OK. I will, I promise." She dips to the blow on the table.

"Look, let's not talk about it now. Tell me about that new piece." This will get him off the topic.

"So what it is, I check out the high-end sex shops in the city. *Penthouse* is interested. They pay the best, and it's easy money."

"Well, great, you can buy a new bed and the other stuff you've been saying you need." But she thinks, *No way, it'll go straight up his poor nose.*

"Let me show what I found today! Research!" Red leaps out of the chair, displacing the alley cat Ferd, who almost lands a blow before streaking for the dark hole of the bedroom. Red follows him, returning with his arms around what Erica thinks just can't be, but what is, an anatomically correct life-size blow-up doll.

Erica drains her beer without thinking. "Fuck, Red!"

"You got that right!" Laughing his gone coke-laugh, Red clutches the doll, planting a kiss on her sculpted pink cheek. *This would make a good painting*, Erica ponders, *a naked pink plastic female, pert-breasted, round of ass, clutched by the lovelorn Red.*

"Call her 'Plastic Fantastic Lover.' She's a Real Live Girl product, she comes in three sizes, shapes, and shades. White, brown, and black. I call her Girlfriend. If *Penthouse* wasn't planning on using a photographer, I'd pitch you for some drawings." He props Girlfriend against a wall. "Wait, there's some even more fantastic stuff I picked up."

"Not now," Erica says hastily. "I have to get up early tomorrow, so I'm gonna split."

Walking home, Erica tries to comfort herself thinking about the slowly mounting stash in her savings account, the tip money she has managed to hold onto.

FEELS LIKE FAME

E rica pushes resolutely through the heavy swinging doors into Lenora's. "Hello?" Silence in the anteroom, in the small bar, in the empty dining room. She's wearing armor: her office-worker suit, polished loafers, her hair confined in a sleek ponytail. She won't be mistaken for a scruffy artist.

"Hello?" Still nothing. She starts to edge back to the door, not disappointed. Relieved. She'll go have a coffee at the diner a block away.

A tall, bushy-haired man bustles in from a back room, frowning slightly.

"I'm here to see Lenora," Erica says in a clear voice she doesn't associate with herself. "She asked me to come in some afternoon around three. With my portfolio." The new canvas, carefully rolled up, is under her arm.

"And you are?"

"A friend of Theo Friedlander. And Red Nottingham." Sweat prickles at her hairline; it's all she can do not to wiggle around. "Stop fussing," her mother used to complain when she was little. "An artist . . . "

"Take a seat, I'll see if Lenora's free."

Erica removes her Army-Navy coat, folding it on her lap. She badly wants to smoke, but doesn't. She watches a tiny Latino busboy lug a heavy crate behind the bar, then another. Eventually,

Lenora, in one of her oversized tunics, this one tie-died, comes in from the kitchen.

"So? Theo's friend. Come."

Erica follows her into the dining room to what is clearly Lenora's table, piled with papers, a ledger, also a couple of drawings. "So how do you know Theo?" Her eyes peer, grey pebbles behind thick glasses.

"Through Red Nottingham."

"Red! Well, lemme see what you got."

Erica opens her sketchbook, swallowing. "This is—"

"I have eyes. Hmm . . . " A movement of her mouth that may be a smile. She points at a sketch of salsa dancers. "You like Latin music?"

"Yes, actually, I lived in Mexico, in Yucatán and Oaxaca . . . "

"This is not so bad. So what is the other one, a painting?"

"It is. It's here. I mean, this place. People who come here."

Heart jabbing, longing for a drink, Erica unrolls the canvas and spreads it on the table.

Lenora looks. And looks. And nods. "I noticed you at the bar sometimes, sketching. This? Well, now. *Jardín Zoológico de Lenora*," she reads in a hard American accent. "Zoo of Lenora's."

Erica has hoped to capture a Toulouse-Lautrecian quality that Lenora—to her—emanates, along with the Gertrude Stein. She glances at Lenora. The restaurateur is either grimacing or smiling at herself as a bulldog with a tiara; Erica can't tell which. At last, Lenora pushes *Jardín* aside. "OK," she says. "I'll look at some more." She flips through sketchbooks of the jazz people, the Cleaners in the Dark, sketches of Carmen and Edie Desmond. Stops at one of Jimmy Loveness. "Great loss," she says. "I knew him from downtown." Lenora closes the book. "How come I never hearda you?" she demands in her deep, smoker's voice.

"I've only been in New York a couple of years. But, mmm, here's something about me that was in the *Times*." A xerox copy of her precious and only review.

Lenora sips from the vodka and tonic with lime that is part

of her legend; Red has told Erica it is always at hand, that Lenora can outdrink anybody. "Tell you what I'll do, Ms. Mason, I'll take one of these drawings and the painting—it's a sly hoot—hang them here for a month or two, see if they sell. Maybe you'll get lucky. Fifty percent, that's your take." Lenora is also renowned as a hard-assed businesswoman. She points to the sketch of Jimmy Loveness. "And this one I want."

"Oh, that's fantastic, that's great, that's so generous of you." Erica knows she's babbling. Any minute she'll be kissing Lenora's hand.

"Yeah, it is. Now, let's talk prices. What are you asking for the painting? Nooo, dear, double it. This is New York, people don't respect cheap."

Erica has been avoiding Red since the repellant Girlfriend evening—no more cozy pre- or post-Mojo sessions over beer or brandy. But she must thank him for opening the door to Lenora, so she invites him over for a celebratory dinner—roast pork and potatoes, a big salad, chocolate cake. He brings a bottle of Courvoisier and, she's certain, some coke. This will surely sail him into the winds and have him regaling her with new dark happenings in the lower echelons of New York's literary world. They have a couple of drinks before he pads over to the easel and turns it around, Erica's palms itching with irritation. She hates when people do that. She always keeps her work turned to the wall when not painting *for a reason*. OK, a superstition, but one she believes. No one can see a work before the last stroke, smudge, line. Before it's born.

"Self-portrait?" he guesses. Erica shrugs. She's already torn up several.

"You're hard on yourself," he says. Then he lays out some coke.

"I've got news," Erica tells him after a quick snort (while thinking that she should not be doing this, there's always the memory, though dim now, of her old drug dealer buddy Frenchy who unraveled on coke). "I went into Lenora's with my stuff."

Red stops mid-straw. "And? She liked it? Yes! I knew she'd go for it. What'd she take?" Erica feels the tangy poison spread through the crevices of her head, a wonderfully frightening feeling. "Two things. A sketch of Jimmy Loveness. And the Zoo. She didn't even blink at herself as a bulldog. In fact, I think she likes it. *And* she told me to double the prices."

"Bloody *mar*velous." Since his London trip, Red has tended to drop bits of Brit into his speech. "You'll see, my girl, even if they don't sell—and they *will*—the exposure will be priceless."

It is a merry dinner, though they only pick at the roast pork and the cake, fueled as they are on cognac and coke. Red too is in an especially good mood, expecting any day a hefty check for his sex toys article.

"You wouldn't believe some of the stuff that's out there," he says, pushing away his barely eaten plate, "I didn't get into gay toys, not the audience, but some of the S&M and fetish shit! God!" He gulps some cognac and explodes with laughter. "They have these giant blow-up dolls. Life-size, made of heavy-duty plastic and anatomically correct? Fat ones, skinny ones, black, white. With wigs. And these babes do not come cheap."

"Yes, I, um, heard of that stuff." Does he not remember showing her his Plastic Fantastic Girlfriend? Ah, those pesky blackouts, chunks of time down the rathole. She'll never bring up to him how horribly he exposed his loneliness without being aware of it, kissing and cuddling a blow-up girl. Instantly, something shoots out of her own blackout rathole into the light and she remembers a night when, barely able to stand, she went with some people she'd just met at a bar to what she thought would be a party and was, but one full of whips and chains. It's a vivid, hateful retrieval of lost time, and Erica is going to throw up at her kitchen table. She gags and runs to the bathroom, Red saying, "Shit, Erica, what the fuck?" She almost misses the toilet.

She sits on the lid, remembering. She'd been drinking a glass of wine in some apartment that was very dark and this guy started to grab her. She remembers laughing and saying, "No man, not in the mood," and then he was pulling her wrists together to hand-cuff her, and she started yelling. She made so much noise that he let her go, but not before he slapped her and she fell to her knees. The others were laughing but she kept screaming. "Fucking little cunt, shut the fuck up!" and he actually, yes, *threw her out of the apartment into the hallway*, where she lay for several seconds. When she got to the street, she felt the blood on her face. Pathetic drunken female.

She splashes water on her face in the bathroom and stumbles out. "I think I got food poisoning. You better go. Go!"

Red packs up his blow, gets his jacket. "You sure you don't want me to stay?"

"Just go," she groans. "I need to be alone."

There's still a little cognac left, so she drinks it. She always finishes whatever bottle is there, no matter what.

LIKE FATHER

Claire and her boyfriend, Tim, are sitting in Erica's living room drinking margaritas and listening to Stan Getz on a warm spring afternoon. They'd flown in from Arizona late the day before and went to bed early on the foldout couch, then checked out the city today. It turns out that Tim loves art, or at least wants to collect it, and has offered to buy several of Erica's sketches for his office. And Erica plans to take Claire and Tim up to Lenora's to see her pieces hanging there.

Claire is quiet, with the furrowed look that Erica knows means she is upset about something. Erica reaches for the pitcher and pours another margarita. "These are really festively good, Claire."

But Claire's face narrows. She stands up and goes into the bathroom, shutting the door sharply.

Erica shrugs at Tim. He smiles back. Like a lot of men, Tim doesn't like fuss and tends to defer to Claire. Erica feels her synapses snap; she loves the richness of tequila, lime, and salt. The drinks are powering her through any anxiety about Claire's darkening mood. She and Tim sit listening to a Paul Desmond album. Erica is turning the record over when Claire comes back, wiping her eyes. "You know what? I've got to get out of here," Claire says, putting on her coat.

Tim stands up. "Claire?"

"I just need some fresh air. And—oh, nothing."

"Have a nice time," Erica says, reaching for her drink, which is almost finished.

Claire throws her jacket down as if Erica has said something outrageous. "Don't you want to know why I have to get out of here? Aren't you the least bit curious, Erica?"

"No. You said you needed some air." But Erica's hands and face are tingling and she is a little breathless.

Claire sits down heavily on the couch. "Oh my God, it is so painful seeing you like this."

"Like what? Sitting in my apartment, relaxing?"

Poor Tim doesn't know what to do, where to look. "Claire," he says again.

"Tim, I have to talk to my sister about this. You know."

"But I thought you weren't going to—you decided."

"No. I have to."

Erica folds her hands in her lap, where they beat against each other like tiny birds. She imagines herself moving up and away, out of the room like one of Chagall's angels. She's momentarily comforted by the image.

"*One day.* I've been here with you just one day. You've already had like four or five margaritas." Claire looks at her watch. "It's six-fifteen, and you're already smashed. Yes, you *are*, don't you think I can't tell? But that's not even it."

Erica holds herself completely still, her drink momentarily abandoned. Like being in a storm on a plane, slapped around by the elements. And this had happened to her, on the plane trip (a graduation present from her parents) to Mexico, when she actually had to use the vomit bag. She grips her hands in her lap, fear threatening to crack her like an egg, all her bits ready to ooze out. *Hang on,* she whispers.

"You know what? You're just not nice when you drink. You make fun of people. *Me.* You say sarcastic, hurtful things. Erica, I just hate seeing you like this."

Erica feels a vein throbbing in her forehead. "It's just my wacked sense of humor, I'm *sorry*." *Divert, deflect; whatever you do, get*

her on another topic. "And let's face it, Claire," she adds, "you've always been high-strung. So I'm sorry if I hurt your feelings."

"Oh, Erica." Claire's face is streaming. "I'm so worried about you and the drinking."

Into the silence that follows, Erica rushes in. "Remember that time," she says, "when we dropped acid in college, it was your first time? You thought you had bugs crawling all over you? And it turned out you had *crabs* and you insisted on going to the drugstore even though it was like midnight? And then we started dancing to Country Joe, or was it the Doors? Yes! We ended up laughing our guts out on the floor? Remember? And . . . and that time we went to hear Jefferson Airplane trashed and you met Grace Slick and she was trashed and she wrote her name on your hand when you asked for her autograph? And the time—"

"Erica! Stop! I'm talking about now, not back in college in 1969 when we were kids and everybody was experimenting. But it was for kids, it got old, except you haven't stopped."

But Erica doesn't want to hear another word. She rushes to her bedroom and slams the door, lying on her bed until she hears Claire and Tim leave.

After they do, she changes into a blouse that looks clean enough and her other, still not paint-stained pair of jeans. She'll go up to Mojo's or, no, to a movie. She hasn't been to a movie in ages. There's this new one people are saying is really good, though creepy, *Looking for Mr. Goodbar*. Yes, she can look in the paper—Claire brought one—but the multiplex is eight blocks away and she's a little dizzy, a little tired, maybe she should have skipped that last margarita. She'll just walk two blocks to Benny's and sit at the bar and relax. She leaves the apartment door unlocked because Claire doesn't have a key and, screw it, if someone wants to rip her off they'll find little of value, except for her art, which at the moment she doesn't give a shit about.

She's on First, where she realizes it's too early for the singles action, the crowds of twenty-somethings who act like kids freed by recess, though some early birds are settling in at the best tables near the tall windows looking onto the street, girls with big hair, girls with long, straight hair, who have shed their suit jackets and lean back so their breasts can be admired by the guys with early-Beatles haircuts and mustaches, as close as they dare to looking hip. At Benny's, Erica sails in, soothed by the familiar glow of the bottles, the tired, efficient bartender Bill who knows what all his regulars want. But she deflates instantly. There are only two other people at the bar, pudgy middle-aged guys who glance at her but are more interested in drowning whatever sorrows pudgy middle-aged guys have. As Erica orders a cognac, she slips off the barstool and falls, banging the side of her head. One of the guys comes over and helps her up.

"You OK?"

"I'm fine. Fine, thanks." She doesn't look at him.

"Your forehead is bleeding."

With a wad of tiny paper bar napkins pressed to the side of her face, Erica reaches for her brandy snifter. She wants to get the hell out of the bar, away from Bill the bartender's seen-it-all blankness, the pudgy guys. But she's bought that expensive brandy and has to finish it. Erica is steaming with resentment; so she has a few festive margaritas and her sister goes into an uproar, making her so upset that she loses her balance at her local hangout. "Another?" suggests Bill in a monotone. "No," she decides. She's gone through several sets of cocktail napkins, cramming the bloody wads in her bag. She leaves a dollar tip and walks to the door with the careful, underwater stroll of the inebriated. The singles crowd outside is thickening now, cheerful. Hours later, there'll be the shouts, crying, and arguments when the daily dream turns sour. But she won't hear them; she'll be passed out.

Meanwhile, Claire has been back and gone again. She's left a note. She and Tim have moved to a small hotel. "I'm sorry, Erica, I don't want to fight with you, I care about you. I'll call you tomorrow." Erica crumples the note and wraps herself in a quilt on the fainting couch and is out.

She wakes the next morning feeling awful, which is strange

because she hadn't had *that* much to drink the day before, had she? By noon, she has pushed through the nausea and is resolutely at work at the easel. The doorbell rings. It's Claire, by herself, carrying a bag, which she empties at the kitchen table: fruit, a baguette, chicken salad, cheese, two cans of iced tea.

"I thought we could have lunch."

"Oh?"

"Erica? Please? We're sisters."

"Right." Erica sighs. "I made some coffee."

They both light cigarettes, although Claire—*naturally*, Erica thinks—is that strange animal, a social smoker, never having more than a few in a day, able to go for weeks without one. Now she looks like she needs one.

"Before you say anything," Erica tells her, "promise me you won't say anything about my face." She's sporting an unattractive bandage over her mustard-toned head wound.

Claire nods sorrowfully. She's all put-together, glowing skin and hair, beautiful little sweater, no doubt a designer label. Erica is wearing her paint-spattered man's shirt and jeans, her hair piled up carelessly.

"Look. Erica," Claire says. "Can we start over? I'm sorry about yesterday. I guess maybe I was out of line." She is biting her perfectly lipsticked lips.

Erica tries to blow a smoke ring, fails. "Sure," she says warily. This could be a trap. Claire may sucker punch her still. "That's all right, then."

"What I mean is," Claire goes on, "I shouldn't have said what I did when Tim was there. I meant every word, but it wasn't fair to do it in front of him. So I apologize for that."

"Oh, I see! It's fine to ream me out, just not in front of the boyfriend." Not quite a sucker punch, but Claire has grazed Erica with her knuckles. And damn if Erica's hands aren't trembling again like yesterday.

"Let's not fight, Erica. I am truly concerned about you."

"And humiliating me is the way to show it?" Erica begins to

walk around her kitchen, touching her little Mexican artifacts, the colored plate with a tiny peasant village scene, the embroidered wall hanging. She's thinking that Claire has always landed on her feet. A well-paying job (though who would want to work for a drug company, peddling their wares to doctors' offices in those neat little suits Claire collects), a good-looking boyfriend with money to spare, a nice condo, trips, restaurants. While she, Erica, has to live on secondhand everything in a crappy tenement.

"I'm not humiliating you! I'm just not going to pretend everything's OK anymore." Now Claire does her crying thing again. "I've joined Al-Anon, Erica; I have to learn to take care of myself and stop worrying myself sick over other people and their drinking problems. And all the stuff that probably happens to you that I don't see, like that gash on your head."

Erica says swiftly, dodging that bullet, "Al-Anon? What is that, some cult? This is just crazy."

"It's *not*. What's crazy is the way I've been worrying about you and Dad. And Al-Anon's not a cult, it's people helping each other with the people they love's alcoholism."

"You've got to be joking. Alcoholism? And what's Dad got to do with that?"

"Of course, Dad! You moved away a long time ago, you haven't seen how bad it's gotten. He crashed the car twice lately when he was drunk, he and Mom are barely talking now."

"That *is* crazy. Really over the top. They were here not that long ago, he was fine. They were the same as always, he has a responsible job."

"Barely. Erica, he doesn't drink all the time. It's called being a periodic. I learned that in Al-Anon. Don't smirk. Sometimes he pulls it together, but then, off he goes again."

Erica is still. She is remembering a night, maybe six years ago, she was still in college. Home for Christmas vacation. She'd stayed up late watching old movies one night, the house asleep except for her father, who'd gone out for some celebratory evening with his best banker pal. He came home in the middle of *Casablanca*, and she said "Hi, Dad," from the couch where she was curled up. In a whiney voice she'd never heard him use before, he said, "Who? Who? Oh, it's my little girl. My little girl," and then he kind of stumbled towards her, arms extended. "Come to daddy." Erica jumped off the couch and rushed past him. She heard him whimper, "Don't be afraid of me." She ran to the bedroom she'd shared all through school with Claire and slammed the door. Claire was staying at a friend's that night, and Erica lay huddled in her twin bed near the window. In the morning, all was as it always was, her father reading the newspaper at the kitchen table, her mother doing the dishes. Erica forgot the whole thing, until now.

"Oh, God," she says. "Poor Dad."

"Poor *Mom*. I mean, she doesn't know what to do about it, obviously."

But sympathy for their mother is out of Erica's reach. She is perennially calm, cool, collected, her preferred weapon the disappearing act. Come to think of it, Erica has not until this moment realized she has never seen her parents argue, yell, fight.

"Oh, Mom will be all right, because—you *know* this is true—she never confronts anything. So she'll go to sleep with her back to him, she'll carry on making pot roasts and mashed potatoes and having a martini at five. But she won't *do* anything, I mean, like kick him out or threaten divorce."

"But it doesn't mean she's not hurting just because she can't admit it or talk about it!"

"Well, maybe you can get her to join that Al-Anon," Erica snaps. And then, out of nowhere, she feels like a complete shit. When she and Claire were little, Mom had made their Halloween costumes for them, baked their favorite cakes on their birthdays, read them bedtime stories, soothed them when they got chicken pox or bloodied their knees. It was when Erica's feisty and Claire's tearful adolescence roared in that Marjorie had slipped into the shadows, unwilling, at least as Erica had always seen it, to face down their defiance and find out the source of their hurt. Marjorie just couldn't face things that frightened her.

Claire comes over and wraps her arms around her sister, and Erica hugs her back. They are both crying.

When Claire pulls away, she wipes her eyes and says, "Please, please do something about your drinking. Promise me."

Erica remembers Benny's the night before. She touches her forehead and winces. "I promise." And then they have lunch.

Everything has been put in its proper place. Floors polished, woodwork scrubbed, windows cleaned, cobwebs removed. The bills paid. Clothes laundered, buttons sewn on, shoes polished. Stew is bubbling on the stove. There is nothing left to do. Showered and shampooed, Erica watches the world outside her window on this afternoon in early May. It has begun to rain and people hurry past with collars turned up, the lucky ones with umbrellas. Erica picks up her library book, something by Elizabeth Jane Howard, whom Red had recommended. He had met her as the wife of Kingsley Amis during his London trip. "*Très formidable,*" he described her. But Erica can't get into the book, as deeply, bitchily intelligent as it is. She's tired of all the damaged contemporary heroines fighting their way out of the paper bag of chauvinist society. No, it's no use. She can no longer put off the phone call she has avoided all day with this manic spurt of cleaning and sorting.

"Hello, Dad? It's Erica."

"Well, hi there, honey. How are you? Is everything all right?"

"Yeah, sure. I just thought I'd call and see how you're doing. Claire told me about the accident. I'm so sorry! How are you feeling?"

"Well, thank you. I've been better. Right arm's in a sling. It was that darn black ice, you know how bad the long winters are here."

"Jeez, and you're right-handed. What a drag." She has a sudden memory from her late teens, driving home after being at the bars in Milwaukee on a freeze-your-ass night, one eye shut to foil the double vision, wipers furiously shoving away the fast-falling snow.

"Well, fortunately that was the worst of it. And the arm's healing."

Silence. Erica thinks, *He'll never, ever talk about it. It.* Her dear old Dad, another mystery parent. Once, when she was a teenager and he'd grounded her for sneaking out of the house after curfew, she'd gone to her mother to try to get out of it. Typical bratty, acutely self-centered teenager. "Dad's so—erratic!" she'd complained. "One night he's all, let's play Scrabble after dinner, and the next he sits there chewing his nails in front of the television." And for some reason, the conversation had veered into the black hole of her fifties' parents' pasts and ended up with her mother near tears, giving her a pearl: "Well, you know, your Dad had a very hard time of it in the War. Very hard. Captured by the Germans. He almost lost his feet to frostbite and he only weighed ninety-some pounds when the Camp was liberated. So sometimes he's well, *moody.*" The War, the Prison Camp, she'd heard of them before, in low-toned conversations between her parents that stopped when she entered the room. Once when she was small but just old enough to remember, she'd seen her father *crying on the phone* and ran to her mother, who didn't seem to realize she was there. Something about her Dad's Army pal Eddie, who'd died from "combat fatigue."

"Dad . . . "

"Erica . . . "

"You go first."

"How's the job?"

Erica thinks, *oh that.* "Oh," she says, "good news. I have a show, well, a few things I've done, at this kind of famous restaurant, and the owner's bought a drawing."

"Well, honey, isn't that great! Isn't that just great! You'll have to tell your mother, she'll be so proud of you. She's at work now."

"Sure, yeah, I'll call her. So, it was nice talking to you, Dad."

"You too, honey. We're very proud of you, you know. And don't worry about me, I'm fine, just fine."

Erica sits at the kitchen table, staring at the telephone. *This is how it is,* she thinks, *everything is fine, all the crap is ignored, packed away under layers of Eisenhower fifties blandness, her smart, college-educated mother stacking books at the library or encased in an apron cooking meat and potatoes, her father in the suit and tie, slowly growing a paunch and jowls, going to church every Sunday, biting his hands or sipping martinis.* She knew from Claire that the cops had driven Ken home shit-faced and deposited him with Marjorie because he was a good citizen, a white guy in a suit. And everything's fine! She feels a sob coming. Just one, for her father, who is not fine.

The first glass of wine after the phone call is nectar, so smooth after weeks of being good. Plus it will stimulate her appetite for the stew, which she eats while reading the paper propped on the table. Another glass, then. Placing it beside the easel, she arranges her brushes, her pencils and ink and pots of paint. She regards the cruel but exciting blankness of the canvas and a picture slowly unfurls, taking its bloody time, a drawing that hunches into the middle of the page. A plain man, in profile, wearing a hat, a tweed jacket, sitting at a table with a pencil and a pad. What is he doing, is he filling in a crossword, a racing form, writing a letter? There is a glass of whiskey too. He's absorbed in what he's doing, he absorbs the light so that the room around him shrinks into itself, he's like someone reading by candlelight during a storm. He's marooned, utterly alone. She wonders about this man, whether he is old or just tired. What is his occupation, who does he care about, what are his obsessions? The shading of the pencils, the rubbing out, the spare layering of colors, the cobalt blue of his jacket, the browns and yellows. At last Erica puts away her pencils, cleans her brushes, turns the easel to the wall and, yawning, goes to bed. And realizes she has been painting her dad.

Sadness doesn't bring crying, not this time. Erica folds her hands together without thinking, a reflex action from childhood. *Now I lay me down to sleep . . .* She thinks of her quiet father, lively and curly-haired when she was little, taking her and Claire fishing, taking them to the Dairy Queen. And now he's that man who is impossibly lonely, crashing cars . . . *I pray the Lord my soul to keep* . . . She squeezes her eyes shut, wishing she could pray, wishing she didn't know exactly how impossibly lonely her dad is.

A package arrives from her mother after Erica's finished the man in the hat. Having taken the position that everything about her family is so lacquered in averageness as to be impossible to penetrate with paint, until the recent image of the solitary man, that is, Erica reads her mother's accompanying letter with mild astonishment.

> *Erica dear,*
>
> *When I was cleaning out the attic recently, I came across these papers. I was going to throw them out along with lots of others. I wonder, did I save every single project and report that you kids ever did in school? I even found that suspension bridge you built with Dad for your fourth-grade science project! Do you remember that? With the little toy cars on it? Anyway, then I found these at the bottom of a box: Grandma Mason's diary and your Paga's sketchbook. I couldn't throw them away. I think they may be of interest to you. If not, do what you want with them. Would love to hear from you more often,*
>
> *Love,*
> *Mother*

First a musty, plain spiral notebook written in the spidery fine handwriting of the past by Grandma Sophie. Her round little foreign grandmother, who tended flowers and baked the best bread Erica has ever tasted, who had great white breasts like the swelling dough always on her kitchen counter. Erica had seen those breasts when she burst into her grandparents' bedroom one hot summer's morning during a childhood visit. She had gaped at her grandmother's hidden, massive, secret flesh. Grandma Sophie's diary is entirely mundane, but Erica finds this touching. Clearly the impulse behind it was to give some kind of larger importance to what was the most ordinary of lives. Erica thumbs through entries about house cleaning and cooking and church services, almost missing the entry midway through. She reads it, then again. It is so different from the others.

> *"Visited Harold's grave with Pa, the twenty-fifth anniversary of his death. I wanted to bring roses but Pa said no, they were not in season and cost too much. I brought chrysanthemums from the garden, the same color as the trees turning in the graveyard. I cried a little. Pa didn't."*

Harold Mason: August 5, 1914–October 6, 1946
Beloved son of Arnold and Sophie Mason.

Erica calls her mother, wanting to know more about this entry.

"So Mom, Grandma's diary, there's this really sad passage about visiting Uncle Harold's grave." The first-born son, dead before Erica was born, tuberculosis.

"Yes, that was always sad for them."

"The thing is, something seems off. I remember writing this report in school about relatives, and having to get all the dates and stuff. And I remember Dad told me his father was rejected by the army in World War I because of flat feet, and then he met Grandma at some church social. When did they get married?"

Marjorie Mason always has had family matters at her fingertips. "Let me see, I think . . . well, of course, the wedding will be in the old family Bible."

Marjorie returns to the phone, a little breathless. "Yes, here it is: April 8, 1914, at First Presbyterian Church in Cedar Rapids, Iowa." Sophie Bjornson had emigrated there to live with her sister in the Scandinavian community. "Sophie worked as a maid, you know, to repay her sister for her passage from Norway. And she met Grandfather Arnold at the church."

"Right. So, Mom, Harold was born in *August* that year. That means Grandma was like four months pregnant when she got married."

Her mother says slowly, "It was never talked about, you know."

"In other words, it was a shotgun wedding."

"Erica, please. They had a long marriage and raised four children. Buried the first one, of course."

"But were they happy together, Arnold and Sophie? I mean, they had to get married."

"Well, people looked at things differently then. It was the family that was important." Her mother sighs. "But, well, they bickered. I think they—well, they tolerated each other."

For Erica, Sophie has finally come alive. She had been a young woman, attractive, healthy and lonely. New to a foreign country where she barely spoke the language—Sophie would always speak with a thick Scandinavian accent, to the delight of her grandchildren. Sophie had laughed and flirted with a young American guy. They had found stolen moments to kiss and fool around. And, pretty quickly, make a baby. She must have been terrified when she missed a period, then another. She would have gone to her married sister and confessed. Probably her sister's husband had approached Arnold, a clerk, to tell him to do the "right thing." In those days, people did the right thing and it was for life.

When Erica lived in Mexico, she'd met an eccentric old woman who lived in a crumbling adobe house just down the dirt path behind Erica's rented cottage on a paved street. Erica had taken her sketchpad to wander around the neglected area, just like a village, with chickens and children running heedless in the dust. She heard the unlikely sounds of a piano being played in a hut; she knocked at the door and met old Carlota, who was delighted to show off her prize possession. Like its owner, the piano was missing some of its teeth. It seemed that the piano was all that was left of a prosperous childhood. Carlota, who told her she had never married, practiced every day. And as Erica was leaving, promising to come back soon, the old maid Carlota told her something wonderful in Spanish: "*Remember, every woman has her history.*"

Now Erica knows, after all these years, a bit of her grandmother's history. But what about her grandfather, that quiet man who always wore a mustard-colored cardigan and spent his leisure time either reading a newspaper and sipping coffee in an old armchair or tending his little vegetable garden? Saying little, Arnold had acquired the habit of invisibility. But it wasn't an unpleasant or hostile withdrawal. And for his small grandchildren, he always had had time, drawing delightful stick figures for them, taking them on walks or to the drugstore for milkshakes.

Erica opens his sketchbook. Crosshatched, meticulous pencil drawings of flowers, fruit, birds and animals. She imagines him sitting alone on a log or a rock, absorbed in the world around him. She calls her mother again. "Did you know about Paga's art?"

But her mother doesn't know, she has no idea. And neither, she thinks, does Erica's father. "Paga never mentioned it to us, they were just for his own pleasure, I'm sure."

"And he never drew people. Not a single one."

Her mother sighs. "Well, your grandfather was a loner. He didn't dislike people, but he didn't seem to—well, need them, I suppose. And I know it made your father uncomfortable, the way Paga and Grandma used to snipe at each other. Those drawings must have been his escape."

"And now I know where the artist genes come from."

Erica decides to paint her grandparents in their little living room, side by side on the plump little sofa, Sophie with her crocheting in her lap, Arnold with his sketchbook, a pencil in his hand. Two grey old people, with splashes of color around them in the red and white of the Norwegian wood carvings, the blues and mauves of Sophie's beloved African violets. Two old people side by side, not touching, not looking at each other.

TOO BLOODY BRILLIANT

But what if you could see this, Claire? Erica thinks. *You only focus on the negative about me. You should see me now. Selling paintings, networking with the glamorati. I'm better than fine.*

"Too bloody brilliant!" Red lifts his glass of red wine. He's not talking about the wine, which is mediocre. It's after hours, Mojo's is closed but for the staff. Red and Erica are friends again and he has gathered the staff to congratulate Erica on *Jardín,* which has had an offer. Nothing firm, but it's movement. "Bring your sketchbook to Mojo's. Show Mortis what you can do, babe. Strike while the iron is hot, for Chrissake, get him to commission a picture for the place."

Homer, the line cook, taps a spread of Mexican sketches. "This is my country! *Mi nieto . . .* "

"Grandson," supplies Erica, switching back and forth from Spanish to talk to Homer. The language feels wobbly but good, like getting on a horse again. Beaming, Homer tells her his grandson is an artist too, studying at the National University in Mexico City. And Homer, to her delight, knows about some of her favorite Mexican artists, like Rivera, Orozco, Posada, Tamayo, Kahlo. "*Le felicito,*" he congratulates her, with the formal elegance of Latin Americans, be they line cooks or diplomats.

The others compliment her too before jumping off to talk about the Off-Broadway show or dance company they'd just auditioned for. Red makes a toast, trumpets his long-lived hope for a contract for his new novel. And Mortis, presumably impressed by Lenora's reputation, agrees to Red's urging that Erica paint something to enliven the walls of Mojo's. She can come in on nights off to do some sketches, Mortis says. He draws her aside. "We'll talk money later."

Everyone should have a night like this in Manhattan, even if it's just one, Erica thinks. An early summer night, not too hot yet, when you own the city, you're the star in a Woody Allen movie, the one who slides into the taxi and commands the driver to take you anywhere you want, and the warm wind on a June night whips through your hair. In her case, it's downtown to the Tin Palace, a new club, to hear jazz, with Red in tow. Afterwards, late, they go up to Lenora's, where Theo Friedlander is having an intense conversation at his table with *David fucking Halberstam*, who is famous! The guy who went to Vietnam and wrote about it the way it really was, to President Johnson's fury—and also? Are you shitting me? It's that Smith woman, the darling of CBGB's, with the underground hit "Because the Night." Smith has the androgynous look currently in with the out crowd and everybody's fawning over her. Erica, sipping brandy, thinks, *So maybe I'm a little jealous of her and her entourage, scruffy downtown guys on the uptown scene.* Erica's at her usual spot at the end of the table, trying to make herself invisible, when Red butts in and makes her want to crawl under the table, telling the whole table about *Zoo* —over there on the wall—and how fabulous Erica is, and a few of them (not Halberstam or Smith, though) actually go over to look at it— *hanging on the wall!* And Theo slips her a little tinfoil-wrapped packet. "Congratulations," he drawls. "Knock yourself out with this in the ladies." She's the uptown wallflower who's been allowed into the cool crowd. For at least one night. Even Lenora says hello.

Red's still in the thick of it with the famous and the infamous when Erica decides she has to leave, as her head feels like a balloon getting dangerously tight from Theo's gift of packaged goods. Nobody notices her slip away, they're all joyously, druggedly carrying on about what a shit Mayor Beame is and whether New

York is permanently fucked. Well, she's had her Fifteen Minutes, Erica thinks as she stands breathing the dirty air on the dirty streets of crime-ridden Manhattan and decides to walk home along its harmful, wrecked, beloved streets. It's the middle of the night down Second Avenue—thirty blocks to her hidey-hole, the city still going, but the blare of horns less energetic now, the gritty intensity is lazier, there are plenty of lone souls walking somewhere or nowhere like her and clumps of homeless Vietnam vets and mentally unmoored folks tucked in on pieces of cardboard in doorways. The saloon doors are all disgorging now, disco blaring from some, rock from others. And then she's outside Benny's, and it's doesn't feel like the place where she was 86ed not so long ago, or the one where she fell off the barstool and cut open her face. It's her oasis, her little temple of hipness, with the kind of music that lights her up, where musicians really *play*, so she's sliding—carefully—onto a stool catching the very last set. A guitarist with wild black curls, wailing like Django with a healthy slug of Clapton, and the stalwart little band of listener-drinkers yelling their approval, like they are not in the white heart of the Upper East Side. When the music is this good, you don't even care if you have a drink or a line or a pop, it's like fucking, it's like rafting down some beautiful, wild river and somehow, there's a drink before her and Erica, who hates whiskey, lets it burn its way down.

"Who *is* this dude?" she shouts at the woman in skintight jeans next to her.

"Some young guy from France—some gypsy."

And when the little dude crashes the last chords, there's silence, acknowledging what he's done: rocked and testified and breathed fire. The sparse, unsober audience lets out a roar.

Back at the apartment, Erica whirls around to an invisible gypsy tune and finally collapses on the fainting couch. She pulls a shawl over her and closes her eyes. *Crash,* she begs herself, *just crash,* but of course the coke has other ideas. So she lies there, feeling something unfamiliar, but not a bad feeling. It's been a long time, but isn't this kinda, sorta, happiness? Maybe? She's done good work, she'll selling it—she has a nice check from Claire's Tim for the three sketches he bought for his office in Arizona. And it's the first time since the "park thing" that she hadn't looked behind her as she made her way around in the city, that she didn't feel her breath squeeze and rasp. She'd forgotten to be afraid.

The next day the phone rings. Red. "Have you seen it? I got you onto Page Six! Everybody reads Page Six!" He reads it out to her: "'Lenora's famous walls get an add, artist Erica Mason's amusing painting of the denizens.' I've got an extra copy, I'll give it you at Mojo's. But don't," he adds, "quit your day job. Yet."

The phone rings again and again. Philip. Aaron Hill. Anders.

"Anders?" Erica closes her eyes.

Who would have thought Anders would read it, he's purely the *Times*. He wants to see the painting, he wants to see everything she's been working on.

"Let's have a drink, catch up."

They make a date later in the week to meet at Lenora's for an early drink at the outcasts bar. He may have broken her heart but he's a valuable source of contacts in the art world. She must be turning into a real New Yorker.

To celebrate all this good fortune, Erica buys a bottle of cognac—Korbel, a cheaper American brand, not the good French stuff. She buys a steak, albeit the cheapest cut. Puts on her favorite Billie Holiday record. Smokes a joint left over from somewhere after her dinner party for one. Ends up sitting in front of a blank canvas. Page Six, she thinks. Lenora's. Anders in two days. The art world.

And then her mind goes blank, like a white canvas, whenever she sits down to work. She has no ideas.

ASK ALICE

Erica has little time to try to paint in June; she's always going to some opening at little galleries in the remoter parts of Manhattan or even Brooklyn, where she drinks the free wine, eats the canapés, and looks at Warhol-inspired Pop Art and abstracts which so often appear to be depictions of entrails, bits of machinery, or nothing decipherable. And of course, she meets a lot of people, who hang around the Chelsea, Max's Kansas City. At one of these art shows, she runs into Anders again. She gets hit on a lot by his friends. By Wally, the bearlike sculptor who is currently working on a series of tiny welded maimed Vietnam vets; by Kitchings, the radical lesbian feminist she'd met at the cafeteria in SoHo; by a tall, thin etcher who calls himself simply Smithers. She goes home one night with Smithers, who shows her his very good imaginary bird etchings, but is impotent. Kitchings invites her to be in a group show of feminists. Erica says she'll show her Cleaners in the Dark series. When she shows up in the afternoon at the gallery for the show, Wicked Women Do Art, at somebody's ground floor apartment on Avenue B, she thinks SHIT! MISTAKE, but Kitchings, a short woman brimming with confidence, takes charge and helps Erica hang and label Cleaners. Wine is handed out and by the time people, mostly but not all women, trickle in, she's well-insulated. She wanders around the apartment, trying to see what excites this enthusiastic band. A group has crowded around Kitchings' work, four large paintings, thematically the same, of a headless woman, with a different kind of fur glued over each pudendum—rabbit, mink, fox, and squirrel.

Kitchings is weaving a little. Of course she's been drinking, everybody has. "Damn if I couldn't find beaver," she says to Erica. "Gotta have some beaver!"

"Well, can't help you there." Erica slides away to the drinks table in the tiny kitchen with now mostly empty half-gallons of the cheap wine she used to drink in college. A guy in jeans and work boots is busily drinking.

"Are you a radical feminist too?" she asks.

He laughs as if she has said something hilarious.

"Guess not. Well, that makes two of us."

Erica nudges her way back into the hairy crowd, stopping before the large Pop Art canvas of what at first seems to be a coke bottle, but which she sees now is a dildo. She moves on, to an installation, a purple bidet with a painted mirror in the bowl with a picture of a vagina.

She thinks of Wulff and his crotch shots. Boy, they'd fit right in here. *Enough.* There is no art here that depicts a being with a beating heart. Beating genitals, yes. She starts to laugh and a woman bumps into her, spilling some of the vinegary wine from her brimming glass onto her Mexican shirt. It's a momentous encounter.

"Sally Rogers?" Erica exclaims.

"Erica Mason!" Sally's foghorn shriek turns heads even in this exuberant crowd. "Far fucking out! *You* here in New York?" A long hug.

"You here too! Actually, I'm in this show. Sad to say."

"What!" Sally shrieks again. "Show me!"

"Not radically feminist, just people portraits," Erica demurs.

Sally stands before her five sketches and one watercolor.

"I love these. This is *poetry!*"

"I'm gonna buy one—this one!" Sally, her old college friend, a hardcore Socialist Workers Party member before gender politics.

Epifania, stocky and dark, hair in a thick braid, right off a stony *milpa* in Mexico, solemnly wafting her can of Pledge. "It's *mine*. I've gotta get it before anyone else tries to."

"Like that will happen here."

But now she has a red dot: Sold! One at least. Good old Sally, stalwart as ever.

"Now for a refill of the slop they're serving here." They wade over to the table and carry their glasses to a relatively uncrowded spot next to the purple bidet, plopping down on the floor with wine and cigarettes. Erica is vastly relieved. Sally! Her old partner in the good old anti-war marches, armed with vinegar-soaked handkerchiefs against the tear gas, yelling "Pigs!" at those overweight cops who were also overworked since the Math Building at Madison had been blown up. Beautiful, plain Sally, who always wore a man's oversize white shirt and jeans, and still does. She holds her head up, sharp-eyed even behind bottle-thick glasses. Her mouth is the most fascinating thing about her; it's shaped like a frog's, incessantly moving, and most of her talk is intelligent. Reddish-yellow hair (you couldn't call her a strawberry blonde) snaking down her shoulders and back. Just as it did back in the day.

"I'm not Rogers anymore." Sally twirls her left hand with its silver and turquoise ring. "Got married on a Hopi reservation two years ago. Sally Rogers Nevins."

"To *Kevin*?" Her shadow, her foil, her valet: big, good-natured Kevin Nevins. Erica had always thought she'd move on to bigger game. Or female game.

"Yup. And I got this job in the art department at NYU, just pushing papers really, but it gets me close to the action. Alice Neel, above all. And Kevin's working at a bookstore."

"Didn't he want to be an organic farmer?"

"Still does. We're taking turns, a couple years in New York while I do the Alice book, then the farm thing. What about you?"

"I was in Mexico for a couple of years, which was great. Tough, too."

"And now you're a New York artist."

Erica winced. "I wouldn't say that."

"Would you get off the floor, OK? People can't get around you to see my installation."

Sally fixes her sharp pin-eyes on the woman speaking, a rotund person in a sort of hemp smock. "But we've become *part* of the installation." She gestures behind her at the purple bidet. "The human part."

Erica begins to laugh. She has a friend at last. She decides to stretch out on the floor for a little rest.

"This is my piece!" the hemp lady proclaims. "So fucking move."

"Think of us as an added attraction," Sally urges.

Erica rolls around laughing.

The woman leaves, returning with reinforcements.

"We're guerrilla fighters for the humanist tradition," Sally declares. "And we won't be moved!"

Erica suggests, "OK, I've got an idea. Let's get some more wine."

"Well, is that slop worth moving for? Yeah, I guess. The bidet," Sally adds graciously, "is all yours."

Lying down hadn't been such a great idea, Erica realizes as she stands up. She has reached a critical mass of booze, if liquid can be mass. She feels it sloshing around; the next glass of wine may topple her. Well, that's never stopped her before.

"Kitchings," she says, "I want you to meet my friend Sally, the world's greatest fan of Alice Neel, whom I assume you've heard of because she is a female artist. Who said—I mean Alice did, and I quote: *I never followed any school or imitated anybody.* Now how did I remember that? No idea. Also: Alice doesn't live here."

Teetering, she continues, "What's with all these vaginas, anyway, Kitchings? You say it's—what, liberated? But you know what? Some perv actually offered me a job painting *flower vaginas*—no heads, no arms, no legs. Just vaginas. How is this any different, what you're doing?"

"Whoa. Back up! Men degrade women; we celebrate ourselves. That's the difference."

"Bullshit. I spit on your sleaze."

Sally takes her arm and leads her outside into sharp cold air.

"I hate this shit," Erica says fervently. "Those feminists are pervs too." Erica loses her balance and Sally nearly goes down with her. They stand up with difficulty. Erica peers at her old friend. "But you're in New York, Sally, and you came to this show."

"Which you're in," Sally reminds her, calmly. "It's part of my *job*, Erica, I cover the feminist art scene for the department. But I agree, this show *is* not up to *your* stuff. So? Let it go. Let it go, my friend. Let's go get something to eat. There's a diner nearby, if we don't get mugged by the junkies on the way."

"Good idea."

A skinny grey cat slinks by, then another. Erica hears the crunch of discarded syringes under her sandals, passes tired old buildings that look like hers in Tiny Italy. A skinny guy, feral like the cats, moves down the other side of the street. Miraculously, a cab appears.

"Better idea, we'll go to the Village."

The next day, Sally calls. "Did you recover yet from last night? You were really angry!" she adds, admiringly. Sally has an idea; she wants Erica to bring her portfolio to this guy called Sam Klein. "He's an important dude in the downtown art scene, I hear he's putting together a show of young artists *at this very moment!* I'm going to call him and tell him about you—about Mexico, that *Times* review, that painting you have in—what's it called?"

"Lenora's. You've heard about it, the place where all the writers and models and shit hang out uptown? But how do you know about the review?"

"You told me last night in the diner, don't you remember?"

"Oh yeah." Erica doesn't remember.

Mortis keeps asking her when she'll have "his" painting ready. They'd bargained hard, she'd wrested four hundred dollars from him in advance. It's almost done, Erica keeps telling him, a pure lie. She still hasn't started it. Finally, on a Monday, a slow night for

Mojo's, she comes in on her night off and forces herself to start doodling jello-assed Karen the actress-waitress; Mortis, in his Italian suit, who leaves early because the place is dead; the wiry little Puerto Rican Carlitos, who is dragging out trash as big as he is, probably heavier. It's after ten, only two customers in the place, a dawdling couple. There's a crash from the kitchen, screams and yells.

Karen flies in, followed by Erica. "*Homer!*"

The way Karen screams the Mexican cook's name, Erica knows she's sleeping with him. Karen holds him, groaning, close to her chest. Nobody's paying any attention to this tender scene. Carlitos grabs a bag of ice and presses it on Homer's arm, onto which a pot of boiling water had cascaded and is already turning his skin magenta against brown. Jesus, the other fry-cook, wets and wrings a cold towel. It is up to Erica to dial for the ambulance.

They move Homer, groaning and gasping, into the dining room. The couple there stares at him.

"You a doctor? No? We're closing!" Erica says sharply.

"Can we get our bill?"

"Just *go.*" After the couple scuttles out, a dead silence fills the room until the ambulance guys swoop in, curtly efficient. Karen insists on going with Homer. The Latinos stand around, looking at Erica.

"The keys," she remembers, "who has the keys to lock up?"

"Mr. Mortis." Carlitos shrugs.

"Oh, shit. Well, you guys finish cleaning up, then go home. I'll wait for him. On second thought, no, one of you stay with me 'til he gets here."

Erica sits down and takes out her sketchpad, arranges her pencils, brushes and ink and begins *Wounded Cook.*

Carlitos comes in from the kitchen. "I finish."

"Well, Jesus can leave, but you stay, OK? Carlitos, you know what Karen does to close? The tablecloths, napkins and so on? " He nods reluctantly, his face tightening. It is one thing to mop the floors and take out the huge smelly trash bags, quite another to do a woman's job. But Erica is on a roll, she's got to keep working on *Wounded Cook*.

"I'll make sure Mortis pays you overtime, Carlitos."

"He never pay that."

"Well, I *promise* he will."

She has to get Homer's classic mestizo features down, above all his expression after he'd been scalded. That millennium of oppression of the brown-skinned that has molded his features into a masked, seeming acceptance of pain.

At midnight, Erica relents and lets Carlitos leave, wedging a chair under the back door and then the front. Thankfully, Mortis arrives soon after to close up. She tells him about Homer.

"Oh hell," he says, gritting his teeth. "Jesus can't handle the line on his own. I'm fucked."

"That's all you have to say? Not, poor Homer, what hospital did they take him to? Nothing but *you're* fucked? The man has third-degree burns, Mr. Mortis."

"And I've got a restaurant to run, young lady."

"Oh how could I forget? Well, try Carlitos. Who by the way stayed until midnight with me to help close."

Mortis blinks rapidly. "All right, all right. So, you go home now too."

Erica finds a taxi, as she's too exhausted to walk all those blocks, and flops back against the none-too-clean cracked leather. From shock to shock, like the cab hitting potholes festooning the poorly maintained streets of her adopted city. From job to lowly job, from sleaze to greed. How long before Mortis fires her or she quits? Then another rung of absurdity.

"Stop here, please!" She has changed her mind about going home. Benny's is right here, and never has she felt a stronger desire for a drink. Or three. Or seven. Or whatever.

BE WHERE NOW

Sally has done it. Erica's precious portfolio in hand, Sally has met with the hot new downtown art man of the moment and got him to include her in a new exhibit, opening in a week. What she doesn't tell Erica is how she wheedled her into it. Sam Klein says yes only after Sally promises him the full weight of the university publicity machine. And at least one "edgier" picture from Erica.

"Edgier! Like what, vaginas covered in old rabbit fur? Shit, Sally."

Sally cools her down. "It's the *perf*ect location! This cool space in SoHo. Just do something wild to satisfy Klein's super-hip neurosis."

Erica's idea is do something about Thomas Thomas. It's intrinsically political, right? A muscled, scarred black boxer. True, Miles Davis had done his great tribute to Jack Johnson a few years before, but Erica's T.T. is the other side of the panther, blank-eyed like a kid with punch drunkenness. She knows she can easily persuade T.T. to pose. Right in his *Shaft*-inspired little apartment, on his zebra-striped couch. She *sees* the picture already like a gift being unwrapped, its slashes of red, black, grey-white. T.T.'s pebbled friendly, vacant eyes. And the title? *Ex-Fighter*. The problem is that she's blown T.T. off for months; also she doesn't want to be tempted to get high and drunk with him at his place. There's something creepy about T.T.'s place, the way he's always hurrying to get the phone or peeking around the living room curtains to check out the street. Shit, he's dealing dope. So she'll go in clean, stay clean, sketch him fast, and get out.

It is one of those swamp heat, pavement-bubbling, garbage-cooking New York days. Going outside, the air is a Deep South zone of hell. Going a few blocks for groceries leaves her soaked. She takes a shower and sits in front of her old air conditioner, which T.T. had found in the basement of his building and installed for her recently. He wouldn't take anything for it so Erica had made him enchiladas; he was thrilled by this new foreign food. There's a lot of stuff she got from T.T. in her apartment, she realizes: a bookshelf, a coffee table, a fern. She had bought a six-pack at the grocery store and pops open a beer. Being good can't mean foregoing a cold beer on such a tropical afternoon. She decides she'll call T.T. later; first she'll do some preliminary sketches for *Ex-Fighter*. She draws him sitting. Standing. She has another beer; she's in the groove. T.T. can't be static, she sees, he must be between motions, the way he always is in reality. One more beer.

The last one makes her sleepy and it's past seven when she wakes up on the fainting couch. She's breathing hard from a dream where she'd been in a subway station and couldn't find her train. All the signs were in a foreign language she didn't recognize at first, great ugly scrawls and colored slashes. She realized in the dream that these were the hieroglyphics of the Graffiti language and all the commuters rushing around her were speaking in Graffiti too, although she herself knew not a word. It was impossible to make herself understood as she fought her way through the thickening crowd and she woke wheezing.

Erica dawdles over coffee and a cigarette, lazy from the heat, which the old air conditioner doesn't do much to alleviate. Over its rattle, she hears a bunch of sirens nearby; nothing unusual about that in Manhattan. She finally gets ready to stroll over to T.T.'s next door with her sketchpad. Tell him, what? She's been super-busy with work. Which is not exactly a lie. And tell him she'll immortalize him with this painting. No, not *immortalize,* he won't understand that. *Make him famous.* Everybody understands famous.

She pushes the street door of her building open and instantly wilts. And everything has gone crazy outside. Police cars with those revolving blue lights are just up the block; frustrated motorists are responding in New York fashion by laying on their horns. She sees an ambulance. A crowd. And a draped stretcher coming out of T.T.'s building. She thinks it's one of the old Italians. But then why all the cop cars? She sees Anthony, the man from the deli down the block, in his white apron.

"It's the super, that black guy, you know him?" Anthony tells her. "He got offed."

It's not quite dark but soon will be. The Italians are talking excitedly. Erica's body feels light, desiccated. Her lips crack from dryness.

"What?"

"The cops found him in his apartment after people started complaining about the smell. They're sayin' he was sliced up like a salami. Some drug thing, I figure. Well, he seemed like a nice enough guy, used to come in for a sandwich every day. Turkey and mozzarella on white, mayo, no mustard. Slice of tomato. But you never can tell."

"No, oh no, oh no."

Anthony catches her as her legs buckle. "You don't look so good. You should go home. There's nothing left to see here anyway."

But Erica goes to the wine store that stays open late and replenishes her stock, which is nonexistent except for a couple of bottles of beer. Then she goes home and thinks about Thomas Thomas, but mostly things like: *It could have been me too. Sitting there on the pimp couch, drawing him. It could have been me.*

Erica is up on a ladder in the bookstore shelving copies of *Be Here Now,* which sells out so frequently that she wonders if everyone in the world except her wants to learn how to be here now. She's been afraid to drink since the night T.T. got murdered, but she's managed to get ahold of some Valium. She likes its floaty, being-in-a-vacuum effect.

"Um, can you help me find a book for this friend who has a problem?"

Erica climbs down. The girl is one of those fragile-looking, no hips, streams-of-brown-hair types on college campuses everywhere. She's twisting strands of her hair around and around.

"This is Self-Help, right?"

Erica nods, waiting. As soon as she finishes shelving, she's off on her break: double espresso and a cigarette. She shifts impatiently. "Yeah, everything here is about personal problems."

The girl stops fiddling with her hair. "The problem is this friend of mine, she's been getting into, like, trouble. She's not a *criminal*," she rushes on, "but like, when she has a little too much to drink, she doesn't seem to know what she's doing. And when you try to talk to her, later on, she denies it. What she's done."

"So, a book that would help her, uh, drink better?"

"Yeah, cut back."

Just then Ron, the assistant manager, sticks his head around the corner. "Hey, Erica, break time, I'll take over for you. How can I help ya?" he says cheerfully.

Erica hurries off to the café across the street. She knows exactly where two copies of a certain blue-covered volume are shelved in "her" section. When she goes back to the store, she checks to see. Yup, Ron had found them. There's only one copy now of the ominously titled *Alcoholics Anonymous*. Seems like overkill, but the poor girl obviously needs some help with her drinking problem.

"You're Portraits? Over by the far wall. Sam, Portraits just walked in."

"Ah, Rica Maison, right, hello. Just check to see there aren't any fuck-ups on your titles, OK?"

Erica returns within seconds. "Sam! My name is spelled wrong."

"What the fuck?" Sam Klein combs his thick mane maniacally with long, pale ringed fingers. "How could they screw that up?"

Erica points: Rica Maison.

But that is your name."

"No, it's *Mason.*"

"Yeah but *Maison,* that has a better ring to it." His French pronunciation is excellent from his years of scuffling in Paris before going into the business end of art.

"It's not *my name.*"

"It's serendipitous."

"But . . . "

Sam whirls away to attend to a tall, shrill redhead who is mad about a dent in one of her assemblages, doll-house-size cages made out of junk food trash. Each cage has a red-haired doll imprisoned within.

Erica weaves through the growing crowd of artists, friends of artists, staff, and possible critics, wishing Sally was here. She would have held firm on the name change. Stopping before a painting—just swirls of ruby red, that's it—she notices the triumphant black dot on the bottom. Sold! Already? An identical canvas hung beside it, except the swirls are emerald green, has drawn a knot of admirers. And the show hasn't even officially opened yet.

Sally, Sally, I understand nothing! There I am over in Siberia, exiled with my old-fashioned and unfashionable portraits, where no one has gathered. And now I have a fake name! Perfect, I guess. You could explain this to me . . . like I don't exist.

Sally had helped select what Erica is showing in this Sam Klein extravaganza. Six portraits: *Jimmy Loveness*—those limpid, LSD-infected eyes. *Wounded Cook, Carmen, Plastic Fantastic Lover*, a *Brownstone Brothel* sketch, and *Ex-Fighter In Memoriam.*

"OK, people, let's wrap it up. We hit at six and we're gonna rock!" Sam Klein's eyes shine, he's wearing a red velveteen vest over tight, tiny jeans: a speed-freak impresario.

Erica has a ghost of a hangover, as she and Sally had sat up late talking about the show at Kelly's Grill. Sally's told everyone she knows about the show, down to the janitors in the art department at NYU. But Sally herself isn't going to be here. Sally is in the hospital.

Kevin had called her that morning and Erica stopped by St. Vincent's before she went to the gallery. Sally was asleep. Kevin, watching football on mute, was downright loquacious: She'd fainted at work and her boss insisted she go to the E.R. where it turned out she had untreated mono—maybe. "All I know for sure is the doctor says she's got to cut back on the booze. She won't be happy when she wakes up," he added. "Especially about missing your show." Kevin wished her good luck. "I'm gonna stay here," he added.

"Of course." This odd couple, joined at the hip. "Tell her I'll come by tomorrow with every scrap of gossip, I promise."

"Well, break a leg or whatever they say in the art game."

"And you are?"

"Erica—Maison. Portraits."

"Ah . . . the *figurativist*." The guy who looks like a critic smiles meanly and moves on.

"Philip!" Erica cries out shrilly, relieved to see a known and friendly face. "God Bless the Child for coming. Want to get some wine?"

"In a minute maybe. Listen, I had a phone call last week from this guy Sonny something. About that painting you did of his girlfriend Carmela?"

"Carmen! Why was he calling you?"

"I don't know, the whole thing sounded a little weird, he said he got my number from her and he wanted to know if I knew how he could get hold of the picture. So I told him I thought it might be in this show."

"Weird." A vein pounds in her forehead at the mention of Carmen.

"Yeah, well. By the way, where's your stuff?"

"Banished to the far corners since I'm just an old-fashioned figurativist."

"Says who?"

"A critic with a ponytail and an American flag tie."

"So that should tell you something. I'm gonna go look around. See you at the refreshments table."

Erica insinuates herself into the little crowd, who all seem to know each other—*if Sally was here, she'd have a receiving line organized for me, but yeah, I prefer the anonymity.* Sandwiched against a wall, Erica closes her eyes. *Figurativist.* Damning with faint praise? Yeah, this is what people want to look at, that woman over there coated in raw meat, those red swirls—sold! What about actual people, real people?

"You're not falling asleep at your opening, Erica?"

It's Anders. Erica shrugs off the nice numbness of Valium plus wine, a new one for her. She's been "good" all these weeks since she got loaded the night T.T. died, painting his portrait, until she met with Sally and the cycle ended . . . Anders. Here. "I was just having an imaginary conversation, telling off this art critic. He sneered at me. Of course I said nothing to him at the time."

"You're an artist; you don't need to defend yourself."

He's smiling at her. "Anders, thanks for coming." Philip too, and Sally in spirit. Red hasn't shown yet, but he will. And Larry Lopez, Claire, Sandra, even her parents have called to wish her luck. And here is the gorgeous fucking Anders.

"Of course I came. I want to say I knew you when you were a starving artist in a garret."

"Don't see that changing anytime soon."

"All you need is luck, some good reviews."

"You think? Any really old-fashioned critics around?"

"A critic with taste, you mean. Who can appreciate your delicious mix of sophistication and naïveté." Anders smiles.

"Perfect. From figurativist to naïf." She's trying to impress him. When has that worked? Anders the prodigious brain. Bored by other brains. Her brain. When they had half lived together, he had floated trial balloons—Wittgenstein and Sartre, Musil and Hegel—but Erica couldn't possibly ascend.

This had bothered her terribly. He hadn't really cared at first; it was her talent that intrigued him, in the same way he loved to listen to those old blues guys. An escape from the ozone of his ceaseless high thoughts. Erica had always known she was a diversion for Anders, something to warm his chilly erudition. What he really wanted from her, she got, was this: a casual meeting in a gallery or a bar. *Anders, I want to touch your skin, the back of your neck where your hair curls up a little. Heat and ice. Will I always be so in love with you?*

"Anyway, thanks for coming. And for not calling me Rica."

"Any time, Erica."

"Anders?" a woman calls.

"Deme! You made it. Erica, Demeter Winestock, a colleague. Erica Mason, the artist I told you about."

"*Rica Maison* now, Sam has reinvented me. So glad you could come, Ms. Winestock." *So this is my replacement. I've seen you before. Dark and lush.* "Well, excuse me, I'm off now to fight the figurative-naïf wars."

Erica passes the new Kitchings display, this time it's headless women in long ball gowns. *Sally, Sally, what am I doing here? And what am I looking at? You could explain the significance of this teeter-totter, for example, a good job of welding, curves of metal bolted to the base. Covered with glitter and hair:* Desesperada, *it's called,* Hopeless Female. *So many fantastic negative words start with "des," don't they: desperate, desolate, destitute, despair? And I feel them all. I want you to be here, Sally, I'm not going to think about you lying there in that hideous hospital "gown" exhausted and ill. But I'll describe Demeter Winestock to you; I promise I'll make you laugh. The well-named Demeter. In a golden field with skirts spread out, the harvesters bringing in the wheat, tiny figures in the background. She's a platter of Mediterranean stuff —olives, figs, strong cheese. Humid black eyes and heaving breasts. God, I hate love; what terrible jealousy it inflicts.*

Approaching her, Deme points at *Desesperada*, wrinkling her nose. "Too much teetering here, don't you think?"

"Yes."

"I want you to know, Rica, I really like your portraits, they have so much *life* in them. You're very perceptive."

"Yeah, maybe too much for my own fucking good." There has been, of course, a good deal of winebibbing before the show opened and since. Erica finds it pointless, suddenly, to be civil— or at least, not offensive—to her replacement. She stares openly at Demeter, thinking of the imaginary painting of her. Behind the juicy foreground full of dripping pungent Mediterranean food, a dark, gluey background, plundered fields like heaps of crumpled sheets.

"I have a particular interest in the therapeutic role art can play in treating my mentally disturbed patients," Demeter is actually saying. "As a psychotherapist," she clarifies.

"Is that so?" Erica replies more loudly than she has intended. "Well, as a mentally disturbed *artist,* I have a particular interest in the therapeutic role my hand can play in slapping you on the face. So would you please *fuck off?*"

"Hey dig, a *fracas* between artists!" someone comments in the small, interested group that immediately forms, including, soon, Philip. And Anders.

He approaches. "Erica, stop this." He speaks softly, encircles her wrist. "Don't."

"That bitch is not an artist, she's a shrink! *I'm* the artist!"

"Erica, you've been drinking. *Don't.*"

"Why, Anders, why? Why, why, why?"

Anders, of course, backs away.

"She threatened to hit me. In the face, Anders!" Demeter's cheeks really are pomegranates, her eyes black olives. But Erica will never, ever paint her.

"What I *said* was . . . what did I say? Oh yeah, I remember. I'd like to *slap* you. Not *hit* you. You fake Fertility Goddess!"

So, Sally, the audience had their little thrill. Anders and his new love were gone then, and I went to get another glass of wine. And Philip told me he was tired of my "antics," what a quaint word, right? After he left, I wound up leaving with some people who knew about a great party and we all squeezed into a car and went to this abandoned factory with enormous windows. The people living there are clever; they've rigged up electricity and have this sort of camper toilet that doesn't need plumbing. A band was playing. I got into an argument with a Spanish guy in black who had long, thin teeth, which naturally made me think of fangs. So naturally I referred to him as Dracula when he tried to touch me. I kicked him in the shins. He was lucky I didn't kick higher. Somebody took me to this little room. I lay down under some blankets or coats. In the morning, I had all this subway switching to do to get home.

The next afternoon, the phone rings. Sam Klein. "I've got news: bad news and good news."

"I'm breathless."

"You should be. We sold two of your six, Rica Maison, the first night! *Plastic Fantastic Lover* and that *Carmen*. That's fabulous, darling! Now the bad news. The guy who bought *Carmen*? He *slashed it with a knife*. On the sidewalk. No, I don't know his name. He paid cash, a light-skinned dude with an Afro, looked like a professor or something. Now the good news. You can't buy better publicity than that, Rica, like when that woman shot Andy Warhol? Fame, Rica Maison!"

"But did he say why he did it?"

"What?"

"Why he slashed my painting?"

"What I heard was he called you a cunt. That's all I know. Then he just walked away. We still have the canvas in the gallery; maybe it can be repaired. But of course, technically, it's still the slasher's since he paid for it . . . "

Several days later, Erica buys purple tulips and sugar cookies from an Italian bakery to take to Sally, who is at home now, sitting on the couch with her feet up, drinking tea and smoking. She looks pale and tired and Erica thinks she'll leave soon, but Sally of course wants to hear everything about the show.

"I can't believe what that man did to your beautiful portrait! He should be arrested, the crazy fuck. Why would he do that?"

"No idea," Erica lies. She shifts around on the beanbag, longing for a glass of wine. Why are they drinking tea like characters out of an English novel? "Sam Klein thinks I'll get all this publicity, but there's been nothing. I'm still unknown."

"Not quite, Erica."

"Tell me about you, Sally. What's this all about, you just had a stomach ache?"

"Turns out my liver's 'compromised.' The doctors said I have to stay off the booze."

"*Compromised?*"

"Actually it's kind of a relief," Sally goes on. "Sometimes I've wanted to do something besides sit drinking in a bar—like work on the Alice book or take this night class at NYU on Great Women Writers, Lost and Found. But I always ended up at some tavern. Not that I didn't enjoy it; well, *you* know that."

"But aren't you being, well, a little *melodramatic* here? Shit, Sally, it's not like you're not productive—you have a job, the book, all the art stuff. You just have a few drinks to relax." Erica adds defensively, "And I just had a successful show, sold two paintings for Chrissake!"

"I'm not talking about *your* liver. It's mine that's fucked up. Look, it's hard to explain . . . But I just feel, like it's over, it's *done*, that part of my life. When the doctor told me I can't drink anymore, I actually felt *relief*, like someone gave me permission to stop. And he told me I should go to A.A."

In the silence that follows, Erica hears the muted constant blare of traffic outside, the labored hum of the refrigerator in the closet kitchen and her own breathing, faster now.

"You can't be serious. Isn't that for seedy old men, Lost Weekend types, that kind of thing?"

"Not in New York, anyway. Which should be no surprise,

when you think of it. I went to one of their meetings last night. With Kevin. He's agreed to stop too, to support me."

"Shit, Sally."

"Don't look at me like that! There were ordinary people there, like us. OK, not ordinary! But people in suits, people in jeans, and, this is the Village, even in drag. Young, old, and lots of women." Incredibly, Sally smiles.

Erica says in a clipped tone, "Well. If that's what you want." How terribly sad for Sally. This is dreadful: Her best friend has joined a cult. And abandoned her. Of course, everyone knows someone who's ended up in Scientology or EST or the Moonies, one of those weird mind-fucking organizations. But not *Sally*.

"We can still hang out, Erica. Go to exhibits. *Coffee shops*." Sally giggles.

"Oh, right."

"Oh, Erica. We will."

Out on the street, jostled by streams of blue-jeaned students, her sense of outrage blooms. *Sally a teetotaler, in A.A.? Her merry old pal, her partner in crime. Well, not crime, but they had thumbed their noses at the world, laughed at its pretensions in some booth or on bar stools and, best of all, in that cozy little box of an apartment.* She walks over to Bradley's, needing comfort. There, she meets a jolly guy who's happy to buy her Four Star Courvoisier, so that's all right.

The show ends. Erica's sold yet another piece, the *Brownstone Brothel* thing, and has an offer to show at a gallery, an obscure place that serves Red Zinger tea and homemade muffins, run by two women on Avenue B, with paintings hung on dimly-lit walls. Sam Klein is also talking about another show; that is, she thinks, if he survives his speedball habit long enough. But Erica is fresh out of ideas, as if even minor success has made her impotent. She faces the blank canvas with a sense of bored unease. There've been dry spells before, but she's worked through them—doodling, playing with paint, waiting for a line to grow legs, a color to connect with another and pull her into the blank whiteness until she is once again blind to everything but the slowly inhabited picture. But not this time. She hunches on her stool in front of the easel; she moves to the couch with a sketchpad. Nothing.

Nothing but a vague sense of doom, like a storm gathering, like—a return of an image that used to haunt her in Mexico—one of the constant vultures called *zopilotes,* beating soundless wings as it came at *he*r; she's the prey. She imagines it zooming into the room from the open window, smashing through the screen. *OK, this is nuts, stop it.* So she thinks about Sally and not drinking. *How can Sally be doing this? How can she spurn the thing that lights up what is otherwise an unbearably ordinary reality? The thing that keeps the* zopilotes *from crashing through the window. What else can take the fear away?* Erica mourns her lost friend. But when Sally calls her, she doesn't sound sad. She is unbereft, a foreigner.

Lying back on the chaise longue with wine, Erica confirms the truth for herself: the relief of drinking! Then, by the fifth or sixth glass, she remembers another truth, the one she always forgets until it is too late. Which is, *oh shit, not again*! Because once again, not intending to, she has overdone it; she is captive once more to the bottle. And all she can do is drain the thing dry and wake up with the hangover of her greed, her weak will, her shameful lust for the stuff. She has only wanted, once again, to relax and forget (tonight about Sally and the non-drinking thing), but here she is, again, lost in the desert of drunkenness. Ending in some pointless fall, some crying jag, some late-night phone calls. God help her if she goes out on the streets.

BLACKOUT, SQUARED

To Lenora's again, in a little black skirt and a tight, watermelon-colored t-shirt, to meet with Red, who has some guy with art connections he wants her to meet. Erica wants to meet some guy badly, with or without art connections. She wants to meet some guy who will erase Anders, who will heat her blood, who will move his hands slowly over her body, who will take her like a prize.

It's the middle of July in the smudged brightness of early evening. After a "meal" of yogurt and several glasses of red wine, Erica walks uptown to save cash, her beloved old Mexican sandals flopping block after block, the 60s, the 70s, the 80s. Just a few more stifling minutes to go. A fire hydrant is open on 81st, kids squealing. She sticks her arms in the gush of water, splashes it on her face, almost sick with relief, almost a kid again for a few seconds.

She shivers at the impact of entering Lenora's saloon, which Lenora apparently likes to keep at ice-making temperature and pulls on her beloved white cotton shawl, another Mexican artifact, which she has, thank God, remembered to bring, then heads for the ladies room to wash her grimy face and give up on her tangled hair, a protest of frizz. She dabs on powder, red lipstick. Ready for action. But there's no sign of Red yet. She waits at the cramped little bar. Has a glass of wine. Another. Red still hasn't shown but someone else has, a guy named Mike. He has the kind of slightly battered, world-weary face of a native New Yorker. They trade creds: Mike is a reporter for the *Post*, she painted *Zoo*, they both know Red. The place is starting to fill up and they move to what she thinks of as Theo's table, where for a few minutes everything is as it always has been at Lenora's. Lenora moves among her subjects in a muumuu, like some vast Hawaiian queen (painting idea?), but the action is still slow-mo, the stars aren't out yet, and the drinking and trips to the men's and ladies' haven't begun.

"You wanna hamburger or something?" Mike invites and Erica realizes she is very hungry. Sure, this is a promising evening. And then, the lights go out. Someone claps. Someone laughs. A baritone booms, "Turn the fucking lights on, Lenora darling!" But the lights don't come on. Waiters bring flashlights, candles. But without air-conditioning, the place quickly becomes a hot mess. People call for their checks. "Let's go," Mike says, flinging down some bills.

Lenora, though, is standing at the door in the dark. "Champagne on me outside!" It's party on, in what they see is not just a power outage in the saloon. A total blackout. No lights in windows, no streetlights, no traffic signals. Cars and cabs leaning on their horns. *The bedraggled city,* Erica thinks, *is like some hulking great beast in the darkness.* But Lenora is making a party out of it, waiters lugging crates of champagne into the blackness. Corks pop, bottles and plastic cups are passed around. Cigarettes glow, joints. People sit on car hoods, on the sidewalk. Erica stands with Mike, drinking cups of cold and then warm champagne, which Mike passes on. "There's Woody!" somebody yells, and improbably, Woody Allen it is, with a little entourage. George Plimpton arrives, Al Pacino, Cheryl Tiegs—dazzling in white—climbing out of limos, back to the womb.

"I gotta find a payphone, find out what's happening," Mike tells her. "I'll come with you!" Erica says, not wanting to be left alone. Someone passes her yet another bottle; she's lost her plastic cup, so she gulps it down. She's lost Mike.

It's like having a blindfold ripped off, is Erica's first thought when she comes to the next day—she assumes it's the next day; anyway, it's very bright and very hot. She checks: She is on her own bed, still in the clothes she wore last night. Even her sandals are still strapped on. She's soaked with sweat, she has to pee urgently, and throw up, of course, but it takes several gingerly-moving minutes to get to the bathroom. She vomits pink bile and sinks on the toilet. She is afraid to get up and look at herself, but she has to check for damage. Her face is pale, ugly, dirty, but there are no fresh scrapes or bruises. She pulls off all her clothes. A couple of fresh bruises on her legs. Nothing serious. She turns on the shower—nothing. Scrubs herself with a towel. And kneels at the toilet again.

Once again, she has lost a chunk of time. Ten hours, twelve? No memory, nothing after looking for Mike outside Lenora's in the dark. On her knees, Erica clenches her teeth and squeezes her eyes shut, as if this might force something of the last lost night to the surface of her brain.

In the kitchen, she finds a coolish Coke in the dark fridge and gulps it down, then finds a crumpled cigarette in her bag. You've had your little lost weekends before and here you are, safe. But she does not feel safe. Something has changed; she feels different. She needs a drink, of course, and she needs something to eat. Milk, eggs, bread, cigarettes, beer. Get to the deli.

Throwing on a sundress and shoving on sunglasses, Erica grabs her bags and keys and attempts to unlock her front door. But it is already unlocked. And maybe, she'll think later, it is this small fact, this detail that changes everything. She begins to shake so hard she has to sit down. Her door had been unlocked since she got home the night before; she had left herself completely vulnerable in this breaking-down city.

Get down the street, she tells herself; *you can make it to the deli.* People are walking around with the aimless saunter of a weekend crowd though it's the middle of the week, with no jobs or schools to go to. Anthony stands at the doorway of the deli, fanning himself listlessly with a newspaper. But inside, he's got a little generator fiercely growling to keep his precious salamis and cheeses alive.

"Who can believe, no power in this kinda heat?"

"Do you know when the power's supposed to come back on?" They shout at each other to be heard.

He shrugs. "The paper it say, lightning striked the Con Edison plant. Very bad. So, New York has dropped dead, like that President Ford, he tell us to do. And the blacks, they riot everywhere, destroy the shops, the buildings, like animals."

Erica, thoroughly unsurprised at the shopkeeper's political views, which she would normally protest, holds her tongue. She needs Anthony to give her bread, milk, ham, eggs, cigs. On credit, until the power's restored and she can get to her pitifully small checking account at Chase. Also she doesn't care about anything now; she can't be bothered with some immigrant's comic book racist views.

There's just one paper left for sale, the *Daily News,* not Mike's *Post.* She puts it on the counter.

"And a six-pack of Bud, right?" Anthony booms over the generator. Ah, he knows her well. "Not cold no more, though." He shrugs.

Erica shakes her head. "Not today," she says. *Maybe if the beer was cold, maybe if I had locked the door, maybe if I knew what I was doing last night when the lights went off inside me.* "And a bottle of water. And a Kit Kat, thanks."

Back in the apartment, she devours the candy bar, first food in uncountable hours. **BLACKOUT!** says the *News* headline, and inside are vignettes of chaos, neighborhoods in Brooklyn and the Bronx getting trashed—shades of all the riots in the Peace and Love sixties— people trapped in elevators, subways. And, a mention of Lenora's champagne bash, or rather the celebs who showed up. The "officials" can't say when the power will be back on. Meanwhile, New York roasts and waits in fear of another night of destruction, starved of basic services, and just about ready to collapse.

And Erica thinks, *I'm part of it, I'm falling apart too.* She feels like she's in some slow free fall, a bird whose wings can barely flap, a parachute with a frayed cord. Mechanically, she eats some bread, drinks coffee, smokes. Lies down on the chaise longue with the barred window open to the street, the stifling air. She dreams she's dragging a heavy suitcase somewhere, turns around in a panic: The case is open, spilling her possessions on the ground. She'll have to go back and collect them, but she can't, because she has to keep going although she can no longer move—

"Hello?" She pushes out of the dream to answer the phone.

"Erica! Red. You OK?"

"Yeah, sure, just groggy. Red, are you? OK? You bailed on me last night."

"I know, I know. I'm sorry, I got hung up on this piece I'm doing for *New York* and then, when I realized the time, the lights go out. So I walk over to Lenora's with my flashlight and there's this party. Everybody's there, but I didn't see you."

"Well, I was there."

"No, you weren't Erica. I ran into Mike Mandelbaum, he tells me my friend the painter? She flips out and starts throwing plastic cups at people. *You.*"

Silence.

"So there's this cabbie who's stopped to join the fun and Mandelbaum gets him to take you home. Shit, Erica, what happened to you?"

"What happened is I'm a sorry bitch. Also, I must have given that cabdriver all my money."

One minute I'm standing outside Lenora's drinking (warm) champagne with the beautiful people and the next I'm wilding out and throwing things. I've been put in a cab somehow and wake up remembering nothing. "If you happen to see that Mike, tell him I'm sorry. Tell him I'm an asshole."

"Jesus, Erica," Red says, "you don't sound too good."

"No. I'm not. But I gotta go now, Red, probably talk to you later."

Erica hangs up, stares at the phone. The thing is, something is different this time. And then she calls Sally.

There is a meeting, she has learned from Sally, who found it in her A.A. meeting schedule, right down Erica's very street in the old brick Catholic school. If she turns left outside her apartment, it's less than five minutes. Turn right and it's less than five minutes to the deli. Which has cold beer again. It's been three days since the blackout and things are back to normal, at least in her part of Midtown. The Friday night crowd is already easing along towards the singles bars. Erica looks at the blush of red above the street, the beginning of sunset. Her bit of nature. She remembers her dream about the suitcase, not being able to move then. Or now. One of the old Italian women comes outside the building. She's wearing an apron—Christ, don't they ever take them off? She probably wears it to bed—and says pleasantly, "Nice-a night, we got the lights back, eh?" and trundles off towards the deli. And that decides it. Erica doesn't want to be standing at Anthony's Deli, while the nice old lady, who will hang around to shoot the breeze with her *campagnolo,* watches her get her six-pack—no, two six-packs tonight. For starters. She turns left and into the Catholic school, straight ahead to an assembly hall that becomes the A.A. meeting on Friday nights.

Of that first meeting, Erica will remember:

Wading through what seems a huge, chattering crowd that is settling on bleachers, and finding an aisle seat in the last row.

A man who stands in the front and stuns her by saying his name, then adding, "And I'm an alcoholic."

Wanting to crawl under her seat.

Wishing she had her sunglasses.

A lot of clapping.

Walking outside and a woman asking, "Is this your first meeting?" and handing her a large blue book and a "meeting list."

Another woman saying, "Remember, throw out all the booze."

Erica replying, "I don't have any booze, there's nothing left."

Someone—the same woman?—writing her phone number on a matchbook just like at a bar. For some reason, she wants Erica to call her.

What Erica will not remember:

Names or faces.

What all those people talked about during the meeting.

They're in the Greek coffee shop on the corner before what has become her regular meeting. The booth in the corner is their usual, and often the next booth too, because they are good tippers, these A.A. people, who are always gone by seven, when the meeting starts. Tonight there's another little group. Erica, Sally, and Maggie at a table together. Sally and Maggie hold hands under the table, breaking one of the non-rule rules of the program: No new relationships in the first year. But Sally, sailing sober with about six months under her belt, and Maggie, with her awesome three years, don't care. Apparently neither does Kevin, who Sally says is happy on the farm. Sally's and Maggie's "home group," down in the Village, has no rules anyway, unlike Erica's on the Upper East Side.

"You'll be fine, you'll see," Sally is saying. "In fact, knowing you, you'll be amazing."

Maggie, almost a redhead—she has the coloring, the freckles, but her hair is brown—nods and smiles from her vast three-year experience.

"And we'll be there in the first row, with your sponsor and your friends from the group."

Erica forces herself to eat the grilled cheese sandwich and the lousy coleslaw that Sally is paying for since Erica can't. She's thinking of everything she doesn't have since she crashed into A.A. three months ago: She's never been this poor, she can't paint, she doesn't have a boyfriend.

"More coffee?" Aitalas, in that greyish-white shirt with great circles of redolent damp under the arms, refills their cups. Bad coffee, which she drinks amazing amounts of.

Maybe Aitalas will ask her out and she can become a Greek housewife. Like—a little chunk of Erica's recent past lights up— Mary Gorgonis of Mr. Geiger fame.

"Don't look so glum!" Sally exclaims. "Think of everything good that's happened since you stopped drinking. For Chrissake— like not waking up with a hangover, knowing what you did last night. And you've started working again . . . "

"Yeah, yeah, yeah. Cleaning three A.A. people's apartments, lucky me. A cleaning lady who can barely make the rent."

"It's just the start, Erica."

Erica looks at her. Sally has kept her job in the art department, with vacation, benefits. She has found love. "A rousing first act."

"You're a gifted artist; things will fall into place."

"Former artist. With no ideas. I know: 'Give time time.'"

In six months, Erica will find a well-paying part-time job for a translation company; start working on a new series, self-portraits called "Cleaning in the Dark II;" have a problematic love affair with an Argentinian boss who fibs about being divorced. And she'll stay sober. Right now, in the Greek coffee shop, she has to get herself together to go tell her story for the first time at an A.A. meeting, at the magic ninety-day mark.

"My attitude sucks, doesn't it."

Sally and Maggie say together, "Ye-ah."

"Well, don't throw any of those corny A.A. slogans at me, please."

Addie spends hours with her on the phone, as does Sally, of course, and two new friends, Roy and Marsha. When she wakes up, she goes to the bathroom and washes her face without vomiting; feeds her new cat, Little Thug, a stray she found at the deli; makes coffee. She shows up at the three apartments to clean and does a thorough, thoroughly unenthusiastic job. She remembers the ending of books, movies. and TV shows. She calls her parents and her sister. Her money doesn't disappear down the blackout rathole.

"I am fairly glad to be sober, OK?"

The three of them head for the meeting nearby, which is three flights up in the large church meeting room, immense numbers of rows of chairs set up and a table in front from which Erica will have to cower soon. The leader, Guy, about her father's age, in a grey suit, arrives and gives her a hug and the room is right-sized again, with all manner of people coming in, the regulars like it's a cocktail party, the newcomers sitting in the back with haunted, averted faces. Addie is there in front, gorgeous. She knows a lot of people, Erica realizes. And they don't think she's an asshole. The day has faded, a crisp October evening is beginning, but the last light streams in through the banks of windows on either side of the room as Guy starts the meeting with the usual business of greeting new arrivals and those who have come back after a "slip." The Preamble is read.

And now it's showtime. Erica, sitting next to Guy at the little table, is it: tonight's show. Her mind goes blank. She looks at the dozens and dozens of faces turned to her and they become fuzzy, and her own story of drinking and trouble is waiting for her as she says, "My name is Erica . . ."

ABOUT THE AUTHOR

After graduating from the University of Wisconsin with an honors degree in Latin American Studies, Linda Dahl worked as a freelance journalist in Mexico, Ecuador, and Brazil, with a particular interest in the arts. Based in New York since the mid 1970's, her books reflect her interests in the arts and love of research. *Stormy Weather: The Music and Lives of a Century of Jazzwomen* (Pantheon, 1984) was called "a brilliant work of oral history" by *Publishers Weekly*. *Morning Glory: A Biography of Mary Lou Williams* (Pantheon, 2000), was a *New York Times* Notable Book of the Year. *Haunted Heart: A Biography of Susannah McCorkle* (University of Michigan Press, 2006), wrote Leon Wieseltier in *The New Republic* "is vivacious, tender, saturnine, industrious and deeply intelligent." Her novel, *Gringa in a Strange Land* (Robert D. Reed Publishers), won the Writers in the Sky Award for Best Creative Writing of 2010.

9 781938 314384